SIDI

CHRISTOPHER BRYAN

Diamond Press

Siding Star

Christopher Bryan

Printed in the United States of America.

The Diamond Press

Proctors Hall Road

Sewanee, Tennessee

For more information about this book, visit:

www.christopherbryanonline.com

Edition ISBNs

Trade Paperback 978-0-9853911-0-2

e-book 978-0-9853911-1-9

Library of Congress Cataloging-in-Publication data is available upon request.

First Edition 2012

This edition was prepared for printing by The Editorial Department

7650 E. Broadway, #308, Tucson, Arizona 85710

www.editorialdepartment.com

Cover art by Jay Libby

Book design by Christopher Fisher

Diamond Press logo by Richard Posan for Two Ps

For Wendy, with love

SIDING STAR

PROLOGUE

Twenty seven thousand years ago, at the center of a barred spiral galaxy now known on earth as the Milky Way, a star was growing old. All stars grow old: but this one grew old before its time. Hydrogen that should have burned in glory for another hundred thousand years was failing, and without it the star would die. Nuclear fusion held it a little longer—held it until there was nothing left to fuse, nothing to defy the gravity that pulled the star in upon itself. Then, in a hundred billion degrees of heat, the core collapsed. In less than a second, ten times the mass and gravity of earth's sun were compacted to a pinhead—and so compacted, recoiled and exploded.

The shockwave burst into the galaxy, plunging outward, spreading, widening, for twenty seven thousand years, until at last its edge drew near to a modest solar system on the Orion Spur. And so to a small, moist planet that was a part of that system—a blue and silver planet, with a single moon.

ONE

Tuesday, October 7, 2008. 5:35 p.m.
Exeter Cathedral Close, Devon, England.

A tall, bearded figure in a rough black habit stood on the lawns to the north of the cathedral and gazed. Nikos Kakoyannis was not gazing at the statue of Richard Hooker to his right, nor at the few late-season tourists who were scattered about the grass. Several people stared at him and a couple of small boys giggled, but he had eyes for nothing but the cathedral.

At last he picked up an old carpetbag that lay beside him on the grass and began to walk along the path towards the north door. His eyes never left it.

He entered.

Coolness and gray-green light, pierced by the sweetness of treble and counter-tenor exchanging the awful solemnities of the *Nunc Dimittis*:

… a light to lighten the Gentiles,
And to be the glory of thy people Israel.

For a moment he stopped. *Glory*, the choir sang, *Glory be… Glory…Glory…* echoing and teasing. Then in response came a single voice, the spoken word sounding with somber power after the revelry of organ and choir —

I believe in God...

—and Kakoyannis moved on.

He walked slowly along the north ambulatory, past tombs and chantry chapels, on into the east ambulatory and so to the Lady Chapel. Lights burned before the icon of the Virgin of Tenderness, but the chapel was deserted, as he had hoped it would be. The worshippers were all at Evensong. He approached the side of the altar, glanced around, then slipped behind it and waited, crouching.

Evensong ended. The grace was invoked. The final cry for peace was sung. Now there was fumbling for coats and the gentle murmur of Anglican piety ready for its supper.

Gradually the murmur died. A portly verger glanced into the Lady Chapel and walked around to check the lights in front of the icon. His footsteps died away. A door slammed. Silence. The rich stained glass of the east window was almost dark.

Kakoyannis was alone.

Emerging from his crouch, he walked to the center of the Lady Chapel. There was still light enough for him to see the icon of the Virgin, her gentle eyes fixed upon him. He would like to have broken it, but what he was about to do must be done in a sacred place and perhaps that desecration would impair the deeper desecration he planned. So he let the icon be and walked on, crossing to the north ambulatory and down to the north door. It was locked, but within minutes gave way to his probing. He shot back the bolts, and it opened. He left it ajar. It would be hidden from outside by the shadow of the porch: and it was a means of escape.

Now for quire and sanctuary.

He removed the gold and scarlet crucifix from its stand and placed it face down on the ground. On the high altar he put a single black candle, setting it midway between the golden candlesticks normally lit to welcome the Presence. On the sanctuary floor in front of the altar he spray-painted symbols of power — circle, pentangle, tetragrammaton, and secret names in Hebrew and four other tongues of the black art.

He then took his stand before the altar in the midst of these symbols, and by the light of a small LED flashlight read aloud from a black book, words upon words that denied words, until they died into cackle and finally to an easeless silence.

It was done.

And now he waited, his gaze fixed on the altar.

He had dared the rite. The dark flame was burning, and before it was the place where the demon should appear. And before them both, himself, directing upon the flame the eye-beams of his mind, summoning.

Something was moving, something breathing, something stirring on the fringes of his consciousness.

He redoubled his concentration. Who knew what discarnate entities might ride the storm he was creating? He must concentrate only on the center, the focus of power. His eyes burned into the flame. Faintly, faintly, faintly, it was changing. Something was answering. Slowly. Slowly. The more concentration. The more stillness. The utter direction. The air above the flame was darkening. Now, steadily, there emerged a countenance: almond eyes gleaming in the faint light. It was that which he had willed to encounter. It was the face of the Beast. And now was the time.

He called.

He called with a cry that had once been heard in the court of Solomon: words of power that uttered their command and were what they commanded. And the Beast came, shimmying around the flame and crashing against one of the unlit candlesticks so that it lurched in an arc of gold and struck the sanctuary floor with a clatter that echoed and re-echoed until it died.

Two

*Exeter. The home of DI Cecilia Cavaliere.
A little later the same evening.*

Detective Inspector Cecilia Anna Maria Cavaliere of the Devon and Cornwall Constabulary turned the key in the front door lock and pushed. The door opened with its usual peculiar shudder, enveloping her in yellow light.

It had been a frustrating day.

The frustration had begun that morning: the light on her internal line started flashing before she got her coat off.

It was Sergeant Wyatt, on the desk.

"We've got a dangerous animal at large, ma'am, and Superintendent Hanlon wants you take charge of the Incident Room. You've got 5B."

"We've got a *what?*"

"Dangerous animal, ma'am."

"Isn't that a job for the environmental officer?" DI Cavaliere was officially "serious crimes." "Where's DS Coles?"

"Off sick, ma'am."

"DS Wills?"

"He's off sick, ma'am."

"Oh, for heaven's sake—isn't there anyone who *isn't* off sick?"

"Yes, ma'am. You."

"Huh! All right, then. What kind of animal?"

"A wolf, ma'am. Escaped from the local fair sometime before dawn. Cage wasn't locked, apparently. There's some stuff — hard copy that's not on the computer yet. I'll bring it now. Just wanted to make sure where you were. Thought you might be off sick."

"Ha, ha."

So she'd spent the rest of the day in the Incident Room, coordinating grids, checking maps, organizing volunteer groups from Animal Rescue, putting experts with nets and tranquillizing darts in charge of them, and drinking tea.

The experts, she'd been assured by both the fair and the university (who provided most of them), would have no difficulty at all tracking and finding an inexperienced young female wolf who'd been born and raised in captivity, answered to the name of Katie, and had never spent a day fending for herself in her life.

So she should be back to the delights of Serious Crime by midday.

"What are you doing today, *bella*?" Papa said when he telephoned her mid-morning.

"Looking for a wolf, actually."

"Oh — the one on *telegiornale*? The one the fair has lost?"

"That one."

"It sounds energetic."

"Well, I'm not actually *doing* the looking, Papa. I'm just sitting here telling other people to do it and drinking tea."

"They cannot find you *un buon caffe*?" She chuckled. He always said that. Even though the coffee at the university was just as bad as it was here.

"Here, Papa, we drink tea." Come to think of it, *she* always said *that*.

"Oh. That's all right then. Well, I know you'll be kind to the wolf when you find her. Remember San Francesco. *Ti amo, bella.*"

"*Ti amo, Papa.*"

As it turned out, she'd had no chance to be either kind or cruel.

For the inexperienced young female obviously knew something the experts didn't. And when six o'clock passed and the darkness began to draw on, they were obliged to pack up and go home, their nets un-cast and their tranquillizing darts un-darted.

And DI Cavaliere had begun to form a sneaking admiration for Katie the inexperienced wolf.

But still, it had been frustrating.

And it was good to be home.

Yelps and clattering paws on the parquet signaled that Figaro (her dog) and Tocco and Pu (her parents' dogs) were coming to welcome her.

Here they came! She never understood how three not-particularly-large mongrels could form a tide, but they did. She bent down so as to distribute favors as evenly as possible between three heads, one black (Figaro), one white with black patches (Tocco), and one brown (Pu).

"Thank you! Thank you! Yes, I'm glad to see you too! I've thought of nothing else all day!"

Mama appeared at the study door, holding the telephone handset.

"They've been trying to reach you," she said in Italian. "I think they found your wolf. But they don't sound too happy about it."

"*Grazie, Mama.*" Cecilia took the phone, wondering what was wrong with her mobile. "DI Cavaliere here… All right… If she's done it, she's done it. Who's there? … I take it you've called the people from the fair? … Scene of Crime Officers on their way? … Good. Well, so am I. I should be there in about fifteen minutes."

She put down the phone. Mama was watching her.

"The wolf's all right, more or less. She's in the cathedral. She knocked something over and set off the alarms at the station. That's how they found her. That's the good news.... The bad news is, she seems to have killed someone." She sighed. "Mama, I'm sorry. You heard. I'll have to go."

"When will you eat? You have to eat."

"When I come back. I promise."

"I made lasagne this afternoon. See, I'll cover this and put it on the side here. You can warm it slowly when you get back."

Cecilia kissed her mother, picked up a fork, and helped herself to a small mouthful. *Lasagne con i funghi.* Cecilia stood still, lips closed, carefully savoring the morsel between tongue and palette.

"Mmm," she said at last. "It's good — but... porcini? Or not?"

Mama smiled. "I used a few, but it's mostly English field mushrooms. They're very good."

"It works, Mama! Much too good to rush. Let's do as you say. I'll enjoy it with a glass of wine when I get back."

Mama sighed. "I shall leave you half a bottle of decent Chardonnay in the fridge. Now go and do what you have to do!"

THREE

London. Sussex Gardens.
The home of Charlie Brown. The same evening.

Charlie Brown, sometime Woodward Scholar of Wadham College, Oxford, and presently Sir Isaac Newton Professor of Astronomy in the University of London, couldn't breathe.

He gasped and choked. Something was pressing down on him. Gritting his teeth — or at least trying to grit his teeth, since nothing he did seemed really to work — he managed at last, like forcing himself through mud, to stand upright.

Looming over him was the tower. The domed tower, with sun on it. He knew that tower. Where had he seen it? He couldn't recall, and as always there was no time for thought. Gusts of wind swept him forward like a stray leaf, past the domed tower toward a lofty door that opened as he approached, and the wind carried him through.

Into a hall. White and gold. White and gold everywhere. Floor black and white marble, like a chessboard. And pillars so huge he couldn't see around them. A painted ceiling, pale green and gold, so lofty he could only catch glimpses of it through mists that swirled over his head.

He'd been here before, of course. He knew what was coming. Here he was: the man in the long black robe, waiting for him.

Mist swirled round the robe as the man turned, and now Charlie saw his face, a kind face, with lines of sorrow. But behind the man there was something else, something dark.

"You must," the man said, his voice quiet but perfectly clear. "You must!"

"*Must what?*" Charlie tried to shout, but not a sound came from his throat. He was feeble, a shade, a ghost. He—

Woke up.

He had a crick in his neck, a dry mouth, and a splitting headache.

And the television was babbling at him. He'd fallen asleep in front of it.

But as always, what relief to be awake!

At least the Dream was gone.

It definitely had a capital D. When he was very little it came every two or three nights. Then the intervals had stretched to a week, then two weeks, then, when he was ten, to five or six. That was when Mickey the cat arrived. After that, the dream came rarely. Whether this had anything to do with Mickey the cat, he wasn't sure. Perhaps it did. But in any case, even rare appearances of the Dream were tormenting, and always he woke with relief.

As now.

Except that this time there was something *else* wrong. Something that wasn't the Dream.

Mickey the cat was dead.

He went to the bathroom, winced at the glimpse of his spiky hair in the mirror but didn't comb it. Put on his glasses. Went to the kitchen and drank some milk.

For over twenty years—amazing, really—Mickey the cat had been the one continuing presence in his life. First, through the death of his parents on November 14, 1990. They had been on the Alitalia Flight 404 that flew into a mountain, killing everyone on board and leaving him an eleven-year-old orphan. Then through various aunts and uncles with whom he'd stayed at various times. Through adolescence and growing up, getting and losing girlfriends, discovering that he was quite clever at some things and not at all clever at others. Through grammar school and university and academic successes and accolades. Through thoughts and theories of galaxies and suns. Through it all, whenever he came home, wherever home happened to be, there was Mickey the cat, trotting to meet him with tail upright like a black poker, purring on his lap, gazing at him with whiskery good will while he ate his dinner or watched television or read a book, jumping on his bed and patting his face to wake him up if he overslept.

Then, a week ago, Mickey the cat had some sort of stroke.

For seven days they struggled against it. The vet tried everything he knew, everything. But Mickey was old and finally the vet—a good man who knew his job and cared about his patients—said there was nothing more they could do for Mickey other than end his misery.

So they did.

The hypodermic was swift and, one supposed, merciful. Within a few seconds his old friend was just... a dead black cat. Charlie brought the body home and buried it in the back garden under the plane tree where Mickey liked to sit in the summer.

And that, it seemed, was that.

A dead black cat.

Ridiculous. Of all the miseries in the world, surely this ranked pretty low in the catalogue? One of his colleagues at the University had just lost his *son* to a roadside bomb in Afghanistan.

He looked at his watch. It was only eight. Much too early to go to bed.

He was cold.

He went to his bedroom to get a sweater.

There was Mickey's little bed by the dressing table, just like always. He hadn't had the heart to move it yet.

FOUR

Exeter. A few minutes later.

Cecilia drove into the Cathedral Close to find an assembly of police cars and flashing blue and white lights.

"This way, ma'am. We can go through the north door."

It was young Wilkins, who'd arrived fresh from the Police Training College on Monday. He seemed to be enjoying the excitement.

"DS Sims and a photographer are in the cathedral with the body, ma'am, and DS Jones and PC Venn are in the deanery taking statements."

"Good. All right then, constable. Lead me to the devastation."

She followed Wilkins toward the north door, which was open.

Some lights were on in the cathedral, but the nave was not particularly well lit, and it was a moment before she saw what might at first have been mistaken for a very large dog, lying in a doorway in the wall opposite her. Two constables were standing guard.

She walked across to them. The wolf was on her side, legs stretched out straight.

Alaskan timber wolf, the information sheet said. *Female. Aged two years, five months. Weight, 36 kilos. Height, 0.914 meters to the* shoulder. Name, Katie. Bred in captivity. Keeper: "She's just a big softy. If she isn't frightened she won't harm a fly."

Well, she certainly looked harmless enough at the moment.

"Good evening, Constable Jewell, Constable Langdon. This, I take it, is the alleged culprit?"

"Yes, ma'am."

"And you two are the ones who caught her?"

"Yes, ma'am."

"Good work. What exactly happened?"

"Well, ma'am, we came when the alarm went off and got in through the north door. We had the key, of course, but it was already open. We saw a light burning up at the altar, so we went there and found a hell of a mess…" He hesitated, glanced heavenward, and said, "Sorry!"

Who was he apologizing to? God? The blessed Virgin? The DI?

"Anyway, there was a mess, and in the middle of it we found the old man. Dead as a doornail. PC Jewell checked his vital signs, but it was obvious anyway. Not dead long, though. He was still warm."

"Beyond checking his vital signs, you didn't touch the body?"

"No ma'am. Definitely not, ma'am."

"Good."

"Anyway, then we heard a sort of snuffle and raced back here, and there was the wolf in this doorway, sort of cowering. We could see blood on it. So I kept watch in case it went savage again, while PC Jewell put in a call. Sergeant Stillwell was here in a few minutes and he put it under with a tranquilizing dart, and that was that. It'll be safe enough now, ma'am."

"And you reckon she killed the old man?"

"Looks like it, ma'am. It *is* a wild animal. And it's big."

Cecilia nodded and knelt. This close, she could see the rise and fall of the wolf's body as she breathed. The ear nearest — the left ear — was torn and bloody. And the constable was right. She was big.

"Can you shine your torch here, please?" Wilkins did as Cecilia asked, and she looked more closely.

"What do you think did that?" She pointed to the ear.

"I expect it was the victim trying to defend himself, ma'am. Grabbed hold of the beast's ear in his last desperate struggle."

Cecilia nodded.

While Wilkins followed her moves with the beam of the torch, she picked up each powerful foreleg in turn and peered at it, examining pads and claws. She turned to the wolf's head, pulling back the lips on each side so as to reveal first the dangerous-looking canines and then the rest of the teeth, gleaming white in the beam of the flashlight.

She stood up. "What happens to her now?"

"Well, ma'am, as she's turned killer, the people from the fair are bringing a vet to give a lethal injection straightaway. We'll keep an eye on her until then."

"I see. And you're sure you can keep her safe?"

"Oh, yes, ma'am. She should be out for a good hour yet. If she does start to wake up, we're to yell for Sergeant Stillwell and he'll give her another tranquilizer."

"All right, I leave her with you. But if the crowd from the fair turns up before I've got back to you, you're to tell them *not* to give her a lethal injection before I've had one more look at her. Is that clear? *Not* to inject her. I have something I need to check, and I do *not* want her put down until I've had time to do it."

He nodded. "Yes, ma'am. We'll tell them to hold everything."

"Good. All right, Wilkins, you can stay here. Give the others a hand if they need it."

"Yes, ma'am. Right, ma'am."

Cecilia walked the few meters to the south transept, turned left, and continued until she was opposite the carved gate that led to the sanctuary and the high altar. She paused and glanced west. She was looking at the longest piece of Gothic vaulting in the world, or so someone had told her. It was certainly magnificent. Even glorious. Here one could believe in God. And that, presumably, was the point of it.

She turned east toward the sanctuary, where the cathedral's lighting was supplemented by the bright theatrical brilliance of additional lights brought in for the photographer. The result was an odd mixture of gothic twilight and third-millennium glare. She stood, taking it in — stone columns and soaring arches, the sanctuary a pool of light, and at its center before the high altar, something dark and crumpled.

She sighed. Then she walked slowly forward through the carved gate and between the choir stalls.

The photographer was already at work, and DS Sims was making notes.

As she approached they looked up, and Cecilia nodded a greeting.

"Keith Berryman, isn't it?" she said to the photographer.

"Yes, ma'am."

She'd seen him before. He hardly looked old enough to be out of school, but she guessed he had to be in his twenties. "You're keeping your distance, I hope?"

"Yes, ma'am. I'm just to set up lights around the perimeter so as the deceased is well lit, and take some general pictures. Then I'll take what the Scene of Crime Officers tell me to take when they get here."

"I see they've not arrived yet."

"No, ma'am."

When she came to the altar rails she saw paint marks on the sanctuary floor, curious lines and swirls and symbols. Again she stopped.

"Satanism," Sims said. "Pentangle, circle, the lot. The old fellow was a Satanist. *That's* what he was up to. Be a hell of a job to clean it up."

Cecilia had heard of such things as this, but it was the first time she'd met them. She looked again at the paint marks, then looked up at the altar, and at last lowered her gaze to what lay before it.

An old man, broken and ruined.

She stared, taking in from where she stood the distorted features, the cruelly twisted body.

She looked at Sims.

"ID?"

"No, ma'am. Maybe we'll find out when we can touch the body."

She nodded and looked back at the victim.

"Did anyone *see* the wolf attacking him?"

"Well, no ma'am." Sims said. "When PCs Jewell and Langdon came because of the alarm, they found the corpse, and then the wolf with blood on it, and naturally they put two and two together."

"Blood on its ear. I see. And forensics is on the way."

"Yes, ma'am."

"All right, we leave everything as it is till they arrive. In the meantime, you could go and tell the vet to forget about lethal injections and treat the animal in whatever way she needs for that cut in the ear."

"But surely ma'am, if the creature's a killer—"

"She isn't. Sims, what's in front of us? What can we *see*?"

"A corpse, ma'am. An old man."

"And?"

"Well, the paint marks, ma'am—"

"*Besides* the paint marks, Sims! What about *the body*?"

"It's… it's dead, ma'am."

"Oh, yes, very dead. And that's *all* you can see?"

"Yes, ma'am."

"Right, and it's all *I* can see. *There's nothing else*. There's not a mark on the exposed parts. Not a bruise. Not a scratch. No blood. The robe isn't torn. Does that *look* like the work of a wild animal?"

Silence.

"Um... he could have fallen so as to hide the wounds, ma'am. They may be on parts of the body we can't see."

"Well, yes, he could. He could turn out to be a remarkably *tidy* corpse. And if forensics finds such discreetly placed wounds, we shall look again at our hypotheses. In the meantime, on the basis of what we *can* see, we have no evidence whatever of assault by a wild animal." She paused. "There's something else. I had a look at the wolf's teeth and claws as soon as I got here, and I half expected this when I found no sign of blood or cloth on them. So if the wolf killed him, how did she do it? Telepathy?"

Sims nodded. "Yes, ma'am. I see what you mean."

Cecilia looked back at the corpse. "For what it's worth, when forensics comes I'll lay you odds we're told the old man died of a heart attack. Look at the way he's fallen. His arms. The way he's clutching at his chest." Cecilia hesitated and then went on, thinking aloud. "Maybe he had a heart attack when he *saw* the wolf. It would have been a shock, seeing her suddenly, in the middle of the cathedral. Especially when he was up to no good himself."

"Yes, ma'am."

"Well, then, I'd appreciate it if you'd go and tell the fair crowd that while we've drawn no final conclusions yet—only the coroner can do that—it actually looks as though there's *been* no death by violence, in which case executing the alleged perpetrator would be a bit premature. After that, maybe you could call forensics again and say if they *are* intending to send some people tonight, or are maybe thinking of leaving it till later in the week, or maybe even *next* week, it'd be nice if they'd let us know. Then the rest of us could decide how to get on with our lives."

"Yes, ma'am. Right, ma'am."

"Thank you."

Sims started to go.

"You know where you went wrong, Sims?"

"I should have examined the wolf, ma'am."

"Before that. You went wrong because you got here with your mind made up." She relented. "We all do it sometimes. But the fact is, however obvious something may seem at first sight, if we can't show it, we don't know it. Simple as that."

"Yes, ma'am."

Sims disappeared rapidly in the direction of the dean's door. No doubt he was furious, furious at being lectured to, and especially furious at being lectured to by a young woman. Well, he'd just have to live with it.

She shook her head. *Focus.* What ought she to do now? Wait for forensics, she supposed.

She walked around the edge of the sanctuary. A scarlet and gold crucifix lay face down on the floor. Further away from the altar, a golden candlestick was on its side, obviously pair to the one on the altar. She stared at both, then at a carpetbag that lay at the side of the sanctuary.

She sighed.

Surely even wolves had a right to due process.

Remember San Francesco.

Where the hell was forensics?

FIVE

Heavitree Road Police Station. 7:00 a.m.

Sergeant Wyatt was already on the desk when Cecilia walked in the following morning.

"Good morning, ma'am."

She returned his smiled. "Good morning, sergeant."

Wyatt was an older man, approaching retirement, the son of a soldier. Cecilia figured he'd grown up with all the old British army jokes about Italian tanks having only two gears, reverse and fast reverse, and so on. So when she arrived a few months' back it had been pretty obvious from day one that he wasn't at all sure how he felt about having as his superior a female young enough to be his daughter whose last name ended in a vowel. Then one night a couple of weeks ago a trio of large young toughs with a grudge had jumped him in a road near the Heavitree station. They were starting to knock him about, as luck would have it, just as she was passing. She'd brought her car to a screeching halt, leapt out, and reduced two of them to moaning heaps in about fifteen seconds while he finished off the third. In the process she'd used a couple of Italian street-fighting tricks Papa had taught her—tricks that weren't in the police training manuals. The upshot of it all, she gathered, was that Sergeant Wyatt was now her fan, declaring to all and sundry that DI Cavaliere was "all right," even if she was Italian and female.

"Long day yesterday, ma'am! I gather they kept you hanging about the cathedral half the night."

"Well, yes, it did go on a bit. Still, at least it wasn't like Monday." On Monday she'd had to go out on a hit-and-run that had killed an eight-year-old. In the end the driver turned himself in. Even so, it was ghastly. "I hate it when it's a kid!"

"The day you *stop* hating it's probably the day to think about retiring, ma'am," Sergeant Wyatt said.

She nodded. Of course he was right.

She was hardly at her desk when the outside line started to flash.

"I'm afraid your ex is on the line again, ma'am," the woman on the switchboard said. "What do you want me to do?"

Damn. He'd already called three times, and so far she'd said she wasn't available.

"All right, I suppose I'd better find out what he wants. Thank you."

"Yes, ma'am."

A pause.

A click.

"Hello, Ceci. How are you?" It was the first time she'd heard his voice in… more than two years, surely? He sounded cheerful, even jocular.

"Hello, George. I'm fine, thank you."

"Ceci, it's so good to hear you. It's been too long. Look, I'm going to be in Exeter next week for a conference for the bank. I'll be staying at the White Hart. The thing is, I think there may still be one or two of my things in the house—things I forgot to take. So I thought perhaps I'd drop by one evening and we can check. And then afterwards we could pop out and have a drink together."

She sighed. "George, you took everything in the house that

was yours. Actually, I think you may have taken one or two things that weren't."

"Oh," he said, pleasantly enough, "well, if you're sure. It's just that I seem to be missing a few things, so I thought I'd check. Anyway, I can still take you out for that drink. What would be a good night for you?"

"George, why on earth would we do that?"

"Oh, come on, Ceci! After all that's happened we really *ought* to get together. It's been a long time. Look, I know the situation's awkward, but we were good together once. Why throw all that away?"

That was true. They *had been* good together, or she'd thought so.

But then Freja had arrived from Stockholm to negotiate an exchange of securities with George's bank. In the process, it seemed, George had negotiated her.

"George," she said, "does Freja know about this?"

"Freja? Ceci, this is nothing to do with Freja. This is about us."

"George, there isn't an 'us'. You ended 'us' when you left. Without warning."

"But Ceci, you still have a lot of unresolved anger. I can sense it even over the phone. Nurturing hostile feelings—it's not healthy, you should know that. I still care about you and frankly I'm worried about you."

She very nearly laughed. So now an Englishman was offering to show a southern Italian how to be in touch with her *feelings*?

In a way, of course, he was right. She was still angry. Angry and hurt.

But she doubted that could be resolved by a drink with George.

Unless maybe she broke the bottle on his head? That would show him she was in touch with her feelings.

"Ceci, are you still there?"

"Yes."

"So which evening would be best for you?"

"Best?"

"For a drink."

"Oh, that. Look, George, evidently you aren't getting this, though I can't think why. Anyway, I'll spell it out. Yes, I'm still angry with you on the rare occasions I think about it. Maybe I haven't read the right books, but I was under the impression even cads who leave their wives generally have the good manners to tell them."

"Ceci, what's past is past. You have to let it go. I did what I needed to do. You have to believe that. But we can still give each other a good time if we choose."

Her second phone line was alight and blinking at her.

"There's someone on my other line. I'll have to put you on hold."

She punched the flashing button. "DI Cavaliere."

"Sergeant Wyatt here, ma'am."

"How can we help, sergeant? Lost animals a speciality."

"Good one, ma'am! There's been a break-in at the off-license on Magdalen Road. There are officers there, but Superintendent Hanlon would like you to check it out."

"All right, Sergeant. I'll be there."

She looked back at the other button and realized how much she didn't want to press it. She thought she'd more or less held her own with George — yet the mere sound of his voice brought back that first misery. Misery she'd begun to get over — even to forget.

Damn. Damn. Damn.

She pressed the button.

"George?"

"Ceci."

She took a deep breath. "Look, George, the short and the long is, No, there's absolutely nothing in my house that's yours, and No, I won't let you take me out for a drink. Is that clear? I hope so, because now I have to go. I have a break in to investigate. Please don't telephone me again."

"Ceci, you're not hearing me."

"Oh *please*, George! That's it. That really is *it*. Oh—just one other thing. My name is Cecilia. Goodbye." She hung up, her hand trembling only slightly as she pushed the handset into its cradle.

She sighed, and sat for a few moments.

She'd actually caught a glimpse once of George with Freja: extremely tall, extremely well dressed, and extremely thin, with long blonde hair. He knew what it was like going to bed every night with an Italian sex goddess, and yet he preferred a Swedish beanpole?

According to Papa, that was just the problem. As he'd said to her one evening when he found her weeping, "*Bella*, you're more woman than George knows how to handle, and he's fool enough to think he *ought* to be able to 'handle' his woman. So he finds a Swedish beanpole less challenging. Simple as that! It isn't you that flunked. It's George."

Papa was, of course, hardly an unprejudiced observer.

She looked at her watch. She'd better go and do something about the Magdalen Road break-in.

Still, she reflected as she left her office and walked towards the stairs, it was nice to know someone still thought she was *bella*, even if he was prejudiced.

Six

University College, London. 11:00 a.m. The same day.

"All right then, let's call it a day. Thank you."

The class filed out, keeping their chatter low. They were nice kids.

The fact was, Charlie's lecture had been boring, and he knew it. What was worse, *they* knew it. Not that there was anything wrong with the content. He knew his stuff. But he hadn't *cared*. And if he didn't care, then why on earth should he expect them to?

And now here was Ms. Zaziwe L'Ouverture, graduate of the University of the West Indies, doctoral student and presently also his research assistant, standing by his desk waiting to see if he needed her. He liked Zaziwe very much and generally enjoyed working with her, but just at the moment he didn't want to deal with anybody.

"Okay, Zaziwe, I'm done here. Let's call it a day."

He gathered his notes from the lectern.

"You're repeating yourself, Dr. Brown. What's the matter?"

Charlie looked up at her.

"I'm fine, Zaziwe. Thank you for asking."

She folded her arms and stared at him.

"No you're not," she said.

Zaziwe had challenged him before, but never so bluntly and only on matters of physics. He shuffled his notes together, stuffed them into his computer case and zipped it. Eventually he had no excuse not to look up again.

She was still waiting.

How African she looked! An African princess! That Africa is the mother of all humanity was suddenly something more than an interesting hypothesis, or even, perhaps, an interesting fact. His own whiteness seemed frail and pathetic, his humanity a pale, insipid imitation of hers.

"All right," he said at last. "I'll tell you. But it's idiotic, really. Yesterday, well, I had to put my cat to sleep. I know — it's just a cat. But I've never been without him since I was a kid. And I feel terrible."

She cocked her head. "And you think that's idiotic?"

"Well, relatively speaking. I think of poor Ferguson, who's just lost his son — "

"Sorry, sir, I didn't know we were talking about Professor Ferguson's son. I thought we were talking about your cat."

"Well, yes, but it's ridiculous to be barely functioning just because a cat died — "

"Excuse me, sir, but…" She spoke slowly and distinctly. "*To love something may hurt, but it's never ridiculous.* That includes cats, by the way. And you can't measure out love by kilos. Or grief. So many kilos for a son, so many for a cat. It doesn't work like that."

He blinked at her.

"What's your cat called?"

"Mickey."

"So isn't it appropriate to be sad about losing Mickey, just like it's okay to be sad about losing any friend? Or a son?" She looked at her watch. "I'd better go, if you don't need me, sir. I said I'd meet Thaddeus for lunch."

"Of course."

Halfway to the door, she turned back.

"By the way, you're a Christian, aren't you, sir?"

"I am, actually."

"Well, sir, it says in the good book God will save man *and* beast, doesn't it?"

"I believe it does."

"So God won't have finished with Mickey yet, will he? Death doesn't have the last word. The best is still to come."

"Perhaps it is. I'll try to remember that. Thank you, Zaziwe."

"That's all right, sir. See you later."

He gazed at the door for several minutes after she left.

He'd known for some time that Ms. Zaziwe L'Ouverture from Barbados was brilliant.

But this was the first time he'd realized she was also wise.

Several hours later

Following a late afternoon seminar, Charlie went to his office to check his email and his answering machine. The Lilley Foundation grant he'd been waiting for had finally come through! The news was good — better than he had dared hope. Everything he'd asked for, including the most important thing: complete funding for him and for his two doctoral students.

He looked at his watch. It was late, already starting to get dark outside, but he had a feeling Zaziwe and Thaddaeus would still be around. The Culberton lab, perhaps?

He'd guessed right. There they were, beavering away. He smiled. The truth was, they were the best pair of doctoral students he'd ever had. He knew for a fact that Oxford and a couple of the American ivy leagues had done their best to get the two young West Indians, so he was pleased — and not a little flattered — that they'd chosen to work with him. He put his head around the door.

"May I interrupt?"

He told them the news, and they applauded.

"That's fantastic! *Everything* we asked for!"

"Good old Lilley Foundation! They must have had a brainstorm."

"Who cares?" Charlie said. "The thing is, ANU want us out there as soon as possible—by early next week, if we can. Are you still on?"

"Definitely!"

"Of course!"

The invitation from the Australian National University to use what was in some ways the best equipment on the planet had actually arrived three months ago.

"In particular, they've asked us to work with FLAIR," he'd told Zaziwe and Thaddeus. "Do you know what that is?"

"A bench-mounted fiber-fed spectrograph," Zaziwe said. "You can position it off the United Kingdom Schmidt telescope to access the *entire* 6.6-degree Schmidt field."

"I'm impressed," he said.

"Oh, I only know about it because there was an article in the *American Journal of Physics,* sir. I just happened to pick it up in the library for a bit of light reading."

Thaddaeus gazed at her fondly and then looked away, hiding a smile.

Zaziwe pressed on. "The thing is, you can get up to a hundred low dispersion spectra of stars and galaxies *simultaneously,* working down to about magnitude eighteen. It's brilliant."

Charlie swallowed his own smile and nodded.

So the invitation was accepted with excitement and alacrity.

But thanks to paperwork delays at Senate House, only now, with days to go, was financing finally confirmed. Still, it *was* confirmed, and that was the main thing.

"When do we leave?"

"Wednesday a.m. on QANTAS, I hope. Arrive Sydney

Thursday afternoon, Yanda Airlines to Coonabarabran, and then a quick fifty-mile walk through the outback to SSO."

"Fifty mile *what*?"

"That's a joke, Zaziwe. There'll be a bus. Anyway, Shawn's checked the agency and will book the tickets as soon as I call her. Which, given she's gone home, will now have to be tomorrow a.m. Let's meet here then."

"What on earth are Yanda Airlines?"

"Local."

"I take it with all this money of Lilley's we'll be traveling first class?"

"Dream on," Zaziwe said.

Charlie turned to leave.

Thaddeus went back to the computers, but Zaziwe caught Charlie at the door.

"It's good to see you smiling, sir. And you made a joke!"

"I'm feeling better, Zaziwe. And thanks — you helped."

Charlie walked slowly back to his office, gathered his papers, and started the short walk to the underground, and so home to an empty house. No one with welcoming meows and poker tail would be coming to greet him. No one would be fussing at him for their supper. There was a catch in his throat and he could feel tears starting in his eyes. But it was okay to mourn for Mickey the cat, and he wasn't going to apologize for it to anyone, not even to himself.

And now, of course, there was another side to the Oz trip. He'd been looking forward to it for the research opportunities it offered, but the fact was he was glad to be leaving the house in Sussex Gardens for a while. It would be good simply to be with colleagues in another place, to eat his meals in company, to be part of a little family.

So, like many a better man before him, he was glad to be going Down Under.

SEVEN

Exeter Crown Court. Friday, October 10.

Q uite how or why the wolf had got into the cathedral was impossible to say. In one sense the "how" was clear enough, for the north door was still open when the police arrived. But the precise sequence of events that brought her there remained a mystery. Of course it was easy to theorize: to suggest, for example, that Katie, trying to return to the fair and getting as far as the High Street, might have bolted into the close; how then voices or a car starting might have driven her further toward the silence of the cathedral where, finding the north door open, she plunged through it.

Whatever drew her there, by the time Katie jumped onto the high altar she was surely confused and frightened. Faced by a nasty little flame and a sweaty, bawling man, she appeared to have shied from the flame and in doing so backed into one of the altar candlesticks, sending it to the floor and triggering the alarms at Heavitree Road Police Station.

In the light of what evidence there was, that, or something like it, could reasonably be conjectured.

What did not appear, however, was any evidence that the wolf had attacked Nikos Kakoyannis. Quite the contrary.

"You are certain, then, that the deceased met his end by what you would describe as natural causes?"

In view of the strange circumstances surrounding Kakoyannis's death, the coroner had ordered a post mortem. Dr. James Boswell, who conducted it, was perfectly clear. The deceased had died of a heart attack, the result of immense strain followed by sudden shock.

"And you saw no signs of assault by a wild animal?"

"None whatsoever. Of course the mere sight of the wolf in those extraordinary circumstances could have been enough to bring on the victim's heart attack, and that, I surmise, is what happened. Upon his person, however, it is clear that the wolf itself laid not so much as a claw. The creature should, so to speak, leave this court without a stain upon its character." Dr. Boswell fancied himself something of a wit. He glanced, as he spoke, at the couple of local reporters in attendance.

"So that's all right," DS Sims said in the pub afterwards, supping the pint that DI Cavaliere had just placed in front of him. "Death by natural causes it is." He seemed to have got over his snit in the Cathedral.

Cecilia smiled. She was feeling indulgent.

"There's still the matter of the crucifix, though. Obviously it didn't affect the manner of death. But I'm puzzled, all the same."

When the police arrived at the cathedral, they'd found lying on the ground not only one of the candlesticks but also the crucifix that normally dominated from a stand behind the high altar. But Katie could only have moved the crucifix by knocking down the stand on which it rested, and the stand was unmoved. Not only that, but the crucifix was undented.

"You see what that means?" she said.

"He must have moved it himself, ma'am. A Satanist wouldn't want Jesus on the cross staring at him, would he?"

"But if he did that why didn't he set the alarms off, the way Katie did when she knocked over the candle? They were all on the same system."

"There must be a fault in the system."

"The manufacturers say not. According to them they've checked thoroughly and it's working perfectly. And they say there's no way to beat it."

DS Sims supped his pint and looked thoughtful. Finally he said, "Well ma'am, it seems to me both those things can't be true. Either there *is* something wrong with the system, or else there *is* a way to beat it, and the old boy knew what it was."

Cecilia smiled. "I agree. And unfortunately we can't ask him."

The economy, national and international, and the American presidential election campaign were between them dominating the news that week, and so Kakoyannis's death and the inquest made scarcely a paragraph in the nationals and only the inside pages even of the west country press. The *Express and Echo*'s reporter did draw his editor's attention to Boswell's *bon mot* in court.

"Who gives a damn if wolves have stains on their characters?" The editor settled on DEVIL WORSHIP LEADS TO CATHEDRAL DEATH—with its vague implication that somehow or other the Church of England was to blame for the whole thing—as altogether more appealing.

EIGHT

Heathrow Airport. Monday, October 13.

Charlie Brown looked at his watch and nodded. So far, so good! The minibus he'd ordered had arrived on time. The driver had known the way to the airport, and even how to find the right terminal. There had been no traffic jams, the minibus had not broken down, and here they were waiting at the check-in, actually fifteen minutes earlier than necessary. It was not, of course, that nothing could now go wrong. But he did have the luxury of reflecting that whatever went wrong at this point, it would almost certainly be the airline's problem, not his.

The line moved slowly forward.

Zaziwe was checking in.

Thaddeus.

"See you in the duty-frees!" Hand in hand, they disappeared.

They went well together. When he first realized they were an item, he'd wondered how Thaddeus might deal with the fact that good though he was, Zaziwe was proving to be better. The perceived problem had turned out to be no problem at all. Thaddeus seemed proud of his girlfriend's superior abilities and sometimes introduced her as "the one with the brains." Charlie found it endearing.

And now he was at the counter. Electronic boarding pass, passport, all were in order. He started off after them into the overseas departure terminal.

He didn't hurry. Thaddeus and Zaziwe would find him when they needed him, and he reckoned the duty-frees were a rip-off anyway.

Oh, there they were. Laughing together at something they'd seen on the shelves.

Of course, rip-off or not, the Duty Frees would no doubt be more fun with a girlfriend.

A lot more fun.

NINE

Ministry of Defense Research Establishment,
Harton Down, near Exeter. Tuesday, October 14.

James Drew was something of a raconteur, especially among the lab techs. At the precise moment when he felt the tap on his shoulder he was in mid-flow — indeed, in mid-sentence — of a particularly good story.

"Yes?" He turned to find himself faced by Wheatley — Dr. Henry Wheatley, world-ranking scientist, leading researcher into the art of biological warfare, and vastly his senior. "Yes, sir?"

"Excuse me," Wheatley said. "May I see that?"

"Oh, this!" Wheatley was pointing to a copy of the latest *Express and Echo*, which was, as it happened, jutting from Drew's lab-coat pocket. Drew pulled out the paper, which was folded to the editorial page, and being of a tidy mind he started to refold it.

"No, no. Leave it. That's exactly what I wanted to see."

"Oh, sorry. Here you are, sir." Drew gave him the paper, and waited. Dr. Wheatley was not noted for his interest in popular journalism or, indeed, anything else that did not bear directly on his work. He handled the paper now like a tech handling an unpleasant specimen, scanning the editorial quickly, his lips pursed.

"Thank you." He handed the paper back, nodded, and left.

Drew looked after him for a moment, turned back to his friends, and shrugged. He'd quite lost the thread of his story.

That evening, driving toward his home on the outskirts of Exeter, Henry Wheatley stopped at a newsagent. When he returned to the car he held a copy of the paper he had borrowed along with copies of all the other papers. He shut the car door but did not immediately drive on. Instead, in failing light, he sat and read all that the press could tell him of the life and death of Nikos Kakoyannis. It was not much, but it was enough to interest him.

The wolf by no means came out of the affair scot-free. In addition to the cut on her ear, Katie seemed to have picked up a virus. Within days of returning to her cage she began to mope: her nose was dry, her eyes dull, and her appetite nonexistent. Just as her keeper was about to call the vet, she seemed to recover. But then, the fair having meantime moved to Hampstead Heath, she became ill again. This time a vet was called. She prescribed antibiotics for Katie and was against her travelling. So it came about that when the fair moved again, Katie found herself convalescing in an isolated enclosure in the London Zoo.

TEN

"We know then," Reginald Hargrove MP said, "that the method exists. We have, ah, good reason to suppose that this fellow, ah, Kakoyannis found it. The question that remains is, can we gain access to his knowledge?"

"Precisely," Henry Wheatley said, with a glance at the others gathered around the boardroom table.

The governing body of the Academy for Philosophical Studies was assembled at his request. The setting was elegant. Artificial fire logs blazed and crackled beneath the handsome mantel. From beyond richly curtained windows he could hear faintly the hum of London traffic. His colleagues had listened to the results of his research for the better part of an hour, from details of Kakoyannis's career to details of the final scene in the cathedral, pieced together from newspaper reports and discreetly obtained local gossip. He pointed — using a report lifted from the police's own computer — to inquiries regarding a cross that had been moved and a sophisticated alarm system that had inexplicably failed. All, he claimed, pointed in one direction. The expressions of his three fellow board members suggested that they, at least, agreed with him.

The chairman said nothing. As was his custom he watched and he listened.

"There are, I think, two stages," Wheatley said. "First, the Book of the Ritual. We know that Kakoyannis was looking for it. The fact that he undertook the ceremony suggests he found it. That book we must have."

"Do we know where it is?" Tom Hutton, engineer by trade: tough, stocky, elbows on the table, work-worn fingers scratching his ear.

"I think we've a very clear idea." Wheatley touched one of his files and smiled. "A small black book is listed among Kakoyannis's effects in the police report. And the description fits—such as they give. Clearly they didn't examine it properly, for which we may thank them."

"Then we must devise some means of, ah, obtaining possession of it."

This from Reginald Hargrove M.P. Dignified and portly.

Wheatley nodded. "Exactly."

"How?" Maria Coleman, tall, handsome, immaculately groomed, CEO in one of the city's two largest advertising agencies.

"I shall ask for it."

"*What?*"

Wheatley smiled. "I shall go to the police and ask for it. I am a scholar. So was Kakoyannis. Why should I not have lent him a notebook? And why should I not claim it back?"

A frontal attack. Certainly Wheatley had nerve.

Hutton was nodding. "It might work, at that."

"You may both have been scholars, but you were hardly in the same *fields*." Coleman again.

"One may take an interest as an amateur in a field other than one's own. And in any case—" Wheatley was smiling, "how should children distinguish the metaphysic of Plato from that of Aristotle?"

"That's all very well, but there's still a hell of a difference between biological warfare and what *he* was up to."

Still, Wheatley's point remained.

There was a pause.

Hargrove broke the silence.

"And you are saying, Dr. Wheatley, that if we obtained the book along lines devised by you, we should then, as the board of this academy, be in a position to perform the, ah, Ceremony of Power?"

"That's what I'm saying. We could perform the ceremony."

"And yet..." The others all looked at Coleman. "Shouldn't we still need to find the right place? A focus of power? As Kakoyannis did?"

"I don't think so." Wheatley was here sure of his ground. "You're right about the need for a focus, of course. But there's more than one kind. Kakoyannis needed a major site because he worked alone. Nothing else would do. And that caused him a lot of problems. To start with, in this country it inevitably meant a site contaminated with Christian superstition."

"Not inevitably," Coleman said.

"Well, all right. Not inevitably. But in general that's the case. And Kakoyannis, at any rate, chose a Christian site — which, I suspect, destroyed him. Then he had the problem of timing. Need for secrecy limited his choice of time. The night he selected was possible for the operation, but only just. Another disadvantage. Now compare our position." Wheatley was leaning forward. "We shan't be working alone. We shall be five, and one of us" — his voice dropped slightly, and he glanced respectfully toward the chairman — "a Master. This means that we already *are*, in ourselves, a focus of power." He was speaking more loudly again. "If we get the book, we can use a center that has only minor power. We could use our own center, pure of superstition. And we could choose the perfect time."

He sat back.

"What if we don't get the book?" Hutton again. "Suppose we can't manage it? Or it's the wrong one?"

This, the chairman decided, was becoming a waste of time. What needed to be said had been said.

"Almost certainly it is the right book," he said. "You are, however, too sanguine. This is still an on-going investigation, and the police would not normally hand over evidence." He turned to Wheatley, who started to protest. "You need not comment, it is as I say. They would not *normally* hand it over. In this case, they will. I know someone at Exeter. You shall have the book."

ELEVEN

Heavitree Police Station. Friday, October 17.

"It's not on the computer, ma'am."

Cecilia had asked one of the secretaries to run off hard copy for her of the entire Kakoyannis file. Perhaps some new thought would strike her. And if it didn't, perhaps she really should relegate the crucifix puzzle to the realm of the inexplicable but probably harmless and turn her attention to other things.

"What do you mean? It has to be."

"Apparently it's been deleted, ma'am."

That, of course, could happen. Anyone could make a mistake. What was less likely was what followed.

"Then get on to the computer boffins and have them find it on the mainframe," she said. "I need it." She knew perfectly well that virtually nothing on a computer tied into a mainframe is ever irretrievably lost. Weeks, months, even longer, and still it lurks in cyberspace, ready to be found by those who know how to look.

Only this time it didn't.

"I'm sorry Cecilia, but it's gone," Joseph Stirrup said when he called her with the news. "It's really *gone*! If you want an explanation, then I'm left with two possibilities. *Either* for some reason every new piece of data that went onto the mainframe last week decided to land on that piece of disk, and so eliminate your file — which is impossible if not absurd. *Or* — which is what really must have happened — someone has hacked in. And they're good. Beyond good! Because they've stripped out *every* piece of data relating to your file *and* covered their tracks. The encryption is first rate. At present I can't do a thing with it. And I reckon *I'm* pretty good."

Cecilia nodded. She knew very well that Joseph was good. Joseph was a young Bahamian, confined to a wheelchair by the car crash that killed his parents when he was thirteen. As if the universe were somehow making up for the blow, his mental and analytical skills had developed to a phenomenal level. Cecilia truly believed there was *nothing* within a computer's capability that Joseph couldn't do.

"So there's no way to trace who did it?"

"I never said that. I said, 'At present I can't do it.' But there's always a way through, if you have the patience. No one can do this sort of thing without leaving a footprint somewhere. And I'll find it. I'll spend every spare minute I've got on it, and I'll nail the scum if it takes me a year. But it might. I'm going to have to do this the hard way."

Cecilia nodded again. The best detective work is a little like the best scholarship: a desire to find the evidence and show what it means that amounts at times to a kind of madness. She recognized it in Joseph because she had it herself.

"Okay, Joseph. Thanks. I guess I'll hear from you when you've got something."

She could sense Joseph's smile. "I won't be able to get to you fast enough!"

So there it was.

Until the hacking, there had been nothing she could actually put a finger on. Not a single item in the inventory of which she could say, with absolute conviction, "This cannot be, without villainy afoot!" Now there was. All right, she didn't know what kind of villainy, but clearly it was serious enough to inspire a criminal act executed with cleverness and daring.

She grimaced.

There only remained the small matter of finding out what it was.

TWELVE

The same morning.

I n some things, Henry Wheatley was as good as his word.
The day following the board meeting he walked into the
Exeter police station, produced his credentials, and claimed
acquaintance with the deceased, a former colleague albeit an
eccentric one. It was a sad business—a brilliant mind gone
awry. Were there, by any chance, next of kin to whom assistance
should be given? Apparently not. Ah—regrettable. Alone in the
world then. That was how these things happened. Well, never
mind. He was sure the police had done everything possible.

There was one thing he had intended to mention with regard
to the dead man's belongings. A book.

"A book, sir?"

"Yes, just a small thing, rather old. Black covers. It contained
some philosophical and theological speculations. In Aramaic
and Hebrew. I lent it to Kakoyannis at a conference we attended
some months ago. It seemed to be the sort of thing that interested him. Unfortunately, I neglected to put my name in it. But
it's mine and I'd rather like to get it back if I could. Any chance
it's turned up?"

The constable on duty checked.

"There does seem to be a book, sir."

Examination revealed that the book answered to the description Dr. Wheatley gave. It contained no name. He had risked this, sure that no one would be so foolish as to connect himself, even in writing, with such a rite as this book contained.

"I'll pass your request to Superintendent Hanlon, sir," the constable said. "He's the one who can release it for you. I dare say you'll hear in a couple of days."

Wheatley was all urbanity. Of course he understood. He would look forward to hearing from the superintendent. He thanked the constable politely and left.

Wheatley's story held. There were no other claimants for anything that belonged to Nikos Kakoyannis. There remained, however, the unanswered question about the deleted file. The chairman had been right. The unresolved question meant that the death of Kakoyannis was still, technically, an ongoing investigation. So when Wheatley's request for immediate access to the book came to Hanlon's desk that afternoon he was about to turn it down. Wheatley could wait until the investigation was pronounced complete, whenever that was —

Hanlon's telephone rang.

"Superintendent Hanlon," he said.

"I know," the voice on the other end said, "and Hanlon — *Superintendent* Hanlon — you know very well who I am."

"Yes."

"And you know you are in our debt."

"Yes."

"Good. What we need is a quite simple. There is a form of authorization on your desk, for release of a notebook to a Dr. Wheatley. Sign it."

"The book's evidence in an ongoing investigation. I—"

"Dr. Wheatley is a senior person holding a senior government post. It will be entirely proper to release his property to him when he needs it. It would be quite wrong to inconvenience an important man over a detail that is almost certainly a result of police incompetence. Do you understand?"

"Yes."

"Then sign the release."

"Of course."

There was a click, and the line went dead.

Hanlon sighed with relief. He'd feared for a moment that the request might be for something much worse. And of course it was right for a man like Dr. Wheatley to have his book.

He signed.

The same day, Henry Wheatley was summoned by telephone to collect that which he claimed. Of course, he would have to be responsible for it, and in the event of any dispute... but Dr. Wheatley quite understood. He signed the appropriate documents, carefully placed the precious notebook in his briefcase, locked it, and left.

THIRTEEN

That afternoon.

The adventures of Katie, like much else in police work, required a report. Cecilia Cavaliere tackled it as she tackled most things, carefully and thoughtfully. And it was almost by accident that she learned what had happened to the book. The circumstances as described sounded reasonable enough, and the idea that a scientist of Wheatley's stature would be involved in criminal activity was, on the face of it, absurd.

But the fact remained that there was still an ongoing investigation. So why had the book been let go? Surely Wheatley could have — *should* have — been told to wait? So who'd let it go? Hanlon would have the authority to do it. But why would he?

There was an anomaly here, in fact there were two anomalies, and anomalies made Cecilia uncomfortable.

"Is there anything else, ma'am?"

"Oh!" She had been standing there, thinking. "Sorry, Constable! Well, yes, there is one other thing. Do you happen to know who authorized the release?"

"Superintendent Hanlon, ma'am."

She thanked him and hung up. Hanlon, whatever his faults, was a stickler for procedure. So what the hell was going on?

She shook her head.

It was time to go home.

She tidied the papers on her desk and went to take her coat from the hanger.

Then it dawned on her. It wasn't just the anomalies that were nagging at her. It was the name Henry Wheatley. She had a good memory for names. She always had. And she didn't think it was letting her down now. Somewhere, somehow, she'd heard that name before, and not in connection with anything good.

A trial?

A murder trial?

And even if she were right, was that *this* Henry Wheatley?

At last she went back to her desk and called Detective Sergeant Verity Jones. Little Miss Perfect! Verity Jones had been allocated to CID six weeks ago. Small and fair, so immaculate and *à la mode* was she at all times that Cecilia at first decided she'd have been better placed in a fashion house or a boutique. She'd quickly learned that Verity Jones also had a sharp, inquiring mind, a first in classics from Oxford, and no fear whatever of hard work.

"That's right, Verity. W-H-E-A-T-L-E-Y. Anything you can find. Where he's worked, appointments, interests. The lot. You can start with *Who's Who*, I should think. All right? And one other thing, I think he may once have been a witness in a murder trial. Quite a prominent one, if I'm right. Otherwise I don't see why I'd remember it."

"Yes, ma'am. I'll get onto it first thing."

What an asset to the department Verity Jones was! Cecilia had more or less persuaded Verity's parents—quiet, scholarly folk who'd brought up their daughter to take a quiet, scholarly job and so were appalled by her career choice—that there was important work to do here and colleagues to work with who were not unworthy of their child. She just hoped she'd been right. And prayed to God they never learned that

Superintendent Hanlon had tried to grope Verity Jones just as he tried to grope anything female that moved.

Cecilia grinned. She'd not been there, but the story had gone round. Little Miss Perfect, petite and fashionable, had said "DON'T do that, sir!" in cut-glass tones that effectively caught the attention of everyone within twenty meters. At the same time she'd riveted Hanlon with (in Sergeant Wyatt's phrase) "a look that would have paralyzed a bloody basilisk." It evidently paralyzed Hanlon, who presumably wouldn't be in a hurry to try that again.

Cecilia had had no such problem over her career choice. Mama and Papa were proud of her work, and Papa's family had a long history of such service. A Cavaliere had taken part in the charge of the mounted Carabinieri at Grenoble in 1815 that shattered the French line and led the Italian colors to victory. Another was in the charge at Pastrengo in 1848 that saved King Carlo Alberto from the Austrians. Another was among the Carabinieri who helped capture Rome in 1871 so that it might become the capital of Italy. And last but by no means least, in World War II a young Andrea Cavaliere — who would have been Cecilia's great-grand uncle — had been killed in action serving with the second Carabinieri cadet battalion in Rome, gallantly defending *la bandiera Italiana* when, against hopeless odds, the Carabinieri had been one of only two units in the Italian army to resist the German occupation.

With such a family history, naturally she'd want to serve in the *forza publicca* of the country where they now found themselves.

And with such a family history she surely *ought* to be able to get to the bottom of whatever the hell was going on…

Whatever *that* was.

FOURTEEN

Sunday, October 19. Coonababaran National Park,
New South Wales, Australia.

"**B**limey!"

"Now *that* I call impressive!"

The minibus had topped a small rise, and there before them, white in the sunlight, were the two domes of Siding Springs Observatory, one seeming to rise directly out of the trees, the other standing high on a cylindrical tower.

"It should be." Charlie was smiling. "In some ways it's the best facility in the world."

In that earlier project, now some years back, he'd certainly had reason to know. He'd been involved with the observatory's Two-Degree Facility, which quite aside from its innovative technologies was still the largest and most complex instrument of its type on the planet. And how they'd used it! In the course of five nights they'd succeeded in observing and analyzing over a thousand quasars and four thousand galaxies. Nobody before had ever managed to observe and analyze so many objects in such a short time. Certainly without 2dF it would have taken years. Equally certainly, his own contribution to that analysis was what had clinched him his chair at the university—as well, no doubt, as securing the current invitation for him and his students to work with FLAIR.

Thaddeus and Zaziwe were excited at sight of the domed tower, as well they might be. So was he. Or at least he would have been, except the Dream had come back last night, and as always—

Hold on!

The domed tower!

The tower of his Dream, the tower he always knew he'd seen before but could never recall!

How could he *not* have remembered?

It was the tower that stood before him.

The tower of the Anglo-Australian Observatory.

He drew a sharp intake of breath—so sharp that Thaddaeus looked back.

"You okay, Dr. Brown?"

Charlie forced a smile. "Just excited!"

But he wasn't okay.

So was the dream about something he'd found at the observatory, or was going to find? He shook his head. His subconscious was surely muddling things that ought not to be muddled.

The dream had depressed him as always. But now its breaking through into the fabric of his life, his real life, the fabric of his work, the fabric of his passion—that alarmed him.

He must pull himself together. Apart from anything else, he had students depending on him.

He tightened his lips resolutely and looked around him.

Low buildings reared from the forest on either side of the road. The minibus was turning left into a courtyard. There it stopped.

"We're here," he said.

Why did one always say that, when one could not possibly be anywhere else?

Zaziwe and Thaddeus got out of their seats.

Welcome to the Land of Oz.

Damn that dream.

FIFTEEN

Monday, October 20.

The promised report on the life and works of Henry Wheatley was on Cecilia's desk before lunchtime.

Career at grammar school impeccable, crowned with an open scholarship to Wadham College, Oxford. Gained something of a reputation as a marksman at the university shooting club, but academic career as an undergraduate somewhat disappointing, finished with a Second. But then brilliant research paper led to widespread recognition.

From which, Cecilia gathered, Henry Wheatley never looked back.

Among his many impressive positions was his current post with the Ministry of Defense, which involved the highest possible security clearance. There was no record of his ever having had any connection with a murder trial either as a witness or in any other capacity.

The detective sergeant had attached a note:

> As you know, our computerized records don't yet go back before 1985: but in view of your age and Wheatley's, that surely ought to be enough in this case?

Incidentally, DS Sims, who is addicted to reading the grizzlier nineteenth-century murder trials, informs me that there *was* a Henry Wheatley of Old George, Mortlake, who appeared as witness for the prosecution in the trial for murder of Kate Webster, accused and subsequently convicted of the murder of her employer, Mrs. Thomas. Cut her up in little pieces and put her in a box. As this happened in 1879, I doubt it's much help. Sorry.

So much for *that* idea.

And just what, exactly, did little Miss Perfect mean by *in view of your age*?

The inspector shrugged and went to lunch.

Yet her doubt was not allayed. She *had* seen Wheatley's name somewhere. Somewhere suspicious. And *not* in the record of a nineteenth century murder trial.

But where?

Her question persisted throughout the day and into the evening.

She sat in the armchair by the window, an unread book on her knee, and gazed into space. Figaro gazed at her thoughtfully, then came and sat on her feet. It didn't help.

At half-past nine Papa came round. He looked tired, and had obviously called just to make sure that she was all right but she told him her problem anyway. They spoke Italian, and what she had to say sounded even vaguer and more farfetched than it had in English.

"Why don't you pay this fellow Wheatley a visit?" he said when she'd finished. "Then you'll get a feel for him. You have strong instincts about people, and they're usually right."

She nodded slowly.

"Well, yes, Papa. I could do that."

Of course, to ask the kind of questions she needed to ask,

based on no evidence, would require permission from her superior officer.

Damn.

Yet her doubts remained, and Papa's suggestion the only way she could see of doing anything about them.

SIXTEEN

Heavitree Police Station. Wednesday, October 22.

Superintendent Hanlon was destined for great things and in the meantime occupied a position already too small for his many talents. Of all this he assured his subordinates so often that it was impossible they should either doubt or forget it. He had dark, curly hair, a winning smile, and a nice body. He'd been to an expensive school and to Cambridge. He had friends in high places and a beautiful wife. He regularly said all the right things about the contribution of women to good policing and the importance of equality of opportunity.

At their initial interview when she came to work for him Cecilia hoped he'd be all right. Now she knew her instinct that he wasn't had been right. Since he was her superior officer, she in any case owed him respect, loyalty, and obedience, and these she would still give, only slightly modified by the fact that she regarded him as a treacherous toad.

Her appointment was for 10:00 a.m. Knowing that he would keep her waiting for up to an hour—this time it was forty-five minutes—she scheduled no next appointment and tucked a book into her shoulder bag.

Hanlon had no apology for keeping her waiting but was all friendly grins and good humor as he waved her to a chair.

"Good morning, Cecilia! Or—of course, these days I should say, good morning, *Inspector*! Everyone tells me you're doing very well. I'm pleased. And I'm really glad we managed to get it through for you."

She said, "Thank you, sir."

It wasn't easy.

Because this, of course, was the treacherous toad part. The truth was, her promotion a couple of months ago had been a close-run thing, but not for the reason he implied. She too, as it happened, had friends in high places (well, one friend, who'd once been Papa's student) and so she knew that Hanlon had fought her promotion tooth and nail, until he was finally over-ruled by the Chief Constable of the Devon and Cornwall Constabulary.

"Well, Cecilia, what seems to be the problem? How can we help you?"

"I'm afraid I need to question Henry Wheatley, sir."

She explained her suspicions as best she could. Unfortunately, even though she never specifically mentioned the superintendent, she could hardly avoid implying how contrary to normal procedure it had been that *someone* had released evidence pertaining to the ongoing investigation. She sensed Hanlon's mounting defensiveness even before he spoke. His mouth was tightening. This was a mistake. She ought to have known—

"Cecilia, I really am not at all sure that I can allow this. Dr. Wheatley holds a top-secret, senior government post. It was entirely proper to release his property to him. And we really cannot allow ourselves to harass an important man such as this just because of something that will probably turn out to be just a matter of police incompetence."

"I see. So I'm to understand that he couldn't have got his book back and it would have been all right to harass him if he *wasn't* important?"

The words were out before she could stop them. She was at

once aware of his sharp intake of breath. She'd blown it. She'd surely blown it. How *could* she be so —

Brrrrrrrrring!

Hanlon, now looking at her as though he could chew up nails and spit out rust, snatched up the phone, said, "I told you —" and then was clearly interrupted by someone *far* more important than he was.

What followed was something Cecilia could not have hoped for. Even from where she sat she could hear the angry voice, although she could not hear what it was saying. Still, it was evident that someone was (as Sergeant Wyatt would have put it) giving Hanlon a right bollocking, and didn't care who heard it.

Hanlon was squirming in his chair.

"Yes sir... of course sir.... I quite understand sir...."

Cecilia, to tell the truth, was doing a bit of squirming on her own account. She looked up at the ceiling. She looked down at the floor. And all the time she was struggling not to chortle.

Hanlon finally managed to get in a "Just one moment sir" — and then, surely eager to get rid of her at any cost, said, "All right, Cavaliere, do your interview if you must. But be discreet. I don't want any trouble about it. I want that understood."

"Oh yes sir! Of course, sir. Discretion's the word!" *Yes, sir! Yes, sir! Three bags full sir! Grazie a Dio!*

She went back to her office and at once emailed him that she would "act promptly on your recommendation that I interview Henry Wheatley" — thus covering her back should he change his mind or forget what he'd said. (Sergeant Wyatt had taught her a rather more vivid expression for it.)

That done, she decided to take an early lunch.

Mind you, she'd have loved to know what the bollocking was about.

Maybe Sergeant Wyatt would know.

Maybe it was about Hanlon's releasing the book to Wheatley in the first place? He had, after all, ignored procedure. Maybe someone had noticed? Someone who mattered? Someone who wasn't as sensitive about frustrating important people as Superintendent Hanlon was? Actually, that was another puzzle. Hanlon had sounded like an automaton when he trotted out his ridiculous explanation. Did even he really believe it? And if not, why on earth had he released the book? She shook her head. There were too many questions here.

Like the sensible Italian she was, she would go and eat.

SEVENTEEN

London. The same morning.

It was a brilliant autumn day, mild enough for spring. Sparrows chirped around the pavements and gutters of the Bayswater Road. Taxis and buses answered with cheerful honks and growls. On the steps of the academy stood the chairman. It was not his habit to leave the building during the morning and he was not entirely sure why he had done so now. He looked at the elegant Victorian terrace houses opposite him, then along to his right at the trees in Hyde Park, visible at the end of the road, dark, leafless, and barren against the sky — or rather apparently barren, for doubtless life still lurked within them. Directly opposite him were two pretty children with a young woman, the children gleefully riding little scooters in the sunshine. In vain the young woman kept cautioning them — "Be careful, darlings! Not too near the edge, darlings! Mind other people, darlings!" — in vain, for she herself could not help laughing with them in their pleasure, and so her messages were hopelessly mixed. And the "other people" were smiling, happy to step aside and make way for the joy in their midst.

The chairman shook his head. He was glad that from here he could not see into the park itself. He did not like parks, for many things grew in them. He did not like things that grew. He did not like children.

So he stood, looking at the children and meditating his dislike.

Then, as if from nowhere, there came the blue butterfly. Quite *how* it came was a mystery. It was surely the wrong time of year and the wrong place. The color—glowing, iridescent—was fitter for the blazing noontide of a tropical island than an autumn day in London. Yet there it was, fluttering delicately in pale sunlight.

The chairman caught his breath, entranced. To his amazement it came to him. Like a gift, like a benediction, like the breath of an angel, it flew closer and closer until at last it settled, trusting, upon his sleeve. He gazed at it, marveling. It was exquisite: a tiny living jewel, innocent, vulnerable, perfect, its wings trembling, its antennae moving gently. Never, it seemed, had he seen anything more graceful or more beautiful. He smiled. His hand closed over it. Now he could feel the dainty flutter of its wings against his palm, and even, he fancied, the touch of its antennae. His smile broadened. Slowly, slowly, savoring the moment, he pressed his hand against the cloth.

The sparrows continued to chirp. The taxis and buses honked and growled. The young woman and her children went on their way.

Still smiling broadly, the chairman turned and went back into the academy, brushing the tiny ruin from his sleeve.

EIGHTEEN

Exeter. Wednesday evening, October 22.

That evening Cecilia Cavaliere made her visit to Henry Wheatley, taking with her PC Wilkins, who would doubtless benefit from the experience.

Wheatley's was a large, handsome three-storey house, dating from the 1930s and set back from the road. The drive leading up to it was occupied — in effect, blocked — by a blue Lexus LS 600h L sedan. Cecilia parked her own car in the road, and together she and PC Wilkins walked up to the house.

Henry Wheatley quickly made clear the enormous value of his time, and the extent to which he was inconvenienced by unnecessary and thoughtless interruptions. But Cecilia was long past being put off her stride by such a display as that. Indeed, she noticed in herself a tendency on such occasions to slow down rather then speed up. The truth was, it amused her to play the plodding, slow-witted police officer.

"I know sir, these things *are* irritating for all of us. I always think that death is *very* annoying and inconvenient. But, just a few questions, sir. I understand you'd lent a book to Kakoyannis? A notebook that was found among Kakoyannis's effects?"

"Yes, Inspector. I've already told your colleague at the station all this. And your superintendent released the book to my care."

"Yes, of course, sir. But if you'll just indulge me a moment or two longer. You did lend this book to Kakoyannis, then?"

"I just said so."

"Yes, sir. Quite right, sir! Thank you, sir. And when would that have been?"

"Oh, about a year ago. I don't keep a record of these things, you know."

"Of course not, sir. Very understandable. And you were both — where?"

A fraction of a second's hesitation? Of course, he could just be trying to remember.

"We were at a conference together. On religion and science. Organized by the Academy for Philosophical Studies in London. Last... June? I remember now — of course. It was last June."

"Thank you, sir. That's most helpful. You have a note of that, Constable?"

"Yes, ma'am," PC Wilkins said. "Academy for Philosophical Studies. In London. Last June." He was playing along nicely.

"That's right, Constable. Now sir, where exactly is this book?"

"In my desk. Would you like to see it?"

"Well, yes sir, I would, actually."

"Very well."

The book that Wheatley took from his desk and handed to her was hand-written in what looked like Hebrew.

"Well now, this is very interesting sir. Although I'm not a scholar myself, you understand."

"No, Inspector. Would you like to take the book with you? Then perhaps you could get a *scholar* to examine it?"

"That would be very obliging of you sir. There have been a couple of unexpected developments in this matter, and it may be helpful for us to look at it further."

"Oh really? What kind of developments, Inspector?"

"Sorry, sir, I'm not at liberty to say."

"Then of course you shall have the book. I hope it proves useful. I'm always delighted to help the police."

"Thank you, sir."

She and Wilkins started to leave.

"We'll return the book to you as soon as possible, sir," she said in the hall. "And apart from that, I hope I shan't have to trouble you again."

Henry Wheatley looked her in the eye.

"None of us *has* to do anything, Inspector. We do what we choose to do."

"Yes, sir. I dare say, sir. It was a manner of speaking."

"Ah. A manner of speaking. That can be very deceptive, Inspector. Especially self-deceptive." He smiled. "If things are as you suggest, it seems to me that perhaps the police should not have released this book to me in the first place."

For a moment Cecilia considered how pleasant it would be to punch that smug, intelligent face. Still, something had happened. Urbanity was gone. The man was mocking her. Why?

Frowning, she peered at the book for a moment, then looked up at him.

"Are you *quite* sure this is the right book, sir?"

"Of course I'm sure Inspector. Do you think I don't recognize my own writing?"

Touché! Wheatley's voice, somewhat high-pitched anyway, had risen very slightly. And, just caught by her as she glanced up, there had been a second's hesitation, a momentary distancing of the eyes.

Cecilia, flicking through pages, continued as though she had noticed nothing. "And you are fluent in this—Hebrew, isn't it sir?"

"Mostly Aramaic, actually. Some Hebrew. Yes, officer, as it happens, I am. They are just languages, like any other. The fact that some regard them as sacred doesn't change that. Actually, they're rather simple languages once you get past the alphabet, which is a little strange to us."

Voice normal. The crack, if crack it was, had been quickly hidden.

"I see, sir. Thank you."

"Hebrew in particular is also rather beautiful, I think. Would you like me to read some of it for you?"

"That won't be necessary, sir. You're interested in Judaism, are you?"

"I am interested in *superstitions*, officer. Of which Judaism is an example. So is Islam. Christianity, of course, is another — in the case of Christianity, a particularly virulent and dangerous superstition that brought down the Roman Empire."

"Sir?"

"Oh, yes. It's all in Gibbon, if you want to learn about it. Another superstition, of course, is Law."

"Oh, really, sir. Now that *is* an interesting opinion."

"It's not an opinion, officer, it's a statement of fact. Law is a meta-narrative by which successful groups disguise their moves to power."

"Which leaves you feeling free to break it, sir?"

"Good heavens, no, officer. For so long as the society of which I am part is successful, I follow its customs."

"Very wise, sir. Well, I'll see you get the book back. Goodnight, sir."

"Snooty little blighter, that one," Wilkins said as they walked through light rain to the car.

Cecilia nodded.

"Still, at least he gave you the notebook, ma'am."

"Yes, he gave us the notebook. In fact — and make sure you note this when you write it up — he all but *thrust* it at us. He was also, as you point out, snooty. The trouble is, I'm not sure what the snootiness meant. What do you think?"

"He didn't like it when you asked him if it was the *right* book, ma'am."

"You noticed that? Good for you! But what was his problem? Guilt? Or injured innocence?"

"Hard to say, ma'am. He's very smooth."

"Yes. Smooth and yet somehow… not smooth. Erratic. *I* think he's lying, but I certainly don't know how to prove it… yet."

Wheatley watched their departure from an upstairs window. He'd prepared the notebook he gave them against just such an eventuality as this. For a moment he almost smiled at the thought of their bringing in someone who might actually *read* it. Then he frowned. The academy might be asked to confirm his story about the June conference. It would depend on how thorough the police were, but it was better not to take risks. The one who'd done the talking—the one with the Italian name— was obviously not nearly as stupid as she pretended to be. The loose end must be tied up.

Wheatley turned to the telephone.

NINETEEN

Wednesday, October 22.

The first thing Cecilia did when she arrived at her desk the following morning was to face the truth about herself and this case: she was frustrated.

And no wonder.

Every instinct she possessed told her that Wheatley was dangerous, that he had lied to the police and given her a substitute book, that he had committed acts criminal and terrible, that he was up to something criminal and terrible that involved other (criminal and terrible) people. She was sure of it.

Which meant nothing.

Which got her nowhere.

What we can't show, we don't know.

"You know what your trouble is, Cavaliere?" her form mistress had said when she was thirteen, after dragging her out of a fight with a girl two years older and twice her weight who'd said all Italians were cowards, and by whom she'd been getting rather badly knocked about. "You don't seem to know when you're beaten."

She shrugged.

A couple of things she could still do.

She put in a routine inquiry regarding Wheatley and Kakoyannis's attendance at a Conference on Science and Philosophy at the Academy for Philosophical Studies in London during the previous June. Just in case.

She sent the book to Scientific and Technical Services for examination. She felt that she owed that to Wheatley. They'd have Kakoyannis's fingerprints, and his print on the notebook would indicate that Wheatley was telling the truth. Of course, if there were no such print, that wouldn't prove him a liar — enough people had handled the book in the station that his prints could have been eliminated.

Scientific and Technical Services were, of course, backed up. Unless she was prepared to categorize Wheatley's book as urgent, she'd have to wait a week give-or-take for her report. How could she do that, when she didn't have any hard evidence even that a crime had been committed?

The results of her enquiry about the conference were faxed to her within a half-hour of her request. The Academy of Philosophical Studies confirmed that there had been a Cosmos conference in June of the previous year. Dr. Henry Wheatley and Dr. Nikos Kakoyannis had both taken part in it.

For now that seemed to be all she could do. There remained Joseph Stirrup's work, but even he didn't know when he'd have those results.

So she had nothing.

So far.

It was well into the afternoon before the question occurred to her.

What isn't a murder trial but precedes one?

What sometimes *sounds* like a murder trial?

She picked up the telephone.

"About Henry Wheatley," she said. "Would you ask DS Jones please to try 'inquests' for me, instead of 'murder trials'?"

TWENTY

Cecilia had to attend a two-day conference at Middlemoor, so it was not until Friday that she entered her office again. She had scarcely sat down at her desk when there was a knock. Through the glass-paneled door she could see DS Verity Jones.

"Come in!"

Hmm... Perfectly cut navy blue suit, quiet high-necked blouse, black shoes. Cecilia raised an eyebrow.

"I've a meeting with Superintendent Hanlon," Verity said.

Ah. Cecilia nodded, for a moment not DI to DS but woman to woman.

"If you have a problem, I want to know."

Verity Jones gave the faintest of smiles.

"You'll know," she said.

Cecilia smiled. Little Miss Perfect was tougher than she looked.

But the detective sergeant was on a mission. She walked up, took a sheet of paper from a folder, and laid it on Cecilia's desk. She confined herself to one word.

"Bingo."

Cecilia picked it up, and the heading leapt at her. Sir Joseph Loveland. The Loveland inquest. Third of February 1993. The death of the great biologist.

She'd been not much more than a girl at the time, but it had made a splash on the news, and she'd heard all about it. And Wheatley — *their* Wheatley — was called as a witness.

She looked at DS Jones, who was wearing the triumphant grin she surely deserved.

"Good work."

"I've a full transcript of the inquest: it's being scanned and you'll have it on your email this afternoon, ma'am." She hesitated, then went on. "The fact is, I've done a bit of work on my own on this, and I think there's more, ma'am. If you've got a minute."

Cecilia was due at the site of a robbery on the other side of Exeter in half an hour, but this was definitely worth a minute. She waved Verity Jones into a chair.

"Let's have it."

"Well, ma'am, first, I'm beginning to wonder if there maybe *is* something strange about Wheatley's early career. He went up to Oxford with an open scholarship, but then he didn't really do all that brilliantly. Ended up with a Second."

Cecilia smiled. Verity Jones, she happened to know, had achieved a double First in Mods and Greats.

"Then he got a research position with Loveland, at that point reckoned perhaps the most brilliant biologist of his day. And that's the first *odd* thing — that Loveland took on Wheatley when he could have had his pick of brilliant minds."

"Maybe he just saw something in Wheatley the others missed. It's possible."

"Well, ma'am, maybe he did. Just regard me as your old-fashioned positivist." She dropped into a passable imitation of a Scottish brogue. "It is for poets and theologians to offer *interpretations*. I merely exhibit the facts."

She had managed to inject just the right note of contempt into "poets" and "theologians." Cecilia laughed.

"All right. Facts noted."

"Well, ma'am, in any case Wheatley joined him, and they

worked together for two years. Then as we know, Loveland died in strange circumstances. Committed suicide. Hence the inquest."

"As you may remember, and as you'll certainly see when you read the report, the suicide was a mystery. Loveland seemed in every way a happy, contented man. No evidence of depression, debts, family troubles, anything. He'd gone up to London for his daughter's fourteenth birthday. They'd had a little party, he'd made a charming toast. Seemed in the best of spirits. Then that night he wrote a note saying life was too much and took an overdose. Just like that. His daughter found him next morning. In one way the inquest was straightforward enough. All the actual *facts* pointed to suicide, and there didn't seem to be anything that suggested otherwise. Except, as I said, that no one could find a motive."

"And that's where Wheatley came in?"

"Right, ma'am. Wheatley had been in Oxford on the night of the death. He was called to give evidence about Loveland's state of mind. But then both the coroner and a lawyer for Loveland's family started asking a lot of very pointed questions about Wheatley's own relationship with Loveland. Wasn't it true they'd quarreled? And so on. *That* got into the news, and that, presumably, is what you remembered."

Cecilia nodded.

"Well, as you'll see from the transcript, the fact is Wheatley stood up perfectly well. The questions didn't get anywhere, and on balance, the inquest's conclusion had to be for a straightforward suicide... *balance of the mind disturbed*, and so on. But it's evident there was more than a hint of suspicion in the air. And it attached to Wheatley. Just, I think, as you remembered."

"So have you talked to the coroner and the lawyer?"

"No, ma'am, I haven't. Because they're both dead. What's more, they both died within three weeks of the inquest."

Cecilia contented herself — for the moment — with a question.

"Didn't anyone think that rather strange?"

"No ma'am, and unless you happen to look at the thing from the point of view we're taking, I suppose there's be no reason to. The coroner died of a heart attack at his home in Surrey. The lawyer was killed in a car accident in Cornwall, by all accounts his own fault."

"Very interesting." Cecilia picked up a pen and started to doodle, determined to control her mounting excitement. "There's more, isn't there."

"Ma'am, you just wait. Henry Wheatley produced that brilliant thesis on techniques of biological warfare eighteen months after Loveland's death. Since then, he's never looked back. Being of a nasty and suspicious turn of mind, I immediately wondered if there might be any connection between Wheatley's thesis and whatever Loveland was working on. In other words, did he pinch the boss's work?"

"And did he?"

"How to find out—that's the problem. Now, apparently there was a second member of Wheatley's research team, a man called Travers. He'd left about six months before Loveland's death. But he'd have had a good idea where Loveland was heading and to what extent Wheatley's thesis connected with it."

She'd done great work, but she did love to draw the story out!

"Verity, by your tenses am I to take it that Travers is dead too?"

"That's right, ma'am. What's more..." She paused again. Clearly, she had saved the good wine until last and could hardly be blamed for savoring it. "Ma'am, he died on a climbing holiday in Scotland three weeks after the Loveland inquest."

"Good God! Bodies all over the place. Yet nothing obvious to connect them with each other."

"Exactly, ma'am. No *reason* to connect them unless you look at them from this angle, and no one did. Why should they?"

Why *would* anyone have connected these deaths? Why would *they* if not for Cecilia's wild and still largely unsubstantiated hunch, now expanded if not buttressed by Verity's intelligent follow-up?

"Really good work, DS Jones. Now, do we know where Wheatley was while all this was going on?"

"He left England two weeks after the inquest and was in the United States until just before publishing his thesis. While he was away, the three men died. Within three weeks. I would imagine he can account for every hour of those three weeks."

"Yes, I rather imagine he can. Never mind. This is good. Very good. So we've got three men, all dying within days of each other, all having something to do with Loveland or Loveland's death, and all having something to do with Henry Wheatley. Not that there mightn't be some *other* party linking them, someone we haven't thought of or don't know about. Have you considered any possible alternatives?"

"With respect, ma'am, I don't see that anyone else *could* have been involved in the research end. Wheatley and Travers were the only members of the team. And Travers hadn't been replaced. On the family end, it was Wheatley they questioned so hard. Not anyone else. He *is* the only link, so far as I can see."

"I see what you mean." Cecilia got up from her chair, walked across to the window, and gazed out. These facts were all but incapable of innocent explanation. On the other hand...

She came back to her desk.

"Ma'am, I've scanned the rest of the files, newspaper reports, and so on, and I'll attach them to the inquest transcript. Maybe you can get something else from all of it. I don't think I can, for the moment."

"You've done very well indeed. And of course I want to see the rest of your material. I've a feeling about this man."

"I know, ma'am. Me too."

***

During the afternoon, Cecilia read all of Verity Jones's research, then went back and reread the material she'd come up with earlier on Henry Wheatley. It was then that she noticed, in a list of organizations, The Academy for Philosophical Studies. Member: Board of Governors.

Hmmmm.

Wheatley's being on their board surely made their backing up his story about Nikos Kakoyannis a *shade* less impressive?.

Apropos the academy, Verity Jones had added a note of her own:

> Educational charity. Established 1989. Chief business — running evening classes — very MENSA and pseudo-intellectual. Also goes in for fund-raising for other people's educational schemes. Last year made huge contribution to the new Cranston College of Science (govt. sponsored — Hackney). One thing against them — brush with Charity Commissioners in 2001 — use of funds — question of political involvement — put right — no action taken.

It hardly amounted to a criminal indictment.

And yet ...

Slowly, she reached for the telephone. It was answered by one of the others, but she asked for DS Jones.

"Do we know any more than is written here about the Academy for Philosophical Studies?"

"No, ma'am. Not at the moment we don't."

"Well, there may be nothing in it, but I'm starting to get a feeling about them, too. See what you can turn up, will you? Oh — and the notebook. Since Scientific and Technical apparently need forever to do their thing with it, could someone in the meantime at least let me have a photocopy of it?"

"Yes ma'am. On it, ma'am."

Cecilia shook her head. Apparently DS Jones had time to watch American films.

She looked at the clock. She should have been off duty twenty minutes ago. She was to buy fish from the fish shop in Magdalen Road for *pesce alla griglia*.

"Thank you," she said. "But no hurry for anything today! I'm out of here."

Verity Jones needn't think she was the only one who could talk American.

TWENTY-ONE

London, Bayswater. Friday, October 24.

The chairman presided over the next board meeting in his usual manner, reacting to nothing and behaving in general as if he heard nothing. He listened expressionless as Coleman reported on a major project: the academy's link with the new Cranston College of Science and Technology. Most of the plans she unfolded with such conviction he knew to be irrelevant to his own expectations, but there was no harm in letting her play with them for a while, and there was always the possibility of some frustration to his plans that would make what she was doing useful.

Occupying a wide area on the north bank of the Thames below Tower Hamlets and above Limehouse, Cranston would, when fully operational, offer over four hundred places for studies in engineering, applied sciences, sociology, behavioral psychology, management, and related subjects. The facilities would be the most up-to-date and extensive in the country — in some respects, in the world. The project was financed mainly by government, a condition of which had been the provision of considerable additional funds from voluntary sources. The academy had been able to offer an astonishingly large sum from its own funds, in return for which it would have a share in formulating the policies and design of the project.

"I am happy to tell you," Coleman said, "that building is on schedule, and there is every prospect that the plant will be complete in time for the intake of students in October next year. Our own influence on the thinking of the institution grows daily and will amply repay, I believe, our participation in the financial investment. Should the position of this academy be in any way jeopardized in the future, I believe it would be possible, in time, for our entire operation to be transferred there. In any event, both before and after the establishment of the New Order, it seems clear to me that Cranston College can provide, as we hoped, the best young scientific brains available. Whilst none of us would wish to underrate the value of this academy as a recruiting center, we cannot deny that our clientele in general tend toward certain obvious limitations of character and intellect. The enrollment of Cranston College will be altogether wider and more satisfactory in scope.

"There is also another matter to be considered." She paused and looked at the chairman, who reacted in no way whatever. Thus encouraged she sailed on. "It is becoming evident that as we suspected, the area to be occupied by Cranston contains an ancient and valuable center of power—the site known, at least since the sixteenth century, as Hadrian's Grave. Of course, it has nothing to do with the Roman Emperor Hadrian. We can now state positively that it was used as a base for the mysteries of the Mithras superstition as early as the third century. According to several authorities, it vastly exceeds the potentiality of anything we have yet controlled, being entirely free of Christian influence and already affected by a powerful act of reversal at some time in the more recent past—possibly the eighteenth century.

"Naturally, we must proceed cautiously. We have managed to persuade the governors of Cranston that the site is structurally dangerous—as, indeed, it is—and would cost an enormous sum to make safe. At the same time we have pointed out that it is of historic interest and that there might be a public outcry if it were damaged. Accordingly, we have suggested that it be sealed off, and we have offered the services of experts provided by us to oversee the site. The governors have accepted our offer eagerly. The last thing they want is fuss about a historic site. For our part we have virtual control, including control of access."

She shuffled her papers together and sat back.

Hutton introduced the final matter on the agenda: police inquiries at the academy and Wheatley's part in allowing them to happen. The formality that had dominated the proceedings up to this point disappeared. Coleman whipped around to face Wheatley.

"You must have been out of your mind to bring the academy into this. Don't you realize how dangerous that was?"

The chairman stared into space.

Wheatley felt that he'd pulled off something of a coup in getting the book at all, and ought to be praised, not criticized over details. He did not, of course, say so. He assured them that he respected their concern. And regretted the disturbance that had been caused. But he was quite certain that there was no ground at all for alarm. It was, to begin with, perfectly clear that the police officer who called at his home knew nothing. Absolutely nothing. She had been acting on a hunch.

"And what, do you think, caused that hunch?" Coleman said.

"If anything, it was probably the file."

"The file?"

"Yes. The police file. We needed the information in it but I should merely have had it copied. Deleting it from their records was, on reflection, a mistake—for which I take full responsibility. And, in my view, it's the only thing that's made the police look twice at this matter."

The fact was he had deleted the file because he could and

because it had amused him to frustrate the police. But he meant what he said. It *was* a mistake.

"And now that they've looked?"

"Now that they have looked—what good will it do them? What in fact, is there for them to discover?"

"Plenty," Hutton muttered.

"Ah, yes—*but not about this.* We must remember what the police actually *think* they are investigating. The death of Nikos Kakoyannis. We didn't cause that death. We knew nothing of it. There is therefore nothing for them to learn."

"Rubbish," Hutton said. "You've lied to the police. You've given them a forged document. You've hacked into the police mainframe. And you've forced us to lie. What if they find that lot out?"

"And you know as well as we do," Coleman said, "that if the police once really become interested in this academy, there's a great deal for them to discover. It's only a question of time."

"Exactly! *Time.* And time is the one thing they haven't got. Consider the position. Of course I've taken a risk. And of course the police will get closer to us, and to me. *Eventually.* But for the present, they have no idea what they're looking for, and if the inquiry here didn't satisfy them, they'll be running routine checks. On the academy. On me. On you. All of which will produce very little to start with. A question here. A coincidence there. And while they spend time on that, we already have the book, thanks to me. And on Friday, it will be Samhain. The supreme night for the Ceremony of Power. We can do it! And once we have, it won't matter two pins what the police discover."

He thought he'd summed it up pretty well.

"It's still damned dangerous," Hutton said.

"Of course it's dangerous. And so is what we're about. Whoever achieved anything without taking risks?"

***

Once more, the chairman decided this had gone on long enough.

He coughed.

"Samhain. It is fitting. The police" — he looked directly at Wheatley — "suspect something of you, but you are right — it is nothing to the purpose." He looked into space once more. "They also suspect the academy, but of what, they do not know. You are, again, correct. Arrange the ceremony. And inform the agents. At once."

He rose and left them.

Again there was silence. Wheatley began gathering together his papers. He noted that Hargrove had refrained from taking part in the criticism, no doubt suspecting which way the wind might blow. So he wasn't surprised when he leaned forward, plainly poised to capitalize on the situation, and said, "If I may venture an opinion, ah, lady and gentlemen, it seems to me that we owe, ah, a considerable debt to the initiative of our esteemed colleague Dr. Wheatley. I should like to place on record — "

But Hutton had plainly had enough.

"For Christ's sake, Hargrove, you thought he was up the pole as much as any of us. The only difference between you and us for the last twenty minutes was you had enough bloody sense — or maybe were just gutless enough — to keep your mouth shut."

"Mr. Hutton, I must remind you — there is a lady present."

"Oh, Jesus! She'll be here on the thirty-first" — he indicated Coleman with a jerk of his head — "for the same reason as the rest of us. What she can get out of it. Muck and brass. They go together. Or hadn't you noticed?"

Coleman slid a cigarette into her holder and lit it. She had spoken her mind to Wheatley and that, so far as she was concerned, was an end of it. Tom Hutton's outburst troubled her not at all.

In fact, she was rather amused by it. At least he was a *man*, which was more than she'd say for either of the other two...

Luxuriously, she drew on her cigarette.

Wheatley zipped his briefcase, then sat back for a long moment.

Hargrove's wealth and the prestige of his name had made his support worth having in the past. On the other hand, with the coming of the New Order these assets would be comparatively worthless, and Wheatley rated the man's abilities in other directions at about the level of a chimpanzee's. Hutton was different. Rough. Crude. Overly direct. But concerning his intelligence and ability, there could be no doubt. His support under the New Order could be invaluable. In the past, Wheatley had ignored him, having other fish to fry. The time might be coming to change that. Of course, he could do nothing at this moment, save perhaps sow seeds that might be watered later.

Hargrove was blustering on. "One is, of course, aware that the, ah, development of the New Order will require certain individuals taking to themselves certain, ah, burdens of office. Members of this board will naturally be qualified in that direction. But one envisages only the highest sense of public duty — "

"You make me sick," Hutton said.

"On the whole," Wheatley said, "I agree with you, Tom."

"What?"

"I said, on the whole, I agree with you. It's nonsense to talk about high motives and burdens of office. We're all here because we want power. I want it. You want it. Even the chairman wants it — more than he has. And to get it, we need each other."

Hargrove said, "But, good God — "

"I don't like you, Wheatley," Hutton said, "and you'll not win me over by smooth talk. So don't try."

"I'm perfectly aware you don't like me." Wheatley was careful to be as precise and polite as ever. "In general, I regard that as an advantage. Affection is a muddy affair that clouds the true basis of relationship. In our case, the nexus of relationship is quite clear. We want control. As you said. But control begins with control of ourselves."

Hutton flared, as Wheatley knew he would.

"When I want your advice, I'll damn well ask for it."

"Precisely," Wheatley said, rising to his feet. "And that may just possibly be sooner than you think."

"To hear you, one might think you were after the boss's job," Coleman said.

"Not at all. I have as much loyalty to the chairman as anyone here. The facts remain. Until now, in this room we have been playing at power. Soon, we shall have it. And when we do, we'll need to know what to do with it. That means, as Tom says, knowing why we want it. It also means knowing who our friends are, and who are our enemies." He looked straight at Hutton. "Think about it, Tom." He picked up his briefcase. "I must go. No doubt I shall see you all on the thirty-first."

Twenty-Two

London. The Zoological Gardens,
Regent's Park. The same day.

"Hello, what's this?" asked the woman in a white coat who was about to examine Katie.

"It's the new lock," said a scrawny young man in jeans and a polo shirt. "You just press the red button, then walk in."

The veterinarian pressed it. There was a sharp buzz, and she walked in.

From within the enclosure Katie watched, eyes shining, ears pricked with interest.

"I'm not sure I like it," the vet said. "That button's a bit easy to overlook, if you ask me."

The young man shrugged. The veterinarian turned her attention to the patient, led forward by her keeper. She peered down Katie's throat, looked at the injured ear, and examined her, all the while murmuring endearments that Katie seemed to welcome.

"She looks in pretty good shape to me," she said at last.

"I think she's been doing fine," the keeper said. "The antibiotic seems to have done it. I wouldn't mind us giving her another week, though, just to be on the safe side."

"More medication?"

"No, it's just I'd like you to come back this time next week and make sure she's still doing okay. After all, she seemed to recover before, and then relapsed."

The vet nodded. "Well, yes, that makes sense. Same time next week. And we'll sign her off then if she seems all right."

Katie continued to watch as the three of them negotiated the lock and went on their way.

Exeter. Cecilia's house. The same day.

"I think if I were you I'd show it to Michael Aarons. I'm sure he could help you."

Cecilia had told Papa about the black book and asked him if he knew anyone she could trust who could read Aramaic and Hebrew.

"Is he on the faculty?"

"Actually he's a friend of mine in London. A priest. But you're going there tomorrow, aren't you? So I could arrange for you to see him if you like."

"A *priest*?"

The Cavalieres' part in the Italian seizure of Rome in 1871 had led to their estrangement from the church. Pius IX, piqued (as Papa saw it) at losing the Papal states, had by the Decree *Non expedit* forbidden Italian Catholics to participate in the political life of the new Republic—in effect, excommunicating those who did. Thereby (as Papa never failed to point out) the supreme pontiff had at a stroke lost for the Roman church virtually every Italian male who was a patriot—and he had certainly lost the Cavalieres.

So she was surprised to hear of his friendship with a priest.

He read her surprise and smiled.

"Your mama and I met him at a London University dinner. Michael teaches the occasional course. Second Temple Judaism—though I'm pretty sure his doctorate's in New Testament. An interesting man — and not, in fact, a Catholic. He's an Anglican. I enjoy talking to him. Anyway, it's clear to me he's fluent in biblical languages. I'm sure he could help you."

TWENTY-THREE

The Academy for Philosophical Studies. The same day.

"Inform the agents," the chairman had said.

Only minutes after the board meeting ended, text-messages and emails were on their way. Their message was cryptic—a single word, and a date. But those who received the message understood it, and they would be standing by their telephones on the night of the Ceremony. There were forty in all—each member of the board, other than the chairman, being responsible for ten—scattered in key places throughout government, industry, finance, and media. And each in turn was responsible for ten more secondary cells, unaware of each other's existence and unaware of their part in an overall plan.

Those who gathered around the board room table had waited for a sign: the key to a Ceremony of Power by which they should set in motion the next stage, inaugurating a New Order. The death of Nikos Kakoyannis, and their consequent access to the black book and the form of the Ceremony was, it seemed, that sign.

Immediately following the Ceremony of Power, a further code word would initiate certain actions. A great deal of groundwork had been laid over previous years. The economic irresponsibility of the United States' administration under the forty-third president, an irresponsibility in which the rest of the world had cooperated, had already created an international economic depression of unprecedented proportions. In the light of all this, a scenario had been prepared, precisely timed immediately to precede the American presidential election on November fourth, only four days after the Ceremony of Power. Within thirty-six hours of the Ceremony, there was to be a series of crippling strikes, affecting transport, power, and food delivery across Europe. At the same time, a coordinated series of suicide bombings in major United States' centers would produce maximum carnage and terror among ordinary Americans. The effect of this even the Academy did not pretend to know. But surely forces of reaction would be encouraging public opinion to support plunging an already near-bankrupt country and overstretched military into further military adventure. Judging by the evident inclination of some in the present administration to play fast and loose with the United States' constitution, it might even lead them to demand postponement or cancellation of the election itself in the cause of "national security."

Then surely there would be hell to pay. Many would turn to violence—which would, of course, be exactly the reaction that would satisfy the Academy. In any case, and even if the election took place, continuing collapse of world stock markets involving unprecedented runs on the euro and the dollar was planned for the following days, culminating in a parallel collapse of the international automobile industry. This would throw thousands more out of work in the United States and Europe. The workers' frustration would naturally explode into violence: Detroit, Birmingham, Paris, Modena, and Rome had been selected. Racial, ethnic, and religious tensions would all be fed to add fuel to the flames.

There would follow conflicting and impossible demands from extremist groups on both left and right. The academy was very hopeful of the American right, confident that the pundits of right wing television channels and radio talk shows could be galvanized into words calculated to inflame an already anxious populace. Funds the Academy had invested over several years here ought to have played their part, ensuring a virtual hijacking of the American conservative movement by religious bigots. And *that* would mean that what there would not be when the crisis came was intelligent debate, the thoughtful weighing of conservative and progressive options. The loudest voices would be those of hysteria, of accusation and counter-accusation that would (however ludicrous) be believed by those who wished to believe, along with increasingly absurd and contradictory demands.

When this moment came, there would arise also the well-orchestrated "grass-roots" call for firm action; and when that came, the academy had seen to it that there were those under its influence standing by in the United States and in Europe who would be ready to respond.

What part was to be played in all this by the Ceremony of Power? Initially the Ceremony would unleash destructive energies that contributed to the chaos, setting masses against their leaders, leaders against the masses. Subsequently these same energies, focused and coordinated by those who understood them, would give power to those who took control—power to move those masses and their leaders, to influence assemblies, to rule. And in them, a New Order for North America and Western Europe would be born: an *imperium*, an empire, to be based upon boundless wealth and control for a few, material satisfactions for those who served them, and bondage for the rest. Such were the plans of those sat around the board room table. Such their understanding of the Ceremony of Power and its effects.

Only the chairman knew differently.

They all wanted power to satisfy their needs—greed, ambition, lust, a quest to control others or to fulfill the illusion of freedom.

Only he saw beyond such power to its reality, perceiving it

for what it was: *a tale told by an idiot, full of sound and fury, signifying nothing.*

And only he knew the real meaning of the Ceremony.

Of course he was content to let the board members play their games and organize their plots and their coups while they could. Indeed, he would even encourage them. They caused pain and damaged people's lives and insofar as he could still be amused, that amused him.

Until the end came. Then there would be an end of their plots, too.

For the real goal, the final reality, was very much simpler than they imagined.

The Ceremony was not about the establishment of *any* order new or old, good or bad.

The Ceremony was about the destruction of order.

The Ceremony, if performed correctly, would destroy the galaxy.

Twenty-Four

Siding Spring. Sunday, October 26.

At the close of Friday's staff meeting Charlie asked if there was a church anywhere near the observatory. Anglican, he observed, was his usual tipple, but he'd be quite happy with anything reasonable. To Thaddaeus's amusement and Zaziwe's outrage, one or two of the more orthodox atheists among their colleagues made it plain they were scandalized by this lapse from scientific rigor. Still, it turned out that there was an Anglican church within reasonable driving distance, and it had a 9:00 a.m. Sunday Eucharist. Thaddaeus managed somehow or other to charm his way into borrowing an Australian National University minibus, and so, at half-past-eight on Sunday morning the three of them gathered and set off, with Thaddaeus driving.

West Indians, Charlie decided, know how to dress for church. For his part, he felt rather drab and now wished he had made more effort. With his open neck shirt and trainers he was definitely "casual." By contrast, instead of their usual jeans and tee-shirts, Thaddaeus was immaculate in well-cut gray suit, crisp white shirt, and university tie, while Zaziwe was brilliant in black and yellow silk.

It cheered him up just to look at her.

And he needed cheering up.

Part of the reason he'd made so little effort this morning was that last night he'd had the Dream, which now seemed so clearly mixed up with the Observatory. The work at the Observatory was going well, in fact, better than he could have hoped. He liked his new colleagues—even the militant atheists who so annoyed Zaziwe!—and of course Thaddaeus and Zaziwe were a joy. So there was nothing there he could put his finger on to make him uneasy.

Yet he *was* uneasy, more so than ever, and his unease was at its worst after he had the Dream. Because the Dream was now linked to his work, that meant—

"A penny for them," Thaddaeus said.

"They aren't worth it, I assure you." He peered through the window. "I think it's going to be a nice day."

Thaddaeus glanced sideways at him. "Yes, I think it is."

Evidently Thaddaeus had been in the United Kingdom quite long enough to tell when an Englishman wishes to keep his thoughts to himself.

The church was small but pretty. The wardens greeted them with a friendly way, made sure they had prayer books and knew how to follow the Anglican rite, then left them alone. Charlie found himself thinking back to his response last night to the atheist—one of the nicest, he thought—who'd taken him aside and gently raised the question as to how a scientist of his stature found religious faith and science compatible. Of course it wasn't the first time he'd been asked such a question, and it wasn't the first time he'd given the same answer: "When I look at the universe that science shows me, at the staggering complexity of the processes that were necessary for human beings to exist—processes that could perfectly well have gone in millions of other ways, but didn't—why then, even as a scientist I think I can allow myself to be in awe. Of course I can also refuse to be in awe. I can say, the universe has to be the way it is, otherwise I wouldn't be here. And that's certainly true. But still, to be in awe or not to be in awe, that's a choice — an emotional choice — and I don't see opting for one as being any more or less 'scientific' than opting for the other. But if I can allow myself to be in awe at what I see, then why can't I allow myself to hope? And even to trust? And I don't find those attitudes impairing my commitment to scientific rigor — in fact, they spur me on. For if I hope and trust, then why should I fear the truth, whatever it is?"

And his good atheist colleague, bless him, had smiled and nodded, and said he would have to think about that.

Briefly, Charlie prayed for him.

For the anthem, several of the congregation went up into the little sanctuary and sang the Hallelujah Chorus. Badly. Actually, *very* badly. At which point, it struck Charlie how much God must be enjoying this. And Handel too, he suspected. For an instant he felt the divine amusement and delight, the communion of the saints. Joy, sheer, gracious, and compassionate, seemed to surround him.

When it was time, he went up with the others to receive communion. "The body of Christ... the blood of Christ."

If that were true, then Love was true, and nothing else mattered. Not his dreams, not his depression. Not even death would have the last word. As Zaziwe had pointed out to him in London.

It was all so much simpler than one often imagined.

TWENTY-FIVE

Tuesday, October 28.

Cecilia left early and drove to London. She was required to present herself as witness in a trial at the Central Criminal Court. The trial did not begin until Wednesday, but Papa had made an appointment for her for that afternoon with Michael Aarons, the Anglican priest. So, having arrived, booked into her hotel, and eaten lunch at a decent little French bistro nearby, she walked the short distance along the broad, busy street to Saint Andrew's Church—a handsome building from the late eighteenth century. She turned in through green double gates toward the vicarage.

The front door opened as she was approaching it, and a figure in a leather-belted cassock emerged and came down the steps to meet her. Wiry and compact, Michael Aarons, Vicar of Saint Andrew's, Holborn Circus and Archdeacon of Hackney, moved with spring in his step and controlled energy. She found herself at once liking him. His eyes were dark, intelligent, and kind. To be sure, at first glance his clean-shaven features seemed somewhat severe: slightly saturnine, marked with pain. But then he smiled. Instinctively, she smiled back.

He greeted her formally in an Italian that was perfectly correct.

"Good day, Inspector Cavaliere. I'm honored to meet you. I am Michael Aarons, a friend of your father."

She replied in Italian.

"I'm delighted to meet you, Father. It's kind of you to see me at such short notice."

"Please come in. My study is through here. Will you take a coffee?"

She accepted politely, wondering, as she always did with non-Italians, whether he meant the same thing by *un caffè* as she did. But when the coffee arrived it was in *tazzine*, and it was good. She smiled at him.

Michael switched to English.

"You are, I take it, perfectly bilingual in English and Italian?"

"I am."

Taken out of context, he reflected, the words might have seemed like a boast. But as she said them they were simply a statement of fact, as if she'd said, "I have dark eyes."

"Mama and Papa came to England when I was very little," she said, "so Papa could be professor of classics at the university. So I grew up here. School was in English, of course, but even when I was at home they always spoke English with me during the day. But then in the evening, unless we had guests or something like that, we were Italians."

Michael smiled at her little recital of family life. If only he could respond with quite such a recital of his own. He sighed.

"So," he said, "for you English became the language of work and enterprise, and Italian the language of food and family and love."

She looked at him quizzically. Perhaps she had noticed his momentary withdrawal? If so, she contented herself with replying to what he had said.

"You might be right—at any rate, when I was about fourteen, I must have said something like that to Papa. Because I remember him saying it wasn't true. 'In their way, the English are as romantic as we are,' he said. 'Never forget they produced Shakespeare and Jane Austen.'"

"I think your father's right," he said. "We English *are* romantics, in our way." He paused, smiling to himself. "Anyway, even though I speak a little Italian, I, unfortunately, am *not* bilingual. So perhaps we'd better stay with English for our serious business. Andrea tells me you have a document you want me to see?"

Cecilia opened her briefcase and produced her photocopies of the black book's contents. Michael took them over to his desk, sat down, and began to go through the pages.

"Mostly Aramaic," he said after a few minutes, "a few passages of Hebrew. All very mystical and medieval!" He looked up at her. "So far as I can see, they're extracts from the *Zohar*. Do you know what that is?"

She shook her head.

"Well, *Zohar* means 'splendor,' and the *Zohar* is a text that talks about how the eternal and infinite God may be manifested in the creation. Most of it was written by a man called Moses de Leon, who died in 1305. What he produced was a mixture of things—spiritual theology, mystical psychology, myth, anthropology, poetry." He turned back to the papers and turned more pages. "Yes, that's what it seems to be. Parts of the *Zohar*. Just copied out! No comments or notes, just the text. Rather odd, really. Did it come up in a case?"

"Yes Father, it did."

"Please—call me Michael."

"Of course I will. And I'm Cecilia!"

"Thank you, Cecilia!" He smiled and returned to the papers. "Well, yes, evidently you have mystical criminals in your part of the world."

"Would you believe it, Michael, if a man told you he'd lent those notes to someone at a conference on philosophy and science?"

Michael thought for a minute and shook his head.

"I can't imagine what it would be for. If somebody wanted the texts, there are editions. Why work with something written out by hand? I find that very hard to explain. Unless there's some significance in the arrangement or the selection. At a quick glance, I can't see any."

She didn't seem surprised, merely nodded.

"Actually, I have an English translation," he said. "If you like, I could work through your notebook this evening and give you references to it. Then you could check the passages yourself in English. You might see something I'm missing. A common thread, something that links to what you're investigating."

Again Cecilia nodded. "That would be very kind. Thank you. I'd like that. But for now I gather there's nothing at first glance that seems to you at all sinister?"

Michael went back to the text. There were several minutes of silence while he read a page here, a page there. Finally he sighed and shook his head.

"As I say, just quotations from the *Zohar*. But obviously I haven't read every word. I'll read the whole thing through carefully later today—just in case I've missed something."

Cecilia thanked him again.

So Kakoyannis's notebook once again seemed to have turned up a blank.

If it *was* Kakoyannis's notebook. Her doubts remained, now intensified by what Michael had said. If *only* they had looked at it more closely before letting it out of their hands in the first place.

Still, there was no helping that now.

She looked up at Michael.

"It doesn't get me much further, but I'm grateful, all the same. And if you *could* let me look at those references—."

"I'll be happy to. Where are you staying?"

She gave him the name of a nearby hotel.

"All right. I have to see someone now, but I think I can work through your text later this afternoon. I'll give you page references to the translation, and I'll get someone to bring it all round to your hotel this evening. How will that be?"

"Marvelous!" There was a pause. Her attention was caught by a silver-framed black and white photograph on his desk—a man and a woman. "Forgive me," she said, "I hope you don't mind me asking—is that a photograph of your parents?"

He smiled. "Yes," he said. "It is."

She peered at it. "They look lovely," she said.

He nodded. "Yes," he said quietly, "they were. They died some years ago. In a car crash."

"Oh," she said. "I'm so sorry."

He shook his head, but said nothing.

Then he smiled. "One other thing—are you expecting to be still in London on Friday evening?"

"I am."

"Then would you like to come to some supper here at the vicarage? I've some friends from the university coming. They're also friends of your father and mother, and I think you'll enjoy them."

"I'd love to come. I hope you won't mind—I'll just be in my working clothes for my court appearance. I didn't bring anything very exciting with me to wear."

"It really will be just supper—not dinner! Please come just as you are! We'll be delighted to see you."

TWENTY-SIX

Later the same day.

Cecilia walked back across Holborn Viaduct to her hotel and telephoned the station at Exeter.

Scientific and Technical had finally come up with their report on the book. No, they had found no evidence that it had ever been in Kakoyannis's possession — which might prove nothing but at least gave no support to Wheatley's story.

A different approach had proved more interesting. On her own initiative, Verity Jones had continued to make inquiries about others who'd been involved in the inquest. One was Loveland's daughter, who might, she thought, have some explanation to offer about the lawyer's hostility to Wheatley. Another was the doctor who'd originally been called to the scene of Loveland's death.

The daughter, it transpired, was now working for BP in Alaska. After some effort, DS Jones had actually managed to speak to her by telephone at her home in Anchorage. As regards the inquest, she was unable to help. She remembered the lawyer's harping on at Wheatley but had no idea what might have been behind it. She had, she reminded DS Jones, been very young at the time. Then, without realizing it, she revealed a fact that was far more significant to her questioner than it was to her. The detective sergeant, who had transcribed it into her notes word for word, read it out:

> "Of course Daddy had already visited London earlier that week. He'd been up to deliver a lecture. I remember that because he was supposed to buy Mummy some special kinds of plates that you could only get at a shop in Regent's Street, and he forgot! So she was a bit annoyed."

> "Oh, really? That's interesting. I don't suppose, ma'am, you happen to recall where the lecture was, do you?"

> "Where? Um… wait a minute, he mentioned it a couple of times, I've got it on the tip of my tongue… The Philosophical Academy… no, the Academy for Philosophical Studies. That was it."

Cecilia whistled.

"Yes, ma'am," DS Jones said, "I thought that was interesting too."

The doctor was a respected family practitioner who'd retired from practice three years after Loveland's death and lived well into his eighties. There really didn't seem to be anything to pursue there.

Cecilia agreed.

Nevertheless, true to form, Verity Jones had saved the best until last.

She'd initiated an inquiry with her opposite number at Paddington Police Station regarding the careers and present whereabouts of two police officers, a sergeant and a constable, who'd been called to the Loveland house by the doctor and had given evidence at the inquest. The results of the inquiry were now available. She read them:

> "'According to our records, Sergeant Roger Lovell, the senior of the two officers you inquired about, was

admitted to hospital and diagnosed with brain cancer one week after the inquest in question. He died five days later. Police Constable William Crane, the junior officer, resigned from the force three days after that, and at present our records give no evidence of his whereabouts.'"

"Good grief," Cecilia said.

"Yes, ma'am," she said. "That's what I thought. Of course I'm still checking on Crane, but so far no joy. Somerset House doesn't have any record of his death, so he *ought* to be still around. On the other hand, I ran his social security number and there's nothing showing since he left the force. Maybe he went abroad. But if so, he did it without documents—or, at least, there's no record of a passport's being issued to him. Part of the problem is, the records I've got don't show any living relatives—he's a bachelor, or was, and an only child with both parents dead, so it's hard to know where to go next."

Cecilia sighed. "Has Joseph come up with anything yet on that missing file?"

"I asked him this afternoon. He says he's 'plodding away,' but I think he's actually getting a little frustrated. The trouble is, there's really no one around here smart enough to help him. He's been teaching me a bit about what he's doing, and I now have just about enough knowledge to see the problem but nowhere near enough to be any help."

"He'll get there. I've never known him to fail."

"Oh, I'm sure he'll get there. I think it's just irritating him that it's taking so long."

Cecilia sighed. Well, they would all just have to be patient. That went with the territory for good police work.

Still, they now knew of five people involved in Wheatley's life at the time of Loveland's death who might have been a threat to him, and of these five, four had died and one had vanished, all within weeks—indeed, virtually days—of each other and all while Henry Wheatley was conveniently out of the country. It was incredible. Yes — that was it. Despite the lack of tangible evidence against Wheatley, the facts regarding that part of his life, arranged as they could now arrange them, were simply incredible unless there were malicious design in them. And whose design but Wheatley's?

And what of the Academy for Philosophical Studies? Surely this new appearance on the edge of the affair stretched coincidence just a shade too far. Were they involved as a group? Or, was Wheatley using them? At any rate, there was much here that must be followed up.

The telephone call completed, Cecilia drummed her fingers on the table.

And thought.

TWENTY-SEVEN

The same day.

Mid-afternoon, Wheatley received a telephone call from the academy. The chairman required that he come at once back to London. No reasons were given nor apologies offered for the suddenness of the request. And indeed neither the journey nor the hour was convenient. So Wheatley was tired and irritable by the time he entered the academy late in the evening and nodded curtly to the pale, bespectacled young man who sat at the inquiry desk.

Minutes later he was knocking at a heavy mahogany door on the fifth floor. The door bore a brass plate on which was the one word, Chairman. He waited. After a few seconds, a green light glowed on his right, and the lock emitted a faint bleep. He turned the handle and entered.

He had been in this place before and knew what to expect. Heavy oak paneling. Heavy velvet curtains, closely drawn. Deep carpet. Heavy Edwardian furniture. All dimly perceived in the glow of a single table lamp, dark green and bronze, and the flames of artificial fire logs that glowed and crackled beneath an ornate mantel and bathed the room in constantly shifting light. The central heating seemed, as always, to be on full power and combined with the fire to create an atmosphere of stifling heat.

And yet as Wheatley stood in the doorway he was aware of a change. Usually the chairman was seated behind his desk. This time the desk was empty, and at first Wheatley could see his master nowhere.

Then a voice came from a deep leather armchair in front of the blaze.

"Come."

Slowly, Wheatley advanced.

"Sit."

This was an unusual honor. Wheatley sat in the facing armchair, his knees almost touching the old man's. The heat was here quite appalling, and at close quarters the chairman reeked of sickly sweet cologne that did not at all disguise the stench of decay. But Wheatley had long since ceased caring whether another's company gave him pleasure or satisfaction in any normal way—intellectual or emotional or even physical. What mattered was power. And here was a source of it. Clearly, this was to be a special occasion.

The old man leaned forward, his scraggy neck craning awkwardly over the stiff Victorian collar.

"You know why I have sent for you?"

"Perhaps."

"The offering."

"Yes?" Wheatley realized that his voice was slightly breathless.

"You are ready to make it. It shall be part of the Ceremony of Power."

Wheatley waited through a silence.

The chairman spoke again.

"The policewoman—the one who came to you. Cavaliere. She has her family living next door to her. Her mother and father. They shall be the offering. You know what to do?"

"Yes, but—her *parents*? Surely they won't be... virgin?"

"It does not matter. They are wholesome, affectionate, and intelligent. On this occasion it will be enough."

"I see."

"At Samhain. It will be a holocaust. The house. Everything. You and I must make the dedication here. Alone. Before the ceremony. The ceremony will release it, and it will advance you to Mastery. The others will not know. They are not yet ready."

The old man leant forward and laid a bony hand on Wheatley's knee.

"It will also be a vengeance, will it not? A vengeance on foolish women who interfere, and silly parents who bring them up to interfere." His lips stretched in what seemed to be a smile.

Even Wheatley's heart gave a leap at that grimace. But his hesitation was momentary—an instinctive rebellion of flesh against the fixed determination of will. A second later, and he had himself under control.

He smiled back.

The two sat motionless, gazing into each other's eyes. Firelight sent their shadows leaping and dancing around the walls. Suddenly it was difficult to distinguish the old man from the younger.

Or even to be sure that either of them was alive.

Twenty-Eight

London, Hackney. The same evening.

The air in the room was heavy with the smell of cheap cigarettes, Embassy Tipped and Players Number Six. British flags festooned the walls, almost obliterating the fading yellow paintwork.

Maria Coleman's eyes roamed over the dozen or so men and women who sat on folding wooden chairs, listening to the oratory of Joe Clanthorpe and occasionally interjecting questions. Two of them, in their tweed sports coats, old but well pressed cavalry twill trousers, and shoes outdated in style but polished to brilliance, looked to be retired military men. Six or seven others were in their late thirties. A few looked like late teenagers, cropped hair or shaved heads and imitation leather jackets the favored look. One wore a long black trench coat. Several, absurdly, wore sunglasses.

"… the answer is simple. The repatriation of immigrants will free vast sums at present tied to social services for these people. That money will be redirected to our own old people. And what is more, our getting rid of the burden of membership of the European Union will mean…."

She looked discreetly at her watch. She must at least catch some of the other meeting.

She rose quietly from her chair and slipped out the door.

Fifteen minutes later she pulled the black Porsche to a curb in Steadman Street and for a few minutes sat peering into the vanity mirror and making adjustments. When she got out, her hair was combed straighter than usual and she was wearing thick-rimmed glasses. Instead of her white belted raincoat she had on a rather battered mackintosh.

The atmosphere at the left-wing meeting was much like that of the meeting she'd just left, right down to the uncomfortable folding chairs. Even the cigarette smoke smelled the same. The mix of people was slightly different—younger, with several women, wearing blue denim rather than black leather. And there were, thank God, no sunglasses.

In other words, everything looked as usual.

Good.

She moved a chair at the back to a place where she could see better and sat down.

Why exactly she kept this personal watch on her cells, she wasn't sure. She could just as easily—and in many ways more safely—have worked only through her agents, as did Hargrove and Wheatley. But for some reason she preferred this personal check. It kept her in touch. And there was no doubt that if the academy's plans went through, the cells would be important. A scenario of chaos had been planned—but these were the foot soldiers who would have to make it work. Without them there would be no New Order. There was, then, a degree of wisdom and efficiency in keeping her finger on their pulse. And wasn't efficiency what mattered?

Efficiency!

She thought of Wheatley again.

Affection is a muddy affair that clouds the true basis of relation-ship. Pompous little cretin. What the hell did he know about affection? He wouldn't recognize it if he fell over it.

She'd certainly put a shot across *his* bows at the last board meeting. She'd quite enjoyed that.

Still, she'd better be careful. Wheatley was influential in the academy, and the academy offered the surest entrée she'd ever come across to wealth and power. Its resources seemed inexhaustible. As for the ceremonies and rituals? She didn't like the sound of them. She'd never set foot in the "temple" they talked about in the upper part of the building, nor was she looking forward to the moment when, she gathered, it would be necessary. But these things seemed to be the way in, and so long as they were, she expected she could live with them.

At least, she could live with what she'd seen so far.

And just in case one day she couldn't, there was always the briefcase, resting in the safe deposit box at Paddington Station. Only a fool would leave herself with no way out. For all the academy's talk about New Orders and taking power, what it was attempting was risky. Some would call it treason. And even the academy could make a mistake.

On the other hand, the possibility of a rich harvest from the academy still remained, and if she wanted a share in it she must stay in control—above all she must, as Wheatley said, keep control of herself.

Resolutely, if belatedly, she gave her attention to the speaker.

Twenty-Nine

O n their most recent stay in London, Cecilia's parents had found within walking distance of the hotel an excellent little restaurant that specialized in the cuisine of Abruzzo. That evening, having gone through her materials for the court and checked her wardrobe, Cecilia decided to complete her day by eating there.

She was not disappointed.

Bearing in mind her responsibilities the next day, she ate and drank modestly but well: an excellent *brodetto di pesce*, pieces of fish swimming in a delicious tomato and wine and garlic and vinegar and anchovy and peperoncino broth. With it she drank San Bernadetto sparkling water and a single glass of a lightly chilled young Montepulciano. She left the little *ristorante* in a general glow of goodwill, with *auguri* and *complimenti* for Mama and Papa, and the promise on her part—willingly given—that she would return when she could.

On her return to the hotel, she found five large volumes stacked on the desk in her room. The *Zohar*. On top of the books was a note in Michael Aarons's small, neat handwriting:

Dear Cecilia,

Here are the references. I know that you will be careful! These books are something of a treasure.
God bless you.

Best wishes,
Michael.

There followed a list of passages and pages. She nodded with satisfaction, left the books where they were, and went to bed.

THIRTY

Wednesday morning, October 29.

Rosina Cavaliere clattered to the front door with milk bottles and blinked at the early morning sun. Bushes and paths were soaked—there had been rain during the night. Now the skies were clear, and she breathed an exhilarating freshness. Marvelous! And convenient, too—for today was a day when she had to make visits, always more pleasant in the sun.

She was about to close the door when her attention was caught by something fluttering on it, low down. A roughly torn triangle of paper, fastened with a pin. She withdrew the pin and peered at the paper. On it were some words written in what she rather thought was Hebrew. And someone had taken the trouble to pin it there. How very odd!

The kettle whistled. Resolving to "show it to Andrea when he gets back," she laid the scrap of paper on the hall table and went back to the kitchen.

Figaro and Pu sniffed curiously at the bottom of the door and then trotted after her.

Tocco was already waiting bossily by her bowl in the kitchen.

***

Cecilia rose early, went to the fitness room, and worked out for forty-five minutes. By seven-thirty she was dressed and ready for the day, although she was not required at the court until ten. She had at least two hours before she need leave the hotel, which was just what she had planned.

She got some coffee and a patisserie from the decent little French coffee shop across the road (the hotel coffee she regarded as undrinkable), took them up to her room, sat down at the table, and took the first volume from the pile Michael Aarons had sent to her. It was not difficult to see what he meant about their being a treasure. The blue leather binding was beautiful. She opened the flyleaf and was further informed:

> *This edition of the Zohar is limited to 1250 sets of twelve volumes, volume I being numbered 1 to 1250, and 48 special sets printed on Banham Green's handmade paper, volume I of which is signed by the translators and numbered I to XLVIII.*
>
> *Beneath was the number of the copy, followed by two autographs, written (she suspected) with steel nibs.*
>
> H. Sperling
> M. Simon

In the next two hours, she learned something of the experience of Israel ("As the lily among thorns is tinged with red and white, so the community of Israel is visited now with justice and now with mercy"), and even something about God ("For all things are in Him and He is in all things: He is both manifest and concealed: manifest in order to uphold the whole, and concealed for He is found nowhere"). Concerning Wheatley or Kakoyannis she learned nothing.

And perhaps that was something.

For about one thing DS Sims had clearly been right. Kakoyannis was worshipping the devil. That he should have taken with him in order to do so a set of texts that so obviously had *nothing* to do with such worship—texts, indeed, that appeared to be devoted to its antithesis—seemed, at the very least, unlikely. Not, she supposed, that it was any use expecting devil worship to make sense. Nonetheless, she found herself more and more convinced that the book Wheatley had given her was a fake.

In which case, Wheatley was a liar.

Still, though, she had to prove it. She had to find the smoking gun.

What you can't show, you don't know.

Perhaps it would help if she talked to Michael Aarons again.

THIRTY-ONE

The same day.

At the request of the defense, the court adjourned for the day almost as soon as it began. Cecilia might as well not have been there. Could she make use of the unexpected time? She looked at her watch, took out her mobile, and called.

Michael Aarons himself answered.

Yes, he would be happy to talk to her again about her case and could see her if she came round at three thirty. He was tied up until then and had another meeting at five, for which he would have to leave a little early. But that would give them something over an hour.

When she arrived, he already had coffee prepared — this time in the English style, with mugs and a cafetière, what in Italy she might have called *Americano*. But it was good coffee, and she took it gratefully. He waved her to a chair, sat down himself, and waited. "Michael, have you ever come across something called the Academy for Philosophical Studies?"

His eyebrows shot up. "You mean the group in Bayswater?"

"Off the Bayswater Road. So you *do* know about them?"

"A little, yes."

"It's just that they seem to be coming up in this case. It could be important. If you felt free—professionally free, I mean—to say how you felt about them, I'd like to know."

"Would you?" A pause. When he spoke again, it was slowly and even more quietly. "I must confess I find the academy rather tiresome. Some of us seem to have to spend a lot of time with its... failures."

"Can you tell me what kind of failures?"

When he did, Cecilia had the impression that he chose his words with great care.

"The academy seems to expect certain very rigid mental and spiritual standards from those who go far with it. In return, it offers rewards. But those who can't maintain the standards tend to find the experience—well, depressing. And some of us, from time to time, have to help. Breakdowns. Clinical depressions. People trying to commit suicide. That sort of thing."

"You and other priests?"

"Oh, not all priests by any means. I've a friend who's a psychiatrist. Another who's a G. P. Several cases have come through the Samaritans. All sorts of people have been involved."

"You aren't saying that the academy itself refers people to you?"

"Oh no! The academy never recognizes any responsibility in these matters, so far as I know." He sighed. "Sometimes there's a financial side to things as well. I must be careful what I say here. I'm not saying I've any evidence of them doing anything actually illegal."

No one ever had, so far as Cecilia knew.

Michael went on.

"But like other groups, including, of course, the church, the academy does look for financial and material commitment from its members. A few people seem to have got themselves into difficulty. To be fair, when the academy has been presented with irrefutable evidence on that score, they've always cancelled covenants—even refunded money on one or two occasions. But you know how threatened and irrational people become when they feel themselves under pressure."

"I do." She waited a moment, then said, "Of course I'm not asking you to break any confidences, but would you feel able to tell me how *many* of these people you and your friends are helping? I mean, just roughly? Is it well—two or three a year? Or a dozen or so? Or what?"

"So far as I can recall, we're at present working with about twenty-five people. I will tell you that a sister in one of our Anglican orders has had eleven cases passed to her since the summer."

About twenty-five. Out of seven and a half million who populate Greater London, perhaps not many. Yet considering the small size of the academy, more than enough. Nor was there any clear reason to assume that the priest and his friends were the only people helping former members of the academy. Perhaps there were more? On the other hand, perhaps the academy tended to attract neurotic, depressive people. Wouldn't that account for a high number of such people among its "failures"?

Michael Aarons, like Verity Jones, now displayed a slightly disconcerting ability to answer the question she hadn't asked.

"I think I'm also free to tell you that of the cases I've mentioned, only two appear to have any previous history of mental breakdown. The rest may not have been the happiest or most integrated people in the world before they came to the academy, but they seem at least to have coped with life. Which is more than they can do now."

She nodded. What he said about the academy confirmed feelings she already had. But the stronger those feelings became, the more she was troubled by another question.

"But *why* do you think they're involved in all this? I mean, what's in it for the academy?"

He fetched the cafetière and poured more coffee for them both before answering.

"All right." He sighed, as she had begun to notice he often did before starting to speak about something he found distasteful. "I think that at the core of the academy there's a group of people whose approach to life is what I would call 'gnostic.' That's to say, they seek *knowledge*, especially knowledge of the supernatural—what I think they'd call 'spiritual' knowledge. Actually, what they're looking for is *power* through such knowledge. Because they *know*, they'll be strong. Because they understand, they'll be able to use others, to control them."

She was listening intently.

"Don't misunderstand me. I think being Christian means becoming in some sense stronger—at least, more complete, more truly human. But that's not what Christianity is basically *about*. It's like marriage. A good marriage will make you stronger, but obviously being stronger isn't what marriage is about. It's about faithfulness and loyalty between two people. Are you all right?"

She drew a sharp breath. "I'm fine. Please go on. I want to hear what you have to say."

He looked at her for a moment, then continued.

"Well, I'd say that when Christianity—and, incidentally, Judaism and Islam—are true to themselves (of course they often aren't!) they're about mercy and justice in our relationships with God and with each other. But the academy's so-called 'spirituality' isn't about *relationship with God* at all, it's about *the mastery of spiritual forces*. And the Academy isn't looking for *mercy* or *justice*, it's looking for *power*. I imagine it's because those who run the place care only for power that they feel so free to treat ruthlessly those who can't keep up with them. They use them and then throw them aside. As far as the Academy's concerned, the weak have no value except as food for the strong. And the strong, *because* they're strong, have a *right* to control the weak."

He sighed again. Then he said, "Am I answering your question?"

She nodded slowly. "I think you're beginning to. But do you think people can actually *get* power this way? I mean, real power. Power to do things." She thought of the men who had died twenty years ago. "The power, say, to kill people?"

"I suppose that depends on how far they go with it. If you deal with something only for what you get out of it, I suppose generally you get something. Power. Satisfaction. Maybe in this case power to kill people. There's a long tradition of rebellious forces in the universe ready to make use of rebellious men and women. Yes, you'll get something, for a while. In the end, of course, it's nonsense."

"Nonsense?"

"Yes, I think so. This quest for power, for control, all it really means is that we're trying to be gods—little gods! Like the story of Adam and Eve: 'You shall be as gods.' And of course it's nonsense. I admit there are times when it seems as if there's no God anywhere—no meaning, no sense. I can understand that."

For a moment he paused, and though the pain that shot across his face was gone in an instant, she thought she knew why he could understand it. He'd been there.

"Even our Lord had a moment on the cross when he felt abandoned," he said. "But to suppose that through something *I* did I could somehow make *myself* into God?" He shook his head.

"At any rate," Cecilia said, "you personally regard this thing—this false religion—as dangerous?"

"I regard it as diabolic. It takes the best and corrupts it. To use sex or politics as weapons of control is bad enough, but to use religion!"

"Do you think the academy is involved in Satanism or anything like that?"

"I don't know. Certainly people have said strange things, but vague talk by unstable people isn't information."

"No. Of course not." But she was thinking back to that scene in the cathedral. The dead old man in the cassock. His foul-smelling candle. He'd been worshipping the devil, hadn't he? And that inexplicable trail of death following Wheatley? Just what was she up against?

"Tell me, Michael, what would *you* do if you thought you were up against witchcraft—the devil? The real thing, I mean."

He looked sharply at her before he answered.

"First," he said, "I should try not to take my own role in the matter too seriously. If the devil is to be defeated— and he is—then it won't be by you or me or a thousand like us. As Christians, we believe God has *already* won the only victory that matters. Don't misunderstand me. I'm not saying evil isn't frightening and horrible. I *am* saying that nothing—not Satan and all his hosts—can finally separate you from God's love in Jesus Christ if you don't want it to." There was a pause. Then, "Do you believe that?"

Cecilia, who had been contemplating the fire, looked up slowly and met his eyes. She considered. Papa had brought her up to scorn the church, but never the faith.

Still, she was a little surprised at how quickly she answered. "I think I do."

"Good. Because if you didn't, my advice would be, don't have anything to do with the matter. But if you believe? Then, I suppose you must do whatever seems to be your duty."

Now it was her turn to sigh. Again he looked at her quizzically. She smiled.

"Mind you," she said, "about believing, it's not always the same. I say, 'I *think* I do,' because I have different sorts of days. Just now I'm here with you and feeling ever so believing and hopeful. But there are some days when I feel that everything's just meaningless. Then Figaro does something ridiculous, or I hear some lovely music, or... well anyway, suddenly I feel hopeful again." She thought for a few seconds. "The best I can say as to whether I believe is, I suppose, that I'm mostly an optimist. I mean, I *generally* decide to go along with the hopeful feelings, not the others."

Michael was smiling at her. "Have you ever read 'Bishop Blougram's Apology'?" he said.

"I don't even know what it is," she said.

"It's a poem by Robert Browning. Not perhaps the best he ever wrote. Anyway, how you've described yourself is just about exactly how he describes the life of faith. Having doubts, but choosing to take a chance on the hopes."

"Oh."

"The only thing is, to say all this took Browning about a thousand lines of rather tedious blank verse. I wasn't counting, but you seem to have it pretty well covered in about fifty words!"

THIRTY-TWO

London. Friday, October 31.

By noon on Friday justice had been done in the queen's name, and Cecilia found herself with a free afternoon. She went back to her hotel room, laid out on the bed every item of clothing that she had brought with her, and surveyed them. Her suits and low-heeled shoes were elegant, of course — but in the context of a dinner party? Sensible and boring! Looking at them, she suddenly became aware just how much she did *not* wish to appear in a suit before Michael and Papa's and Mama's other friends. Papa would have boasted about her — he always did. So didn't she owe it to him to present *la bella figura*? Of course she did!

A few minutes later she was at the concierge's desk, bag over her shoulder.

"What's the quickest way to get to Bond Street, please?"

In the window of the very first shop she looked at in Bond Street she saw a dress she liked. She went in, tried it on, and loved it. At which point it occurred to her to ask the price. It was far more than she'd intended to pay, but by then she was a lost woman.

Naturally she needed shoes and a handbag to go with it.

***

The Academy for Philosophical Studies, that evening.

"The police-woman in London?" Wheatley said. "But that ruins everything."

"Not at all," the chairman said. "I have known Cavaliere was in London all the time. All that matters is her parents. If anything, her absence is advantageous to us."

"How so?"

"Alone, her parents will certainly be more vulnerable."

"And the parents alone will be enough?"

"Of course they will be enough. They *are* the offering. The daughter, if you will, can be destroyed at leisure, perhaps after she has sufficiently savored their death."

"You're sure?"

The chairman said nothing, and Wheatley bit his lip. The question was superfluous.

Saint Andrew's Vicarage, the same evening

If Cecilia had any doubts about spending all that money (actually, she hadn't) they would have been assuaged when Michael opened the vicarage front door and she saw the look on his face.

"Cecilia, you look absolutely stunning in your 'working clothes'."

"Oh, thank you! I must admit this isn't exactly—I mean, I didn't want to let you down. Or Mama and Papa."

"I don't think there's much fear of that," he said. "Anyway, come on in! David and Naomi are here. They're looking forward to meeting you."

The Academy for Philosophical Studies, a few minutes later.

"There is, however, another matter," the chairman said. "It concerns the ritual, the Ceremony of Power. I have studied it. And

I now see that it must begin in a place dedicated to our enemy. A church, a synagogue, a mosque, it does not matter. But the enemy must be challenged in a place dedicated to his name. To that extent Kakoyannis was right. And you were wrong."

"But I thought—"

"Do not argue. I have examined the rite carefully. Look. You should have seen it."

Wheatley looked. Near an opening section of the text, some words had been minutely inscribed in the margin. This blasphemy, it said, must be uttered in *"miqdash la-miqdash"*—"a holy place for the sanctuary."

"It means what it says," the chairman said. "The rest we can do here, in our own temple, with the others. This part, not."

"I didn't think—"

"No, you did not think. You were careless. But I have a contact, a man who will admit us to a Christian church. There we shall do what we need to do. But it is some distance from here. You will need to drive us there now. At once. Then we must return here and complete the Ceremony in the temple with the others. There will just be time."

"Of course I will do anything that—"

"Your acquiescence is assumed. But first we shall complete your dedication. You have what is necessary for that?"

"Yes, of course. Here. Here it is."

Hands trembling, Henry Wheatley produced what he'd been instructed to acquire—oddments gleaned from the Cavalieres' house and its environs. Paint from a gate. A piece of cement chipped from between bricks. Small items taken from a clothesline.

Together, they considered the pathetic remnants with utter gravity.

"It will suffice," the chairman said. "You left the talisman? As I instructed?"

"Pinned to the door."

The chairman nodded.

"Then it is satisfactory. I shall prepare the chalice. Kneel."

Henry Wheatley sank to his knees and prepared to make his dedication.

Saint Andrew's Vicarage, a little later.

Cecilia found the evening delightful.

For one thing, David and Naomi Cutler, who both taught classics, were admirers of her father's work, and she was always pleased when any spoke well of her Papa.

"That last book of his — *Rome and the Gods* — it's quite the best thing I've seen on the subject," David said. "He's pulled *all* the threads together. I'm particularly impressed with the way he's tackled Gradel's hypotheses…"

Then there was the meal itself. Though normally relying on a housekeeper, Michael enjoyed cooking for his friends when he could. He'd made a coarse duck pâté, which he flanked with black and green olives, bright radishes, and good French bread. When justice had been done to that, he produced salmon steaks in white wine, with small boiled potatoes and sliced cucumber.

"Ooh, lovely!" Cecilia said, once she'd savored her first mouthful. "Wild salmon! Yes? It's getting quite hard to come by in Exeter."

"You like it? Good. I'm always a bit nervous when I'm cooking for Italians. You're all such marvelous cooks."

"Well you needn't be nervous about cooking for this Italian!"

Saint Saviour's Church, Bayswater, about an hour later.

Wheatley did not like churches. In this case the mere sight of the gothic windows and weeping stone angels made him uncomfortable. Still, the chairman walked without hesitation to the side of the building and rapped at the faux medieval arched door, so Wheatley followed.

The man who opened it surveyed them for a moment, then stepped aside so that they could enter. He said nothing but led down a short passage and into the body of the church, which was high, cold, and silent, illuminated by the yellow glare of streetlights shining through Victorian glass. Wheatley shivered. Still their guide said nothing, merely pointed them toward the central aisle that led to the altar.

The chairman walked forward and Wheatley fell in behind him. Their guide remained where he was. Then, when they were almost at the sanctuary steps, he shouted to them, his voice giving Wheatley a shock as it bounced and echoed off the vaulted ceiling.

"You've got one hour. Then I'll come by and lock the outer door. If you aren't out of here by then, you'll be locked in."

Wheatley whipped around, but the man had already gone.

A door slammed.

The chairman did not look back.

"Come," he said.

He advanced to the altar, placed the book on it, and lit a single candle. There was just enough light to read by.

"Begin," he said, pointing to the place.

Wheatley, his voice trembling only slightly, began.

THIRTY-THREE

Saint Andrew's vicarage.

"Thank you for all your help with the book," Cecilia said, after David and Naomi had left. "The *Zohar* and all that. It must be pretty obvious that this business I'm involved in... well, I'm really not at all sure what I'm up against."

Michael smiled. "I'd rather gathered that. I'll pray for you."

"Will you? That would be nice. Thank you!"

He grinned. "Don't mention it! It's what we priests do! And if the academy's involved in Satanism, I suppose tonight I ought to pray for them, too."

"Why tonight?"

"Don't you know the date?"

"October the thirty-first," she said.

"All Hallows Eve. Samhain—'summer's end.' Traditionally it's the night when the powers of darkness do their thing."

"The witches' Sabbath and all that?"

"Exactly."

"Well, yes, I've heard of that. I just didn't connect it with this."

Suddenly there was a kind of awkwardness between them, as if he no more than she quite knew what to say.

"Well, thank you Michael. And thank you for a lovely evening. Good night!"

"Good night, Cecilia. God bless you. Take care."

Cecilia walked slowly back to her hotel. The streets in this part of the city were quiet though by no means deserted, and the evening was mild and pleasant—very mild for the end of October. Once back at her room, she realized that she felt by no means ready for bed. Though she'd thoroughly enjoyed Michael's cooking and his wine, she'd eaten and drunk lightly, as was her habit, and she still felt fresh and alert. Indeed, the evening seemed to have stimulated rather than tiring her.

She looked at her watch. 10:15.

Why not carry out a little surveillance? It was absurd, when she came to think of it, that she'd spent so much time worrying about the academy and yet she'd never actually seen the place. And tonight of all nights was, perhaps, the time to change that. If the powers of darkness were going to do their thing, why not go and watch?

She had the address. She had a decent camera in the car—since once missing some crucial evidence on a case, it was her practice never to travel without one.

She caught sight of herself in the mirror. Well, yes. First, perhaps, she'd better change into something a little more suited to action.

She was amused by the look on the concierge's face when she approached him—not a half-hour after appearing in her finery—wearing a blue track suit, trainers, and a blue baseball cap with a *tricolore* shield and "Italia" on the front.

Surprised or not, in three minutes he'd seen to it that her Fiat was at the hotel entrance, engine running.

Thirty-Four

The Zoological Gardens,
Regent's Park, London. The same evening.

Once again, like the stirring of a memory, Katie was moved by longing to escape. But this time it was different. The former longing had been tinged with other emotions, guilt among them thanks to her keeper's "Thou shalt not." The ardor she now felt was without guilt—wholly righteous, wholly zealous, as if the greatest and truest of all keepers summoned and must be obeyed. She rose, tail sweeping from side to side, ears pricked, her whole being tense with collected power.

Then she stopped.

The gate to her enclosure was shut.

She pushed against it, but it did not yield. She pawed at it, then stepped back with a little whimper of frustration.

Then she grew still, gazing intently, her eyes fixed on the barrier before her. It seemed to her that the great keeper was still calling her—but in a new way. The great keeper was telling her something. Something important.

She tensed.

Listening.

Watching.

Remembering.

Humans coming and going through the gate.

The nice human in white who talked to her.

The nice keepers who fed her and played ball with her.

Always coming and going.

When they came and went, the little box spoke, and the gate opened. Always the little box called, and the gate obeyed.

Katie shook her head and whimpered again.

It wasn't enough. Still the great keeper was urging her. Look at them! Look at the humans. Look at them coming and going.

Katie looked.

The box spoke and they came and went.

They touched the box and the box spoke and — Katie uttered a triumphant yelp! She'd seen! *They touched the box!*

Again she bounded towards toward the gate but this time she did not push at it. Instead she reared on her great hind legs and supported herself on her forepaws, placing one on the crossbar and one on the box itself. And now it was hard for her. Her paw was not shaped like a human paw — but the great keeper called, and she must try. So she balanced herself on one foreleg, thrust her other foreleg between the railings, then pressed her paw against the far side of the box. Once. Twice. Nothing. Again she whimpered with frustration. Again she heard the great keeper urging her, and again she thrust, and pressed her pads as best she could against the box.

Zzzzzzzzzzzzzzzz!

The box spoke! And at once the gate started to yield. Katie gave another yelp of triumph and thrust herself away from it. It swung back, creaking softly.

She was free.

Silent and powerful she loped between the enclosures, heading north-east toward the main gate.

Once she paused and scented the wind, nostrils twitching.

Then she trotted on, a dark shadow moving purposefully and quickly.

***

Cecilia drew up in a vacant space between parked cars, two doors down from the Academy for Philosophical Studies, on the opposite side of the road. She pulled on the parking brake, and switched off the engine and GPS system.

So far, so good!

This was a perfect spot for surveillance: she had an excellent view without being particularly noticeable herself. The street was well lit, but the porch of the academy (clearly indicated by a shining brass plate that she could see even from the car) was brightly lit on its own. Good! She extracted from behind the passenger seat a case containing a camera and a window-mount tripod. She positioned them, set the Sony Digital 800 to "nightshot," and zoomed in to focus on the porch.

Then, taking care to keep herself as far as possible in shadow, she sat back and waited.

Thirty-Five

The Academy for Philosophical Studies.
The same evening.

Reginald Hargrove had been here for only fifteen minutes, and already he was perspiring. He could feel his shirt sticking to his back. His collar was tight and damp around his neck. This was intolerable. He felt like a laborer.

Couldn't they have told him how hot it would be? At least he could have worn something cooler.

In other circumstances he'd have left, but the chairman had said it would mean money—a lot of money—and he needed money.

Even if it meant standing here with the Coleman woman.

And presumably, whenever he arrived, that oaf Hutton.

Standing here perspiring.

Until the chairman came.

Then it would happen.

That was what the chairman said when he'd explained about needing the money.

Where was Wheatley?

If only it worked…

He tried to think of something else.

They'd promised him new children. That was something to think about. They'd sent photographs. A little boy and a little girl. Innocent. Sweet. He could see them now. But he'd have to go to Tangiers. Europe or North America had become too dangerous, they said. Certainly for what he wanted. And it would cost… a fortune. He still owed for the last pair.

How easy it had been in the old days. He'd seen his great great grandfather's diary. For some reason the old buffer liked to write it down—like Leporello listing Don Giovanni's conquests. There were always villagers happy to give up a child—they had too many anyway and the girls were especially useless. So there were a few extra guineas for the villager, a great deal of pleasure for the squire, and nobody any the worse … except perhaps the girl, and even she ended up in a better place. Wasn't that what they said?

But nowadays… it was all so difficult.

He *must* have more money.

If only it worked… this… whatever the hell it was.

THIRTY-SIX

Outside the academy.

Among arrivals, Cecilia already had pictures of a blonde woman she didn't recognize and a large, overweight man who was (she rather thought) an M.P. she'd seen on the news.

Ah! Here was another, mounting the steps: a man in his forties, she guessed. She focused again and let the camera run. As he arrived at the top, he swayed ever so slightly. Was he drunk? She thought she'd seen him on television too. A big union man, very much a left-winger, which went oddly with the M.P. because she was pretty sure he was right wing.

Ten minutes or so passed.

A Lexus LS pulled into the gap in front of the academy's porch. She tensed. Surely it was the car in Wheatley's drive when they visited him? Yes! And there was Wheatley himself, emerging from the drivers' side. Now he was opening the rear door and helping out very old, very frail man that Cecilia couldn't place.

She ran the camera until they made it up the academy steps and inside.

Then she sat back in the shadow again and waited.

***

Inside the academy.

As the chairman entered, with Wheatley beside him, Maria Coleman felt her heart sink. The truth was, she'd been hoping he wouldn't come. Or be delayed, so they'd not be able to go through with it.

Not that even yet she was clear just what "it" was. She only knew that "it" was the ceremony of power, the ceremony the chairman and Wheatley seemed to think was crucial.

She'd been uncomfortable from the very moment she entered the place — the upper room they called "the temple." Here, it seemed, was one of those "focuses of power" about which she'd got into the habit of speaking so easily.

Here it was, and she didn't like it.

At first it was hard to know why. The circular chamber occupied virtually the entire upper story of the academy, but it was not elaborate. Indeed, it was plain. Bordering on austere.

It was very nearly empty.

Around its entire circumference, black brocades hung in voluminous folds from floor to ceiling. There were no windows, nor any other means of admitting outside light. The only illumination came from two great candle-stands that seemed at first classical in style, and gleamed dully in their own glow.

The floor and ceiling were black, etched with the pentangle and other symbols.

At the center was a pillar.

A single black pillar.

And on the pillar, a flame.

At first impression, being in the temple was a little like being in the tiny village church when she was a little girl. Or in the cathedral where the sisters from the convent had once taken her.

Like it — but not the same.

No.

The temple she was in now stood to those other places rather as a caricature. A parody. An intended resemblance wherein, nonetheless, something was deliberately different.

She found herself staring at the intricate patterns woven into the black brocades, at the curves and arches of the candle stands, at the pillar itself—and there, gradually, she began to see the cause of her unease. There was, in fact, something wrong with them. All of them.

The symmetry of patterns on the brocades was *almost* right, but off just enough to be disturbing. The same was true of the symbols on the floor and ceiling. The pentangle was very slightly lopsided, the circle not quite true. The great candle-stands promised classical balance and elegance but instead delivered something that, when she stared at them, became quite *other* than balance.

The pillar wasn't quite straight. Nor was it *quite* in the center.

Actually, as she now saw, even the room wasn't *quite* circular.

Such tiny flaws.

And yet, as she looked at them, they seemed to press upon her.

Insinuating.

Demanding.

Demanding what?

That she accept them.

So why not accept them? They were the reality, weren't they? And she was a realist. So what of it?

It would not do. Something else was here. The tiny irregular-ities and imbalances pressed upon her, each pointing beyond itself to… what?

To something *utterly* irregular.

To the denial of balance.

The refusal of harmony.

She gasped.

She hadn't known it would be like this.

A wave of nausea swept over her.

It passed.

But then suddenly, irrationally, she tried to do what ten minutes earlier would have seemed unthinkable—and here of all places. Indeed, even now she did not *think* to do it: for it was not at all her mind that led her to the attempt but her body, making its own protest.

She tried to do what she had not done for nearly a quarter of a century.

She tried to make the sign of the cross.

She could not do it.

She started to cry out, to object—and could not do that either. Again something seemed to hold her. Something that came from the air itself, clasping her, caressing her, sliding into her nostrils and her mouth and the secret places of her body, arousing her like a lover. A lover she did not want but could not escape.

And now the chairman had come.

Tom Hutton was sweating like a pig.

So this was the temple.

He didn't think much of it.

The engineer in him hadn't liked it from the moment he walked in. Even slightly drunk—and let's face it he was more than slightly drunk—he could see there was something wrong with it. Whoever built it couldn't use a bloody spirit level—that was obvious. The whole place was out of kilter.

It made him uncomfortable just to be in it.

And now the chairman was here, with the little creep Wheatley ponsing along beside him.

And there was silence. Nothing.

Wasn't anyone going to do anything?

He'd have spoken himself, if he'd dared.

At last the chairman spoke.

And spoke. And spoke.

On and on, a dreary monologue in a foreign language, with something occasionally from Wheatley, who obviously understood it. Well, he would, wouldn't he? He was a *clever* little creep.

On and on.

Someone had said something about Hebrew, so he supposed that's what it was. But it depressed him more than the building, and that was bad enough.

Now the chairman and Wheatley passed beyond what at least seemed to be words to what obviously weren't.

And it was worse.

Muttering. Gibbering.

Like a pair of chimps.

Odd little clicks.

Like little bats.

Meaningless.

Yet sort of... *nasty*.

Their gibbering passed into nothing.

Empty. Formless. A void.

How long?

He felt dizzy.

The chairman was conscious of them all.

Their thoughts.

Their fears.

Hutton's revulsion.

Coleman's terror.

Hargrove's greed.

Wheatley's ambitions.

It didn't matter.

None of them could do anything.

Soon they would know good and evil as he knew them, as his master knew them. Even Wheatley would learn that he had been deceived. The mastery he sought would mean nothing. It was an illusion.

And now it was time.

Drearily, he blasphemed the NAME.

And waited.

THIRTY-SEVEN

Exeter.

The attack came suddenly.

Neither Rosina nor Andrea was at any point entirely clear what was happening, though afterwards they could identify certain stages.

The first was emotional.

As Rosina sat at the dressing table, brushing her hair, she suddenly felt utterly depressed. Why was she brushing her hair? Why was she doing anything? What was the point? God knows, she and Andrea had tried, but they couldn't even make their Cecilia happy. Where was it all going? She dropped her hairbrush, and couldn't be bothered to pick it up. She could only bury her head in her hands.

The second involved their senses.

More precisely, their hearing.

The roar of wind. There flashed into Andrea's mind the fleeting memory of a plague of locusts, seen long ago on television. But this rose and fell in blasts of sound that pierced everything — the room, the furniture, his head — reducing him to chaos.

Which blended into the next feature.

His mind.

Everything was muddled.

He could focus on nothing. Dimly he was aware of the dogs barking. He tried to stand, perhaps with a notion of using the bedside telephone. With every bit of his remaining strength he struggled for control and must have managed to get to the bed, for he found himself kneeling beside it, fumbling at the instrument on the bedside table. For a moment he actually grasped the handset but then could not hold on to it. It fell from his hand and crashed to the floor.

Finally, heat.

Stifling heat that came with a stench of decay.

The roaring mounted in intensity to a pitch of physical pain. For an instant Rosina could have sworn she saw huge mandibles and monstrous beating wings.

Madre di Dio, prega per noi! Mother of God, pray for us!

Then she fainted.

THIRTY-EIGHT

The academy again.

Immanuel Soames, part time lecturer at the Academy for Philosophical Studies, had finished with nineteenth-century idealism (there had been no questions) by 8:30 p.m. That he did not leave the academy until about a quarter to midnight was because he'd spent the ensuing three hours and fifteen minutes having "a drink" (each specimen of which had been declared with increasing solemnity to be the last) with the woman who served the bar, she all the while nattering on all about "that lot," who were "up to something" at the top of the building. Of course it had only been polite to listen, even if it wasn't clear *what* they were up to. And anyway it was interesting, he thought (he wasn't quite sure).

All good things come to an end. The woman withdrew to an inner sanctum. Soames crossed the hall, which was still well lit, and after some fumbling opened the main door to the street. Something large and gray and four-legged was waiting on the porch — something that promptly pushed past his legs and into the hall, causing him to stagger.

"Tha's a bloody great dog! Shouldn't do that, doggie!" he called out, then added with some vague sense of public responsibility, "And don't go peeing all over the bloody building!"

Conscience thus assuaged, he turned back to the door and began to prepare himself for the difficult task of negotiating the street and finding a taxi.

Cecilia swore softly.

A small fleet of minibuses had passed by, blocking her view. Now there was a man in the doorway, looking back at something in the building. Had someone gone in past him? If so, she'd missed whoever it was. The man said something and shook his head vaguely in the direction of whoever it was. Then he shrugged and came on out, leaving the door open behind him.

When he reached the head of the steps, Cecilia filmed him. She had plenty of opportunity, since he stood there for several minutes, swaying slightly. Clearly, he was inebriated. At last he came down the steps and set off somewhat uncertainly in the direction of the Bayswater Road. Cecilia, who followed him with the camera until he was out of sight, suspected he was looking for a taxi. At any rate, she was relieved that he hadn't got behind the wheel of a car. If he had, she'd have felt obliged to do something about it.

She turned her attention back to the porch.

Ten flights of stairs Katie mounted in a whirlwind, and there heard once more the call from the court of Solomon, the word of power. She obeyed, finding in that cry her summons from the great keeper—her summons to joy and high adventure. Straining her heart to the utmost, she crashed against the upper door—once, twice, a third time: at which assault the spindly, civilized lock burst, and she entered the temple in an ecstasy.

They had summoned the beast and to them the beast came.

Light streamed behind her as she leapt to the center, suffusing her in gold as she scattered them before her.

The chairman knew instantly Whose servant had come, and for the briefest of moments was shaken from his equanimity.

Mockery!

They were mocking him!

He had summoned the Beast, and they had *sent* a beast. A parody of what he had chosen.

How dare they?

He refused their mockery. He refused *them*.

Deliberately, defiantly, he gave himself to rage. Not hot rage. Not fury. That would be too like genuine passion. Cold rage. Resentment. Dreary, endless, humorless. There he settled.

Tom Hutton had thought he would faint when the door burst open.

Then in a blinding moment of utter surprise he saw that the invader was beautiful.

His head cleared.

Beauty. His dad's Alsatian bitch, Beauty. All those years ago. They'd loved that dog. Dad wept the day she died. Big, strong dad, who was dead himself a month later, drowned when the coal face flooded in the Lofthouse Colliery disaster. And all because the National Coal Board couldn't be bothered to get off its damned backside and do a proper geological survey.

But now it was as if Beauty had come back. Beauty triumphant! Perhaps Dad would come back too.

His ears were filled with the sound of a rushing wind that came with the invader, billowing the hangings and shaking the building. As if watching slow motion he saw, transfixed, how Beauty Triumphant pawed at each of the great candle stands in turn, how they swayed and fell, catching the curtains and dragging them with them. The heavy material must have been highly flammable, for as soon as the candle flames touched it they crackled into fire.

God knows what Dad would have said about this lot. Strict chapel was dad. *Touch pitch, lad, and you'll be defiled,* he'd have said.

Again he smiled. The flames were licking up. Such clever chaps, all of them—and they hadn't even the gumption to get decent fire-proofing.

So the joke was on them. And what a joke! Mining for dirt, they'd tried to drill a hole in God—and what broke out on them was Beauty!

Beauty was spreading fire everywhere. He could feel it, hot on his cheeks. The fire would destroy them, of course, along with their temple. Their crooked little temple! Why shouldn't Beauty destroy them, after the way they'd acted? Beauty would destroy them all—including Tom Hutton.

But Tom Hutton didn't care. It was surely better to have seen Beauty again and die by her than to live on in the desert.

That was what he thought now, anyway. He hadn't thought it before, but he thought it now. It's what Dad would have said.

And he no longer gave a damn what anyone else thought. They could all do what they bloody well liked.

So he fell to his knees, commended himself to Beauty, and waited for the end.

Reginald Hargrove did not believe it was happening.

Surely it was a dream. A very bad dream. He would wake in a minute.

What was the matter with him?

He *liked* fear, didn't he? He loved to see it in their little faces.

And pain. He liked pain. It was what he paid for. All that money.

But this wasn't the same. It was supposed to be *them,* not him.

He could feel heat from the flames.

His bowels were loose, his limbs slack.

His underpants were wet.

He could hear himself screaming but still he could not move.

This was all wrong.

It was supposed to be them.

It was supposed to be them.

THIRTY-NINE

Maria Coleman was standing almost directly in the wolf's path when it crashed into the chamber. Its charge knocked her aside, sending her reeling against the back wall. From there she watched as the wolf leapt at the nearest of the great candle stands and brought it down. The arc of its fall ended inches in front of her. She felt the rush of air as it tumbled and the heat of its flames. But already the wolf had hurled itself against the other candle stand. Then at the central pillar, and brought that down too. Oil gushed from it, spreading towards the curtain opposite in a gleaming pool that was immediately laced with fire. Flames were already licking at the heavy drapery as the wolf sprang to another panel and tugged. The black damask, clenched between gleaming teeth, ripped and tore like tissue.

Hutton was on his knees.

Hargrove was screaming.

The temple was disintegrating before her eyes.

Suddenly she realized that nothing barred her way to the open door. She tried to run towards it—*but her feet would not obey her.* Whatever power had ruled in that place still held her fast. She could not move or even cry out. She was doomed.

And now to her horror the wolf turned toward her and for the first time seemed to see her. It was going to attack her!

It did not. Suddenly it stopped its triumphant progress and simply stood, and so standing, looked at her with great, sad eyes. And in the instant she met those eyes she knew that she was free.

She ran.

Across to the shattered doorway and through it and down the stairs. At the first landing she paused for a second and pulled off her shoes, then plunged downward on silent feet. The descent seemed endless. Flight after flight. At every step she expected something terrible to fall upon her. At every landing she expected to be seized and forced back. And now indeed she prayed. *Oh God, if I get out of here I'll never come back! Oh God, if I get out of here I'll never come back!* Nothing happened. Screams and cries came from behind her, but ahead she saw no one.

Now she was at ground level. Surely here they would stop her? Her luck held. The hall was deserted, the front door slightly ajar.

She opened it and plunged through.

In the street she felt at last able to pause, drawing in great gulps of cool air, scarcely able to believe she was uninjured. But only for a moment! She was still too close to the building. She put her shoes on and started to walk, high heels clicking on the pavement. She was not walking anywhere in particular. She only knew she was walking *away*. At this moment anywhere would do, so long as it was away from *there*.

And now here was her car, gleaming in the street light. The Porsche was, of course, parked where she had left it—but in the same instant that she recognized it she also realized it was useless to her. In her panic she had left her handbag with her car keys and coat in the anteroom to the temple.

It didn't matter.

She wouldn't go back for them. She wouldn't go back for anything. The car would have to stay.

She walked on, quickening her step.

FORTY

Cecilia watched as the blonde woman put on her shoes and left. The front door was still open. Why was the woman not wearing her coat? Why had she taken her shoes off? Whatever had happened, she appeared to be in control of herself and in no particular distress. So Cecilia contented herself with filming her as she walked away down the road.

And now what?

A huge dog had appeared at the head of the steps with something in its mouth. A dog — no? A wolf? *Another* wolf? Or even — *the same wolf?* Cecilia watched in utter astonishment as it descended the steps, trotted straight to her car, and deposited its burden — which she could now see was a book — in the road by the driver's door. It looked up at her for a moment, then bent down and pushed the book toward her. It looked up at her again, head slightly to one side, as if making sure she understood, then trotted away into the darkness.

Only when the wolf had gone did it occur to Cecilia that in her astonishment she'd forgotten to film it. Damn! Had there actually been a wolf? Was she hallucinating? Apparently not, for there on the pavement was the book, solid and dark. She didn't make the same mistake twice. She removed the camera from its tripod, opened the car door, and photographed the book from several angles. Then she filmed it with a five-pound note beside it so its size would be clear. Finally, she put the camera back in the car, took a pair of forensic gloves from a packet in the glove compartment, put them on, and picked the book up by its edges. She felt a surge of quiet triumph. It was a battered version of the one Wheatley'd given her. *It was surely the original!* And if it was and she could prove it, then she'd proved Henry Wheatley a liar.

She got back into the car.

Inserted between the pages at several points were ribbons. Opening at one of them—and still careful even with gloves on not to handle the thing save by its edges—she was presented with what seemed, once again, to be Hebrew. She strained her eyes in the yellow light, oddly fascinated by the curves and lines of the script. Dark and graceful it lay across the cheap paper. Serpentine. Ingratiating. Almost she felt that if she looked long enough she'd grasp its meaning.

She shook her head and let it close.

She looked up at the still open door to the academy. Should she go in? Her curiosity was fierce and the temptation strong—but then, the wiser step was surely not to risk the academy's becoming aware of her surveillance but to withdraw with the spoils she had and see what could be learned from them. Above all, she needed to find out what was in the book. She should have Michael Aarons look at it. Yes, that was the first priority.

She turned the key in the ignition. Then, as was she pulling out of her parking place, she became aware of flashing lights and sirens behind her. At the end of the block she pulled over and looked back. Smoke was streaming from the upper story of the academy. Lights were going on in surrounding houses. Someone must have dialed 999.

Within minutes there were appliances outside the building and firefighters swarming around it.

There was still, however, the matter of the wolf. She didn't know where it was by now, but surely the police should be alerted? A call from her mobile could be traced, and at this stage of her investigation she wasn't at all sure who needed to know she'd been watching the academy, so—

Ah, problem solved! There was a British Telecom call box opposite.

She didn't say who she was: merely gave her information and replaced the receiver.

When she'd left the box (it stank of urine) she stood for a few moments in the night air, looking back toward the academy. Already it looked as if the situation was pretty well under control.

Then she returned to her car, and drove away.

FORTY-ONE

Wheatley was a man who never allowed himself to be without an avenue of retreat. As soon as the wolf entered the temple he perceived the situation, stepped smartly aside, and walked quickly behind the hangings to a door that led to the back stairs. The door was locked, but he had a key. He stepped out onto the landing, closed the door behind him and locked it again. He would not have the creature following him.

He paused for only a moment. Then—since shrieks and crashes from the temple still sounded uncomfortably close—he descended a couple of floors and made his way to the boardroom. Here the noise was muffled, and he could think more clearly.

For his colleagues, he gave not a damn. He doubted very much whether any of them would survive. He had a vague recollection of seeing Coleman making for one of the doors. Hargrove had tripped on the drapes and fallen in a pool of flame, and he recalled Hutton's going down. He couldn't remember noticing the chairman at all.

But it didn't matter.

None of them mattered.

What mattered was that the Ceremony of Power had been interrupted, the precious notebook almost certainly burned, and the inauguration of the New Order now indefinitely delayed. Moreover, the interruption of the ceremony meant that his attack on the Cavalieres had been interrupted, too.

Would the half-completed ceremony have been sufficient?

He doubted it.

They were both intelligent and perfectly healthy, so far as he knew. They were almost bound to have survived. For his dedication he had, at the chairman's direction, pledged two lives to the power he served. If that pledge were not fulfilled, those lives not given — by sunrise — then his own life would be forfeit. The power knew no mercy, and he knew the rules.

So he stood looking out of the window, and pondered his next step. His attention was caught by movement: a dark form slipping along the pavement. It was — yes, it was surely the creature that had attacked them in the temple, the wolf, with something in its mouth. It stopped by a car and — quite deliberately, it seemed — laid the something on the pavement. It was a book — indeed, it was surely *the* book. For a moment the wolf stood, staring at the car. It bent its head and nuzzled the book, looked again at the car, then trotted off.

Should he go down? Perhaps he could retrieve it?

Too late — the car door was opening. And now someone was getting out, someone in a tracksuit and baseball cap. A boy? No, a woman. Then, to his utter astonishment, he saw it was the policewoman. Cavaliere! But how on earth…? He watched as she first photographed and then removed the book. And as he watched, his frustration and his fury mounted. It was *his* book. The precious book he'd taken so much trouble to get. The book, now he thought about it, that he'd lied to her about. The book that undoubtedly had his and Kakoyannis's fingerprints all over it, as she'd soon discover — for the care with which she handled it did not escape him. *Damn* the woman! Screw her. Screw the interfering *bitch*.

But how the hell had she known to come here? All right, he'd told her about the academy. But how had she known to come *tonight*? Did she have information? Had someone betrayed them? Was there a mole? One thing was clear. He'd never thought she was stupid, but even at that he'd underestimated her.

He watched her drive off, then considered his own car, parked nearby. He looked at his watch. First things first: whatever she knew or didn't know, whatever her sources of information, she couldn't possibly know what he was going to do next, for he'd only just decided it himself.

It was her parents who were the immediate concern and if he left at once there was still time to deal with them. He could be in Exeter in fewer than three hours, well before sunrise. Once there, revenge and expediency pointed in the same direction.

Then, armed with new powers from his completed dedication, he would deal with their daughter.

And that would be a pleasure.

Forty-Two

It was now past midnight, but Cecilia drove by Saint Andrew's on the off-chance — it was, after all, practically on the way to her hotel — and sure enough, there were lights on in the Lady Chapel and the rectory.

She pulled her car into the gap in front of the big double gates, stopped, and got out, clutching her camera and the book, now secured in a plastic evidence bag. She walked up to the main entrance to the church and gently pressed the door. It swung silently open. Even dimly lit in the glow from the Lady Chapel, the interior was a marvel of cream and gold elegance. It reminded her of Rossini: warm and joyful. She walked softly through it toward the light. Even if Michael weren't here, she was glad she'd come.

But he was there, in the Lady Chapel, sitting in front of the Blessed Sacrament. Then she saw his face. Mother of God! She'd walked into a conversation between lovers. She ought not to be here.

She drew back and would have left, but as soon as she moved Michael Aarons turned and smiled at her.

"Hello," he said, as if her wandering into the Lady Chapel at half past midnight were the most natural thing in the world.

Feeling suddenly secure, if slightly light-headed, she went and sat beside him.

For a while they sat in comfortable silence.

"I hadn't realized how beautiful Saint Andrew's is," she said. "When I came in it felt like Rossini, but in here it's like Mozart."

He looked at her. "Now that's interesting. I've always thought of the church as Mozart and the Lady Chapel as Handel."

For several moments they sat, each considering the other's perception, then simultaneously they said—

"Well, yes, I see what you mean—"

"Yes, I can see what you mean—"

—and laughed.

"But neither, I think, is Johann Sebastian Bach."

She considered for a moment. "No, not Bach."

"Wagner?"

"Ugh!"

Michael chuckled. "My sentiments entirely!"

These matters resolved, again they again sat in silence.

"May I tell you something?" she said at last. "Would you mind?"

"Of course I wouldn't mind. I'd be honored."

So she told the entire story, so far as she knew it. Of Nikos Kakoyannis and the cathedral. Of the wolf. Of Henry Wheatley. Of the sequence of deaths. And of what had happened now. Finally she produced the book, still in the plastic evidence bag.

"I think this," she said, "is almost certainly the book we found with Kakoyannis's body in the cathedral. If we can show a *trace* of its having been in Kakoyannis's possession—maybe a hair or two from the carpet bag—then we've at least proved that Wheatley is a liar. And if we find *both* their prints... well, you see the point. So I'm being very careful with it. But maybe you could look at it and give me some idea what's in it."

"Let's go to my study," Michael said. "The light's better there."

They began with her photos, which they looked at on

Michael's computer. He recognized Hargrove and Hutton at once and was able to confirm that the former was indeed a conservative Member of Parliament notoriously to the right of most of his party, the latter a union leader of pronounced left-wing views. He recognized none of the others. She emailed the entire set to DS Verity Jones with a note explaining when and where they had been taken, and asking her to find out what she could about the subjects as quickly as possible.

"Verity Jones will have fun with these," she said. "She's an enthusiast. When you ask her to look for something, she *never* gives up until she finds it!"

Next they turned to the book. Cecilia again put on the plastic gloves, and held it by its edges, open so that Michael could see it. "I'm sorry," she said. "Even with gloves on, if I touch the flat surface I might wreck a print."

"It doesn't matter. This is fine." He bent forward and started to read.

"Turn the page, please," he said after a couple of minutes.

Then, "Turn to the first ribbon."

His voice sounded peculiar.

Then, "Go back to where you were. Turn the page, please."

Several minutes passed while he read. As he did so, his lips tightened. After a while—it seemed the gesture cost him an effort—he closed his eyes and spoke without looking at it.

"Cecilia, this book is extremely dangerous. I wish it could be destroyed."

Cecilia waited.

"If I still had any doubts about the evil that is in the academy," he said at last, "that book would end them. And the wolf *brought* it to you!" He stopped for a moment before continuing. "It holds the key. I recognize it. *Beriyt et-Mavet*—a covenant with death."

"You *know* about this?"

Michael nodded. "After I abandoned the faith of my fathers, for two or three years before I became a Christian, I was... I..."

Again he stopped.

Cecilia saw the pain in his face. She put out her hand and laid it over his. "Michael, please," she said, "I'm so sorry. I didn't mean to—"

He shook his head and gave her a half smile.

"It's all right." He took her hand in both of his for a moment. Then he gently relinquished it, got up, and walked to the window. He stood for several minutes, gazing out at the night sky. At last he turned back to her.

"Twenty-one years ago a drunk driver hit my parents' car. I was in the back—I never even saw him and I doubt mum and dad did. I woke up in hospital pretty well unscathed—well, physically. But I was told mum and dad had died instantly. So had the drunk driver.

"After that, I gave up the faith of my fathers. I gave up... living, you might say. I just got—lost." He sighed. "I was an only child. Mum's and Dad's families were European Jews, and they'd been more or less wiped out in the war. My granddad survived, but he was too old...."

"Oh, Michael," she said softly, but he shook his head.

"The truth is, I could have found someone. There were good people in the synagogue who wanted to help. No, I *chose* to be lost. I felt abandoned and filled with rage and I chose madness. I'm not proud of it. It's a part of my life I try to forget."

"But to come to your problem, yes, I got to know about that. Not enough, thank God, to be enmeshed by it, but enough to see it for what it is." He sighed. "Of course I don't know the whole story. Only God knows that. We're talking of what was always kept secret. And some of it's vague, and it's marred by half-truths and buttressed by rumors.

"Nonetheless, there *is* a story that emerges, and it's more or less consistent. It concerns a ritual. Originally, I think, the ritual wasn't evil. It was beautiful. It was meant to draw on the divine harmony and lead those who used it to find their place in that harmony. But then it was corrupted and its power was used to *deny* the harmony. There's a rabbinic tradition that Solomon used it to control the demons so they'd help build the Temple. Even so, the rite turned him to evil.

"After that the story's vague. Some say Alexander the Great had a version. Others say some of the Roman emperors. Then others, later. Barbarossa, Napoleon, Hitler. They've all been candidates. But as I say, it's vague, and the theories often contradict each other.

"I can tell you one thing for certain though, something from my own experience. I was in Marseilles, while I was still in my madness, and I was shown what I was assured on good authority was a fragment of this ritual—the corrupted form, you understand, the attack on divine harmony. That fragment, they said, was a powerful talisman for evil. Because I'd learned some Hebrew I was told to read it though I wasn't allowed to touch it. And I *felt* the evil. Anyone who would perform that rite with serious intent would destroy the earth on a whim. Actually, that was when I realized I wanted nothing more to do with it. And that's why I got out—indeed, it's why I came back to England. I needed to escape.

"But as you see, it didn't entirely work. The rite has found me anyway. After all these years! Cecilia, I recognize it. That book contains it—and I think it's complete."

"And the academy?" She asked the question, knowing what the answer would be. "They were going to do it?"

"I believe they were. You saw the ribbons?"

"Yes."

"The thing's a bit like a missal. Certain passages, certain invocations—prescribed for certain days. The one marked by the ribbon was for tonight—Samhain—All Hallows' Eve. I think was about to be used. Perhaps it was *being* used."

"And you believe that such a ceremony could really *do* something? Something evil?"

Michael sighed. "Yes, I hate to say it but I think it might. Of course God can't *ultimately* be mocked. But in the short run

God does seem willing to put up with our blasphemies." He paused. "The thing is, words are *actions*. They *change* things. Think of saying, 'I love you,' or 'I forgive you.' That's something the ancients seem to have understood better than we do. And those" — he looked toward the book — "those are very evil words."

"And you'd like me to destroy it?"

"I wish you would."

She hesitated. "Michael, we speak here in absolute confidence?"

"Of course."

"This man Wheatley — you know I think he's murdered three or four people. But he's clever. And as I said, this book may be the piece of evidence that'll enable me to catch him out. Not in much, but at least in a significant lie, which is a start. Lying to a police officer is a serious offence. What's more, I just sent a photo of it to a detective sergeant in CID. You see my problem."

Michael nodded.

For a moment, both were at a loss.

She picked the book up, preparatory to putting it back into the evidence bag. As she did so, something fluttered from it to the carpet.

She picked it up. It was a small, roughly torn triangle of paper, with a line written in Hebrew on it.

"What's this?" Holding it by its corner she held it out to Michael, who looked at it, and again his brow furrowed.

"Cecilia, please, never mind the book for a moment! Would please telephone your parents?"

"What — you mean *now*? What's wrong? What does it say?"

"It says, roughly: 'Andrea and Rosina Cavaliere, the whole burnt offering of Henry Wheatley' — and today's date. It looks to me as if —"

"My God!"

Cecilia quickly put the book and the paper back into the evidence bag, and took the telephone Michael was already passing to her. The menace she had long suspected in Henry Wheatley had now become utterly personal. She dialed her parents' number, then held the handset in the air so Michael could hear the engaged signal.

"*At one in the morning?* I don't think so."

She tried again, just to be sure. The line was still busy.

Her mouth tight, she stabbed in another number.

"Sergeant Wyatt? Oh, thank God! Look, Sergeant, I can't get through to my parents on the phone and I'm worried. Is there anyone near who could just check that they're all right?"

A pause. Then a response that Michael could not hear.

"You have? That would be great. Thank you *so* much! Good. Okay—I'll wait for you to call back."

She put the phone in her lap.

"There's a panda car half a mile away. They're getting it to look in and they'll call me back. They reckon it'll be about fifteen minutes."

It was actually only ten minutes before the phone rang.

"Yes. Yes—here.... What? Yes—it should take me, oh, three hours.... What? No, I don't think so.... I'll go straight there.... All right. Thanks."

She laid the telephone on the table.

"Michael, I don't like this at all. There are lights on in the house upstairs, but they can't raise Mama or Papa. And something's on fire. They're going back to break in. And they've sent for the fire service." She took a deep breath. Then said, "I'm going to go back to the hotel, collect my things, and drive home now. I want to be there."

"Of course you do. But may I make a suggestion?"

She looked at him.

"You're tired, and you're a bit distracted: not a good state for a solo drive. So why don't I come with you? I could even spell you part of the way if you liked—at least out of London. I'm sure I'm not as good a driver as you, but I dare say I know the roads round here better. Or if you don't want me to drive, at least I can keep you company. After all, Andrea and Rosina are my friends. I'm concerned about them, too."

"That would be wonderfully kind of you—but then, we'd be going in my car, so you'd be stuck in Exeter with no car to get back to London."

"Cecilia, I can drive quite well but I *love* trains. The service from Exeter to Paddington is excellent, and then there are even ways to get from Paddington to Holborn Circus on London Transport."

Worried as she was, Cecilia had to smile.

"Thank you, Michael. I should like that very much."

"Good! Now, you go to your hotel and do what you need to do, and then you can come back here and pick me up. There are a couple of things I have to do, but by the time you get back I think I can be ready to go."

They decided that Michael would take the first spell as far as Bristol, and Cecilia the second. They fastened their seat belts, Michael checked the rear view mirror, and they set off into the night.

London's main roads are scarcely ever completely deserted, but at this time of night they were at least reasonably quiet. In a little under twenty minutes, they were nearing the M3.

The last time Cecilia had been this way at night she had been with Mama and Papa. They had enjoyed *Don Giovanni* at Covent Garden with Joyce DiDonato as Donna Elvira—a surprise treat for Cecilia on her birthday. Suddenly she found herself overcome by thoughts of how good they were to her. How much she loved them. And if that pompous little creep —

"Steady on!" Michael said. "That's not Wheatley's neck you've got hold of."

Cecilia relaxed—just a bit. And stopped mangling the strap to her shoulder bag.

FORTY-THREE

Sergeant Stillwell conferred with Sergeant Wyatt at the station again on his personal radio, then returned to the front door of the Cavaliere's house. For a moment he stood listening, peering at the upper windows, two of which were lit.

He could hear his colleague at the side, still stamping on those smoldering embers they'd found.

He rang the doorbell one last time and rattled the letterbox fiercely.

He stepped back from the front door and surveyed it.

Now he'd have to break in.

Then, just as he was about to act, the glass panels filled with yellow light.

For a while, even after consciousness returned, Andrea lay perfectly still, unable to make out why the light was on, why he was on the floor, or what the noise was.

Then he remembered.

Good God! What on earth had come over him?

And where was—? Oh, there! Rosina blinked at him.

"You too?" she said.

"Yes. It was… I'm not sure what it was."

He shook his head and got a little unsteadily to his feet. He felt exactly as if he'd drunk considerably more wine than he needed—unfair, since at supper, knowing he wanted to read afterwards, he'd limited himself to a single glass. Even through the curtains he could see bright blue lights flashing outside the house. He could hear an approaching siren. What on earth was happening? The six o'clock news had been gloomy about tensions with Iran, but so far as he knew no idiot had actually started another war.

Then the doorbell gave a prolonged ring and the letterbox rattled violently.

"I'm coming! I'm coming!" he called out—then realized that whoever it was couldn't possibly hear him. "It's obviously the police."

Rosina got to her feet.

"Maybe they know what's happening," she said.

"I'll go and see."

He went out to the landing and switched on the lights. Various dogs appeared from various places. At least two of them looked sheepish.

He could see a bulky figure silhouetted against the glass panes of the front door, blue lights flashing behind him. He went down to the door and opened it—to cold air, a police uniform, and a broad Devon accent.

"Sorry to be disturbing you, Mr. Cavaliere, but we was a bit worried, you see. You seem to have had a fire round at the side. And your telephone was off the hook."

"Yes. Of course. Sergeant Stillwell, isn't it? Well, thank you, Sergeant. I'm sorry to have been slow coming to the door. I don't know what happened. Something seemed to knock us both out, for several minutes. Do you know what's going on?"

"No, sir. But as I say, you seem to have had a fire. There's definitely something been burning at the side of your house. I don't know what it was. You'd better come and have a look. It's made a bit of a mess of your garden, I'm afraid."

Well, at least it wasn't the start of World War III.

FORTY-FOUR

As soon as Wheatley turned into the road where the Cavalieres lived, he saw the flashing lights of the police car and pulled to the side under the shadow of some trees. The house stood back from the road and was fronted by more trees and a high hedge, but he thought he could make out lights at the point where the second story should be.

After a few minutes, the firefighters arrived amid more flashing lights. Lights had gone on in several other houses in the road. None of this surprised him, for the attack was meant to be marked by fire. The question was, how much damage had the fire done? And what had happened to the couple? For the moment, he determined to sit in his car and watch.

There was still plenty of time.

The fire had indeed made "a bit of a mess" of the Cavalieres' garden. That side of the house was flanked by a high stone wall. The entire area from the wall to the house was shriveled and blackened. A wheelbarrow and a wooden frame had still been burning when the police arrived. The wall of the house itself was scorched, and the frames of the lower windows were charred and smoldering. Fearing that the wall might be on fire inside, the police had summoned the fire service. And while they waited, they'd stamped on the embers and suppressed the flames they could see. Fortunately, the effects of earlier rain had kept the fire from spreading.

The firefighters were naturally greeted by furious barking from Figaro, Tocco, and Pu, who had by now entirely recovered their spirits.

Rosina and Andrea soon calmed the dogs, but found the firefighters were as much at a loss to explain the fire as they were themselves. The flames seemed to have had no origin.

"Haven't you any theory at all?" Rosina asked.

"Well, no, ma'am," the senior officer said, "not really. It's like, well, just as if the ground itself overheated all of a sudden. What we *can* do though is make sure it's really out."

So they did, examining the wall with particular care: which in effect meant ripping it half apart and in the process making an unholy mess of the study. Still they found nothing. That side of the house, as it happened, did not even contain wiring. They dug down in the garden and inches beneath its scorched surface found normal Devon earth. It was utterly baffling.

Yet Rosina and Andrea, in the midst of this, were feeling much better. Sergeant Stillwell had told them about Cecilia's telephone call. Initially, they both thought she was foolish to think she need rush home from London in the middle of the night to rescue them. But then Andrea said, "Never mind! She is a daughter who loves her mama and papa," and they agreed there was nothing foolish about that.

The call from Exeter came through on the mobile just after 2:30 a.m. It was Sergeant Wyatt, with good news.

Cecilia listened, sighed with relief as the tightness in her chest eased, and thanked the sergeant.

"Tell everyone that tonight I think you're all marvelous." She added *"Grazie a Dio!"* as she closed the phone. Michael added a quiet "Amen." Rosina and Andrea were all right. Everything else could be dealt with in due course.

FORTY-FIVE

For over an hour Wheatley waited while the firemen checked and double-checked, fetched equipment from their vehicles and returned for more equipment. As time passed any hope he had that the couple might be dead faded. No one brought out bodies, and when at last the firemen and firewomen left, their manner was cheerful, even a bit raucous.

A while later the police also returned to their car, turning at the gate to bid someone goodnight.

There was time enough.

He unlocked the car's glove compartment and took from it a revolver. He checked the safety catch and made sure the road was clear. Then he left the car and walked quickly towards the Cavalieres' gate. He stopped. Perhaps the police had left someone behind? He shrugged and went on. If there were others there, he had the gun and surprise on his side. He'd kill them, too.

What he could not do was go back. Not now.

At last they had all gone.

Andrea and Rosina went back to the kitchen, which was tidier than they might have hoped. Against that, the study was now uninhabitable.

"But that," Andrea said, "we can think of tomorrow." For the moment, they would make more coffee, read their books, and wait for Cecilia.

The dogs had disappeared. Excitement over, they'd gone back to bed—doubtless his and Rosina's bed. He could not be bothered to do anything about it. Tocco's parting look at him as she mounted the stairs said it all: our humans have obviously gone completely mad. Best ignore them. And no point in taking any notice of their rules.

He sighed.

Come to think of it, Tocco, when *did* you take any notice of rules? When did any of them? Our dogs aren't bred out of the Spartan kind. They're *Italians*, every one of them.

He reached for the macchinetta.

The surrounding houses had returned to darkness. The road was silent and deserted.

Quietly Wheatley opened the gate to the house and slipped through. It was his second surreptitious visit within twenty-four hours, and he knew the terrain. There were now no lights visible from the front. He moved to the left and immediately was aware of a glow from ground-floor windows at the side of the house. Further progress found him crouched behind bushes, at an angle to the lighted windows, which seemed to look into the kitchen. He caught glimpses of two people moving about, first a man and then a woman. Presumably, the policewoman's parents.

Suppose they weren't? He'd have to risk it.

But he couldn't do it from here. To have them both in his sights when he fired he needed to get in front of the windows. He began to inch his way forward.

Cecilia had taken over the driving. As they turned into the road where her parents lived, in the house next to hers, to Michael's surprise she suddenly knocked the car into neutral, switched off the lights and the engine, and coasted the last few yards before coming to a silent halt.

"What's the matter?" he said.

She placed a finger to her lips, then pointed.

"Look — the Lexus!" she whispered. "It was parked outside the Academy earlier. It's Wheatley's."

She opened the car door, got out, and ran on silent feet to the low garden wall. Scarcely checking her pace, she vaulted over it, and disappeared into the garden.

Michael got out on the other side and followed her as quietly as he could, but rather less gracefully and via the garden gate.

FORTY-SIX

Wheatley crept forward, gun in hand, safety catch off. He was almost where he needed to be. Another couple of meters would do it. He edged another few steps, watching where he trod, careful to make no sound — only to hear a distinct *thud* and the crackle of leaves behind him. Damn! Had the police come back? Well, too bad! Now reckless of all consequence, he swung around ready to kill whoever it was.

But whoever-it-was was upon him out of the darkness faster than he could have thought possible.

"In your dreams!" it said — and its voice was a woman's.

He could smell her perfume. Exquisite pain shot through his hand as the gun flew into the air. Enraged, he tried to fight back, to grapple with her, to smash her down, but a stab of pain along his entire arm sent him spinning. The earth revolved and he hit it with a thud that knocked the breath from him. Gasping, he tried to rise but was driven down again by a blow to the small of his back that at once became fierce and unrelenting pressure. He could only lie helpless, raging into cold soil and gravel that pressed hard against his cheek.

Brisk, unkind hands ran over him, his back, his arms.

"You just stay there while I make sure you've nothing else up your nasty little sleeve." *It was Cavaliere again!* But how the hell had that bitch known he was coming *here*? He hadn't known himself. *Damn her!* Was she a witch? Was she *everywhere*?

"I take it you're all right." A man's voice. He sounded slightly breathless.

"Oh yes, *I'm* fine."

Furious barking. Jesus Christ, they'd a whole pack of dogs! He *loathed* dogs!

Another woman's voice, "*Cecilia! Madonna! Che stai facendo? Chi è questo?*"

"*Ciao Mama! Questo?*" The bitch switched back to English. "This, Mama, is Henry Wheatley, who's in *serious* trouble. Hello, Figaro! Oh, thank you! A sloppy kiss is *just* what I needed." Wheatley himself was subjected only to a series of fierce growls.

"All right Mr. Wheatley, the rest of you seems to be clean. Let's have you up and into the house!" She jerked him unceremoniously to his feet. "Oh, and Mama, this is my new friend, your friend Michael. He shared the driving, which was very kind of him. And he'd already provided me with an excellent dinner: *salmone al vino bianco alla francese.* Yum. Come along, Mr. Wheatley, I think we need to have you in the light, where we can see you."

Andrea and Rosina, at Cecilia's request, went to telephone the police and make more coffee.

"You sit down," Cecilia told Wheatley. "Over there. On the couch."

But from his expression Michael guessed that Wheatley'd recovered enough to bluster.

He had. "And then what happens? Are you going to keep me here all night?"

"What happens, Mr. Wheatley, is that in a few minutes my colleagues will arrive. Then you'll be charged with various criminal acts, of which the least significant will be illegal possession of a handgun. Of course we all know the law's just a convenient meta-narrative for successful groups — but the law's *my* meta-narrative, and I happen to be successful here, so you're going to have to live with it."

"Successful? You were merely lucky."

"Just as you like, Mr. Wheatley. In the meantime sit down."

"Or what, officer? Will you *make* me again? Thinking of trying a little more police brutality?"

Cecilia looked at him. There was the tiniest change in her posture, the slightest alteration in the angle of her head.

"Why, Mr. Wheatley," she said softly, "surely you're not going to complain I've been *harassing* you?"

Wheatley blanched.

"Or perhaps you'll say the cruel policewoman set her fierce and savage *dog* on you?"

Watching her from the rug and happy to have his Cecilia back, Figaro thumped his tail and grinned amiably at everybody.

"And by the way Wheatley," she said, "if talking rubbish was a chargeable offense, I'd have arrested you the first time we met."

Wheatley looked blank.

"All that nonsense about Christianity bringing down the Roman Empire! Yes, it's all in Gibbon, but anyone who knows *anything* about *anything* knows Gibbon was *wrong*. It was the *western* empire that fell. If Christianity caused it, why didn't the eastern empire fall, too? It was just as Christian as the west. Maybe more so."

Wheatley stared at Cecilia, and his jaw dropped. Michael always thought of the expression "his jaw dropped" as a metaphor. It had never occurred to him to wonder what that would look like if it actually happened. Now he knew.

"If you really want to know what did it," she said, "it was several stupid military decisions plus the economy. The west collapsed because it couldn't pay its bills. Trust me. Papa's professor of classics. I *know* about these things. And Wheatley, guess what? I was trying to make things a little easier for you just now. I can't think why, since you just tried to murder my parents. But the fact is I don't care whether you stand or sit. Just don't move suddenly. And keep your hands where I can see them."

Wheatley sat.

Michael's jaw dropped.

The wait took less than five minutes. Yet they were, for Michael, minutes of agonizing length. Cecilia stood motionless by the door, never taking her eyes from Wheatley. Wheatley sat on the couch and stared into space, now refusing to look at them or say a word. Normally Michael would have felt it appropriate to leave a man in such a position to his own thoughts, allowing him opportunity to come with what dignity he chose to an acceptance of defeat. But this was different, for there grew in Michael's heart a certainty that for this man, time was almost over—that if he did not reach out to him now, there would be no other chance.

At length, with a bluntness born of desperation, he said: "I know what will happen at daylight."

Slowly, Wheatley raised his head and looked at him.

"Well, good for you. And so?"

"So there's help for it. Even now—there's another way."

"You think I'll ask your help while your lady protector stands there, watching how clever you are?"

"Cecilia—I'm sure you would leave us for a moment?"

"It's of no consequence," Wheatley said. "I will never, never ask for help from you. Or any like you. You ask too much."

"I ask for nothing," he said.

"On the contrary, you ask for everything." Wheatley turned away.

Michael was silent. He knew that what Wheatley said was in one sense true, and he had no answer.

A condition of complete simplicity
(Costing not less than everything)

Never had he been more conscious of personal inadequacy. Never more hotly aware of the limits of his own compassion.

There were sirens and lights. Minutes later the room was full of men and women in uniform, and Cecilia was uttering the ritual forms of English law. "*Henry Wheatley, I am arresting you....*"

And now it struck Michael that in this moment Cecilia Cavaliere stood for Caesar. Certainly he, Michael Aarons, stood at times for an authority greater than Caesar's. When as priest he spoke certain words — *this is my body, this is my blood, I absolve you* — being in himself nothing very special he yet spoke with the authority of Jesus Christ. But Christ from the beginning had always recognized Caesar's authority in its own realm. *You would have no power over me unless it were given you from above.* And this was that realm.

The ritual words rolled on.

"*You do not have to say anything but it may harm your defense if you do not mention when questioned something which you later rely on in court. Anything you do say may be given in evidence. Do you understand this?*"

Wheatley grunted.

"Is that 'yes'?"

"Yes."

Cecilia nodded to one of the constables.

Handcuffs appeared, and two of the uniformed figures took Henry Wheatley from the room.

Caesar had spoken.

FORTY-SEVEN

East London. 2:47 a.m.

PCs Roger Jenner and Akhtar Zamir drove slowly from the direction of the Commercial Road. Ahead of them were the decaying splendors of the Town Hall, the Nautical School, and the East India Dock Road.

It had been a relatively quiet night.

"Not long to go now," Jenner muttered.

Zamir, who was driving, nodded—then frowned.

He had noticed something on the opposite pavement. Now Jenner saw it too—moving slowly, awkwardly, with a limp.

"What the hell's that?"

He slowed the car, did a U-turn in the empty street, and drove back.

But now there was nothing.

The two looked at each other. Had it just been a trick of the shadows? Or had it—he? she?—turned off?

Zamir pulled over to the side and stopped.

They sat, listening.

Nothing, except the low chatter of the radio.

They glanced at each other again, got out of the car, and looked up and down the road, listening.

Still nothing.

Except a smell.

Something burnt. Something decaying.

"*Jesus Christ!*" Jenner said. "What the hell died?"

Zamir nodded. It was not the imprecation he would have chosen, for he was a follower of the Prophet, but with the sentiment he could only concur. The stench was appalling.

There was a moment's pause. Then, by unspoken mutual consent, the two men walked slowly in the direction the dark thing seemed to have been taking. The street itself was well lit, but there were doorways and alcoves in shadow. There they shone their lights and peered.

Nothing.

They came to the crossroad, and stared up and down it. Here the smell was worse. But still there was nothing to see. Nothing but a well lit, deserted street.

They looked at each other.

"Maybe it was a trick of light," Jenner said.

"A trick we both saw?" Zamir said. "But I tell you what — the drains round here must be in a bloody awful state."

They stood for a moment longer.

"Let's get out of this," he said.

His partner nodded.

A few minutes later they were again proceeding down the East India Dock Road.

The episode hardly seemed worth the trouble it took to report.

FORTY-EIGHT

Exeter. The Cavalieres' house. At about the same time.

"Sergeant Stillwell, take two others and look in the garden, just outside the kitchen window. There's a revolver out there somewhere. In the bushes to the right. A Smith and Wesson .38, I think. Anyway, record carefully where you find it and be very careful how you handle it. It's got our friend's prints all over it. You know what to do."

"Yes, ma'am."

"Constable Wilkins, you'll find Wheatley's Lexus LS 600h L sedan parked just to the left of our front gate. The latest model. I want a forensic examination. It might tell us all sorts of interesting things."

"Yes, ma'am."

Michael drew her aside.

"Cecilia, tell them to watch Wheatley carefully until morning. I think he'll try to kill himself."

"Why would he do that?"

"Too complicated to explain now. I'll tell you later. But get them to watch him."

"If you say so. They can put a suicide watch on him. The last thing we need's a custody death."

***

By the time Cecilia came back from the patrol cars, Michael was sitting in the kitchen with Rosina and Andrea, drinking *decaffinato* that actually tasted remarkably like the real thing.

Cecilia looked at him and shook her head.

"I'm sorry, but I wouldn't have left you alone with Wheatley! Forgive me. He'd already attempted two murders this evening."

Michael bowed his head. This too, he conceded, was in Caesar's realm.

"Anyway," she said, "I did tell them to watch him. They'll see he doesn't damage himself. Now, I know we're tired, but I need to get some things clear, Michael."

"Of course."

"Thank God you realized back at the rectory that something was happening here—but can you tell me more? Is there more we should know?"

She seated herself by the fireplace, her eyes intent on him.

"All right." Michael put down his cup. "Well, let's take it in order. First, do you have that triangle of paper?"

"Yes. Wait a minute."

She was back in a few minutes with the evidence bag, wearing forensic gloves. Even so she used tweezers to take out the scrap they'd found in Michael's study.

"Oh!" Rosina said, as Cecilia set it on the table.

"You've seen something like it before?" Michael asked.

"Yes. I found it this morning pinned to the front door. I meant to show it to Andrea, but I forgot. I'll get it."

When she returned, "Please, give it to Cecilia," he said. "Cecilia, lay the torn sides together."

They fitted perfectly.

"How extraordinary—"

"It's just what I expected," Michael said. "And I will explain, but first, can you tell me about what happened here earlier? Before the police came? You say you both fainted?"

Rosina and Andrea described what they remembered of their ordeal.

"Now, about what time do you think this happened?"

Andrea shook his head. "I'm not sure. It was pretty late, well past eleven. Wait—now I remember! I put my watch down on the dressing table when I went into the bedroom, and it said half-past eleven."

"And that's when it happened?" Michael said.

"Not at once," Rosina looked at Andrea. "I brushed my hair for a bit after you came into the room. Ten minutes. I don't know. You said you were finishing an article, remember? I said your bath was getting cold."

Andrea nodded. "That's right. Christopher McDonough's review of Lombardo's new translation of the *Aeneid*."

"So then, Papa, it happened?" Cecilia said. "Say, between 11:40 and 11:50?"

"I should think so."

"All right." Michael turned to Cecilia. "Do you know when you reached the academy?"

"About eleven."

"And when did you sense the disturbance there?"

"Eight or nine minutes after midnight. It was from 12:02 to 12:05 when I photographed the book. The camera recorded the time."

"Then I think I can see the timetable. Rosina, Andrea—I know you may find this hard to believe, but I believe you were victims of an attack instigated by Wheatley and the academy. This divided paper is an ancient form of malediction. The instigator keeps one part. The other he passes to the victim—in this case, you. And some kind of ritual inaugurates it."

Andrea raised an eyebrow. "I know Germanicus thought he was a victim of something like that. Tacitus talks about it. But I'm not sure Tacitus *believed* it. Are you saying these academy people could do something like this and it might *work*?"

"Well," Michael said, "I know what these represent"—he pointed to the paper triangles—"and we all know that something unusual and destructive happened here between 11:40 and 11:50."

"I suppose," Andrea said, "we might have hallucinated some of that, or dreamed it, or something."

"Then we both had the same hallucination," said Rosina, "and in any case we didn't hallucinate the fire."

"That's true."

"A fire that no one seems able to explain. But then it all stopped."

"Yes," Michael said. "It did, at about midnight. At just about exactly the time when there was some kind of disturbance at the academy, as we know from what Cecilia saw and from the time record on her camera. And out of the academy at about midnight came the notebook we now have, containing exactly the kind of ritual that's intended to inaugurate this kind of thing. And the notebook further contained the addresser's half of a malediction specifically targeting you. So while I hate to seem like the credulous priest who'll believe anything, I simply can't see a way to fit all that together except by saying that it *looks* as though what we've got is a malediction—a curse, if you like— that actually *was* working. Frankly, I'll be obliged to anyone who can show me a more pedestrian explanation. I do actually prefer the universe to operate in ways that correspond with the normally apparent dictates of cause and effect and common sense."

"No," Andrea said after a moment, "I can't see another way to fit all that together either. And since—to return the compliment—I hope I'm not such a rationalist, positivist bigot as to suppose nothing can happen beyond categories I can explain, I concede the possibility."

"Well, maybe," Rosina said. "But still it seems an awful lot of trouble to go to just to set this house on fire. They could have managed it better by paying a couple of thugs and giving them a few cans of petrol."

Michael shook his head.

"Forgive me—I've already told Cecilia. This ritual—I know something of it. It wasn't just undertaken against you. If completed, there's no knowing what it was meant to destroy. What perhaps it *could* have destroyed."

There was a moment of silence.

"Then on the other hand, if they thought they could do so much with a ritual," Rosina said, "why did your friend Wheatley need to come after us with a gun?"

"Because the ritual was stopped and because your deaths were necessary to him. To someone—or something—he had promised them. You were his offering."

"I see. Charming."

"And in such affairs as this, if the offerer fails to keep his bargain, he must pay the penalty himself."

"And that's what you were talking about to him?" Cecilia said. "And why you think he'll try to kill himself?"

"Yes." He sighed. "And so now, Cecilia, there's still the notebook. I know you can't destroy it. But you've seen how dangerous it may be. Please, please, be careful with it."

"I will," she said. "But don't think any of this is going into my report. That's going to be the facts, man, just the facts. I don't think the Devon and Cornwall Constabulary is quite ready yet for maledictions."

For a few minutes, the four sat in silence. Finally Rosina said, "We're all ready for sleep. Michael, thank you for bringing Cecilia home. You will of course stay with us. Give me a few minutes to make up the bed in your room."

"Much easier with two," Andrea said. They left together.

Tocco and Pu followed them.

Michael, Cecilia, and Figaro were left alone.

"I could phone someone in London," Cecilia said, "and see if I can find out what happened at the academy. I saw the emergency services coming, so presumably there's some information now."

But she did not call. Instead, suddenly, and in Michael's experience quite uncharacteristically, she put her head into her hands. Figaro went over to her and lent against her.

"What is it?" Michael said softly.

She sighed and looked up at him.

"I'm sorry. It's just that…" She began stroking Figaro's head. "Wheatley. He was right. I wasn't successful, I was lucky. He nearly did it. Do you realize? He was just about to fire at Mama and Papa. If we'd been even a few seconds later!"

"I know. But do forgive me—the important thing is, we weren't. The fact is, your mother and father are alive and well. And despite what Wheatley says—or what you say—that's in major part thanks to you! No," he held up his hand as she started to protest, "hear me, Cecilia, please! *Stammi a sentire, per favore!*"

She smiled. Whether because his Italian was so good or because it was so bad, he wasn't sure. Still, he'd made her smile. He continued in English.

"*I* wouldn't have noticed Wheatley's car in the road here when we arrived, as you did. And even if I had, I doubt I'd have realized what it meant. And even if I'd managed *that*, at best the chances are I'd have got myself shot! You, on the other hand, spotted the car, at once realized it meant trouble, and then, unarmed yourself, managed to disarm and overpower an armed man within seconds and, so far as I could see, without even expending much effort!

"So, let's face it, yes, you had a bit of luck. But you appear to me to have been brilliant in your observation and incredible in your reactions. And if you hadn't been *all* those things, then despite your luck, Wheatley would have got away with it. As it is, he didn't. And as we speak" (a thump came from upstairs) "your mother and father are very kindly making up a bed for me. Those are the things that are real. And those are the things that matter."

Cecilia shook her head. "You're very kind, but..."

"Cecilia, I'm not being kind. I'm telling you what I saw. Frankly, you're so good at what you do I find you terrifying!"

She laughed and shook her head and looked not at all terrifying.

"Oh well, thank you! And about the other thing—about concentrating on what *is*, I know you're right. I know you are. It's just that... No. You're right. I mustn't go there. It's no good thinking about it. Thank you." Another thump. She got up, walked to the door, and called up the stairs.

"Can I help?"

"Yes, you can." A third thump. Rosina's voice sounded somewhat muffled. "You can sit and talk nicely to Michael and stop fussing about us."

Cecilia laughed and turned back to Michael.

"Definitely alive and well!" she said.

FORTY-NINE

Cranston College, London. November 1. 5:40 a.m.

Total blackness.

But the chairman, his flesh charred and broken, was already blind. The fire had seen to that.

An instinct that needed no light had dragged him from the academy agonizing miles across London, avoiding people and prying eyes. It had led him through mean streets and dark alleys, by barren sites and builders' rubble, past wire fences and careless watchmen, until at last he had plunged into shadow and come to this place.

Here, eighteen centuries before, iron-hard Roman legionaries had invoked the Light Bringer, consecrating their strength and courage to the best symbol they knew of justice and order. Centuries later, fools calling upon a power they did not understand had dedicated the altar to Darkness. Evil men fought and cursed. And fire gutted the buildings above. Then, for years, the chamber lay silent, hidden and forgotten, waiting.

Now the chairman had come, contrary to his plans, against his hope. His company was scattered, himself dying. He knew well enough what the fire had done to his flesh and realized how little time even his fanatic will could sustain its failing energies.

A way remained.

He would invoke the Destroyer, calling upon him by his many names: Satan, Set, Shaitan, Iblis—and he would invoke him alone, as had Kakoyannis before him.

Yet not as Kakoyannis, for unlike Kakoyannis he had no illusions.

In this place, prepared for so long, what he was about to do would be like a lighted candle held to escaping gas. Undoubtedly he would perish. It did not matter to him. Hell's yearning is to become incarnate. Its frustration is that the flesh is holy. But where there was willing offering, there the power of destruction could, like a cancer, find something to grasp. Then, like a cancer, destroying what it grasped it could spread. That, for the chairman, would be satisfaction enough.

The efforts of those who opposed him would have been in vain, for they served a Lord so limited by courtesy as to be bound by laws he himself had made, one who was therefore unwilling to use the powers he undoubtedly possessed, choosing rather to proceed only by plea, stratagem, and grace. He was held to have said, as his enemies persecuted him, "*Do you think that I cannot now appeal to my Father, and he will at once send me more than twelve legions of angels?*" But what use was that, if he would not appeal? What use to serve a Lord therefore so enfeebled that he could be defeated by his own creature—and would be, even now.

Even if the Chairman had not been blind, he would have needed no book. So many times he had pored over the rite since Wheatley brought it to him, its rhythms and words were part of him.

He had neither symbol nor protection. Desire alone must suffice.

His body screamed in protest, but the will pierced and silenced it, concentrating all on the last preparation.

The mind cleared.

The agony itself was caught up and used.

A focused energy, refusing every distraction of joy or love, directing all to its utter resentment.

Still the sullenness fought to be verbalized. "It was their fault ... it was his fault ... I never had a chance ... it isn't right...."

Even that, he denied.

The very remembrance of words was a tribute to meaning. And meaning also must be rejected. To be perfect, his resentment must be wordless, mindless, and directed everywhere — approaching the Satanic perfection of which Milton spoke:

> *that fixt mind*
> *And high disdain, from sence of injur'd merit.*

He raised his hand, swayed, and might have fallen, but the altar stayed him. Then, in scarcely a whisper, he again began the rite.

FIFTY

Exeter Police Station. 5:50 a.m.

Those on duty, to do them justice, made a serious effort. Wheatley's cell and his body cavities were checked. His belt, his tie, and his shoes were removed. Nothing visible that could be used for self-destruction was left accessible to him, and thereafter he was subject to a suicide watch—which meant in effect that short of manpower though they were, he was never left unobserved.

So now Wheatley lay on the narrow bed, under the covers. He was not sure of the time, but he knew it could not be long till sunrise. He was indeed a man who never left himself without an avenue of retreat.

He was under no illusion that his continued existence was of the slightest importance to the power he served or that the purposes of that power would be halted by his death. Yet even now he would retain what control he could. He would not wait for the dawn.

His jailers had checked his body cavities but not thoroughly enough. As if idly stretching on the bed, he reached down and probed for the tiny crystal cyanide cylinder. Another casual motion, as if stifling an idle yawn, and he raised it to his mouth.

For the last time a faint smile played about his lips.

Then he bit down hard.

Thus it was that minutes after the chairman began the rite that would have completed Wheatley's offering, Wheatley completed it for himself. And so hell, as is its preference, received everything and gave nothing in return.

In the two or three minutes of life remaining to Wheatley after he had crushed the cylinder, there came to him the amazing possibility of another kind of bargain and another kind of universe. Beneath the still eyes of heaven he responded to that possibility.

FIFTY-ONE

East London. November 1. 6:50 a.m.

Slightly over an hour after the chairman began the rite in the darkness beneath Cranston College, and slightly less than an hour after Henry Wheatley took his own life, in a circular area of East London about eight kilometers across with Cranston College at its center, every single source of power failed. Generators died. Underground trains were plunged into darkness and glided to a halt. Traffic and streetlights went out. Tower blocks darkened. Cars, buses, and trucks came to a stop. Everywhere, where there should have been lights and the sounds of the city rousing itself for Saturday, instead there was silence and darkness, punctured here and there by protesting voices, lit candles, and the dogs, as ever, barking defiantly.

Twenty-four minutes and eleven seconds after that, at the early celebration of All Saints in Saint Dustan's, Stepney (this morning said by candlelight as it had been when the church was built) the priest completed the Eucharistic prayer, declaring—any appearance to the contrary notwithstanding—that all honor and glory were eternally the Father's, by, with, and through the Son, in the unity of the Holy Spirit. Three elderly ladies who were the congregation said, "Amen." And at that exact moment the generators restarted and the lights came on. Minutes later the city returned to life.

"Damnedest thing I ever saw," said a chief engineer, standing by a generator that for twenty minutes had baffled his every effort to start it and then appeared to begin running of its own accord. "*Damned* odd!"

The East London blackout, though local and brief, had been spectacular, and at another time might have attracted national attention. As it was, the fate of a quarter of a million refugees fleeing civil war in the Democratic Republic of Congo and the final weekend of the American presidential election seemed the more significant events, leaving scant or no coverage for the blackout.

After all, in the long run no harm appeared to have been done.

Exeter. 6:55 a.m.

Cecilia Cavaliere was drinking coffee when they called her with the news of Wheatley's suicide.

"What in God's name do we train them for?... Of course it wasn't obvious! My God, it isn't just they didn't follow procedure—hasn't any of them ever read a classic spy story?"

FIFTY-TWO

Siding Springs Observatory, New South Wales.
November 1. UT1 (GMT) 06:37.

Charlie Brown pushed the hair out of his eyes and straightened up, easing his back. The others were still peering at the plate.

They looked tired.

Wrrrrhhhhmmmff! Mmmmmmmmmmmmm...

Oh God, *couldn't* the Aussies do something about that air conditioning?

Still, there might not be much point in that now. If he were right, it would be akin to the proverbial rearranging of deck chairs on the *Titanic*.

If he were right.

But was he?

He hadn't said anything yet. He'd wait a minute longer. See if they spotted it. Maybe they wouldn't see it the way he did. Maybe there'd be... what was it the fellow said to his friend in that old Hitchcock movie when they were all being attacked by Nazi storm troopers? – "You know old chap, I'm sure there must be a perfectly reasonable explanation for all this!" There must be, so maybe there would be. And in the meantime he'd be resolutely British and sensible, and say nothing. Let *them* notice the phenomenon and come up with the explanation. The perfectly reasonable explanation.

But not *his* explanation.

Dear God in heaven, not his.

"It's a good plate." That was Tom Daniels. Very Australian. And great fun. Like Crocodile Dundee, only real. And sharp, too. Very sharp. But he hadn't seen it. Not yet. At least, he must have seen it because he was looking at it, but he hadn't *observed*, as Sherlock Holmes would say.

Thaddeus Quinn nodded.

Zaziwe L'Ouverture looked puzzled.

"It's clear enough for what we need," she said.

"It is," Charlie said. "What do you think we've got?"

She hesitated only a second.

"A supernova, I suppose."

He waited a moment or so, and then almost in spite of himself gave her a little professorial prod. "At the center of the galaxy. Sagittarius A. Does that say anything to you?"

"It's got to be somewhere. Why not there?" That was Tom again. All right then, let him have a shot at it. Maybe there *was* a way out of this.

"Point taken, Tom. Where would you start?"

The Australian gestured at the figures on one of the other monitors. "Well, there's the redshift. Pretty extreme. Which suggests it's moving away from us. I guess I agree with Zaziwe. I think we're looking at a supernova way beyond our galaxy."

But Zaziwe was frowning. *Zaziwe* did not agree with Zaziwe. She wasn't saying anything but she'd spotted it. Charlie was pretty sure she'd spotted it.

Another pause. Then —

"Maybe the redshift *doesn't* mean distancing," Zaziwe said at last. "It doesn't have to."

She *had* got it. Before the others, just as he'd expect. Of course she didn't want to, any more than he did. But she'd got it.

"Agreed," he said. "And in that case?"

"In that case—" She hesitated, visibly seeking to resist the direction of her own logic. "In that case there might not be movement away."

"Yes?" he said.

"It might be moving towards us."

"Oh, my God!" Thaddeus and Tom spoke almost simultaneously. "*The Seyfert effect!*"

"Yes." Zaziwe nodded. "Only this time, of course, it would be us."

Charlie swallowed. They'd all got there. And he had so hoped that they'd get somewhere else.

"The Seyfert effect," he said. "I'm afraid that's what I think, too."

They looked at each other.

"Then God help us!" Thaddaeus said.

Charlie sighed. "My thought exactly."

If they were right, the nucleus of the galaxy had exploded.

FIFTY-THREE

London, November 1. 7:00 a.m.

When Katie's keepers arrived at her enclosure the next morning they found the gate open.

"O Lord!" the keeper from Exeter said. "She's gone AWOL again!"

But she hadn't. They found her curled up in a tight ball in her usual place, fast asleep.

"All *right* then! Good old Katie!"

"I guess she knows where she's well off," the other keeper said.

Katie was none the worse for her adventure, and once she could be persuaded to wake up (which did take rather longer than usual) she stretched, shook herself, and finally trotted out to the scrubland that formed the back part of her enclosure.

"Can you smell wood-smoke?" asked the Exeter keeper, who thought he'd caught a whiff as he was rousing Katie.

"Not that I've noticed," said the other, which was not surprising, since he was recovering from a cold.

"Oh well, perhaps I was imagining it." Or it could be coming from across the way, where he'd noticed them yesterday, burning a lot of garden stuff. That was probably it.

Katie sniffed about, chased a gray squirrel, relieved herself, writhed around on her back in a patch of wintry sun with her legs in the air and a grin on her face (looking remarkably silly), then trotted back to the roofed part of her enclosure. There she ate a hearty breakfast, played with the keepers and her ball for a bit, and finally curled up for her usual post-breakfast and post-game nap.

Of course the open gate had to be reported, and later that morning a memorandum arrived from administration. Katie's enclosure was being secured with a chain and padlock and was to remain so secured until the electronic lock could be replaced with something more conventional.

After all, as administration reflected while preparing the memorandum, conventional locks had worked perfectly well since the London Zoo was founded in 1828. There really did not seem to be any particular reason why they should not go on working for another century or so.

FIFTY-FOUR

Exeter. The same day.

Before Michael went to bed, Rosina had produced a time-table and they'd chosen a suitable train for his journey back to London. Cecilia said she would drive him to the station.

When he emerged from the Cavalieres' front door on the fol-lowing morning he was met by bright sunshine and clear sky. Birds were singing. Dogs were barking. A man was whistling as he washed his car. Michael smiled. Happy All Saints' Day!

And here was Cecilia — driving a large white police car, with its distinctive blue and yellow battenburg markings. The pas-senger-side window slid down as she pulled up.

"Hop in!" she said. "My car's having a service, so they've lent me one of these for the day." After a few minutes of nego-tiating the morning traffic she said, "In one of these you'll get to see the great British motorist in a wholly new light. You just watch! No one ever breaks the speed limit. No one ever cuts you off. Even if you crawl along ridiculously slowly very few people have the nerve to overtake you, and absolutely no one would dream of being so rude as to hoot at you. *È incredibile!*" Her lips curved into a smile. "All this you can find either amus-ing or depressing, depending, as dear Jane would have pointed out, on whether you're in the mood for satire or moralizing."

"Jane?"

"Jane Austen. My absolutely favorite author!"

"Did Jane Austen say that?"

"Yes. Well, more or less. She put it better, of course. In *Sanditon*."

"*Sanditon*? I love Jane Austen and I thought I knew her pretty well, but I don't think I've heard of that."

"Lots of people haven't. She died before she could finish it, so all we've got are the first eleven chapters. But they're wonderful, all the same. Jane at her very best! She was able to be funny about hypochondria while she was dying. She was incredible."

Cecilia spoke cheerfully enough, yet Michael sensed she was in a somber mood. He soon learned why.

Radiating chagrin, she told him about Wheatley's suicide.

"So the short and the long of it is," she said, "you were right, and despite your warning us, we've royally screwed up."

Michael sighed. That he'd expected something like this didn't make it any less disturbing when it came. Last night he'd confronted a man who—

"I don't believe it!" Cecilia said.

"Believe what?"

"Forget what I said about everyone driving perfectly—just look at that Fiesta!"

A white Ford Fiesta in front of them had swerved out to pass a truck, and was pulling away rapidly.

"He's breaking the speed limit, isn't he?"

"He certainly is—and that's just *antipasto*," Cecilia said. "Hang on!" She switched on flashing blue lights, producing a strobe that seemed to shine around the entire street, and accelerated past the truck.

The chase was brief. The driver of the other car obviously registered her presence within seconds, pulled to the side of the road, and stopped. Cecilia stopped in front of him.

"Good job we're early for your train," she said. "This may take a minute."

She walked back to the other car and its driver, a young man with a young woman beside him. The road was quiet for the moment, and Michael could hear and see everything that followed.

"Sir," Cecilia said, "turn off your engine, please, and get out of the car, both of you. And you sir, I want to see your license."

The young man looked worried, as well he might, but he got out and so did the young woman.

Cecilia looked at the license briefly and nodded.

"All right. Please just wait a moment, sir."

Michael watched fascinated as she talked to someone on her mobile radio, giving details of the license and the Fiesta. Within minutes, it seemed, she was informed that there was nothing known against either.

She nodded, and turned back to the couple.

"Look, officer," the young man blurted out, "it's my mother!"

"Excuse me, sir," she said, "Did your mother teach you to ignore a stop sign, run a red light, and cross a double yellow line, all the time traveling way over the speed limit? *And* you were not wearing a safety belt."

"Officer, *please*, the hospital just called. *Please*! She's dying. But she's still conscious. They said she might not last the hour. Please. I'll come to the station after I see her, pay a fine, anything you like. Only please don't hold me up any longer."

Cecilia looked at the young woman, who said. "It's really true officer. Please."

"Which hospital?"

"Devon and Exeter."

Cecilia looked at him. Then she looked again at the young woman. "Is he fit to drive?" she asked.

"Yes, officer, really. He's ever such a safe driver, it's just—"

"All right! I believe you. Okay, here's the deal. I'll get you to the hospital. But first calm down! You won't get to see your mother if you kill yourself on the way. Take a deep breath.

Good. Now, get back in the car and buckle up. Both of you! Okay. Switch on your engine. Good. Now, I'm going back to the police car. When I pull out, pull out behind me, and follow me. Stick with me. Is that clear?"

"Yes, officer."

Cecilia came back smartly to the police car and got in.

"Hang on!" she said, buckling her seat belt.

Michael found what followed as exciting as anything that had happened to him for a long time. Lights flashing and siren blaring, the blue, yellow, and white police car whipped through the midmorning traffic as everything scattered before it. Behind them, he could see the Fiesta hanging on grimly.

Minutes later, they entered the hospital car park. Cecilia pulled over, leaned out of her window and pointed the following Fiesta to a vacant space. The young man parked, leapt out, and ran toward her.

"Thank you! Thank you!"

"That's all right. Go! Go! Go!"

He grabbed the young woman's hand and off they ran.

For a moment, Cecilia and Michael sat in silence.

"I hope he gets to see his mother," Michael said.

"So do I. Just wait here a bit, will you."

He watched curiously as she left the car and went into the hospital.

After several minutes inside the hospital she returned, smiling.

"Apparently we did it. His mother's still conscious."

"That was nice of you," Michael said when she got back into the car. "Making sure they'd made it in time."

She raised one eyebrow, gave a half-smile, and shook her head.

"If you really want to know, I did that partly to make sure he was telling the truth. I was pretty sure he was, but he could have been pulling a fast one."

"And if he had?"

"Lying to a police officer? Wasting police time? Believe me, moving traffic violations would have been the very *least* of his problems."

Michael smiled.

"Did you know," she said, "that an amazingly high percentage of people who commit blatant moving traffic violations turn out on investigation to be breaking the law in some other way? We catch people like that all the time. It's really odd. The very people you'd think would go out of their way *not* to get noticed do exactly what's calculated to draw our attention."

"Oh."

"Still, even in this naughty world sometimes a cigar is just a cigar. Apparently that really *was* just a panic-stricken young man trying to get to his mama's bedside. And now I suppose we'd better get you to the train. With no more dramas, I hope."

"Yes, I suppose we had," he said with a glance at his watch. "Though I must admit I did enjoy all that—racing along with the siren and the lights and everything."

She looked at him and her dark eyes suddenly danced with fun.

"Yes," she said, "it *is* rather satisfying, isn't it?"

At normal speed they pulled out of the car park.

Michael watched her as she threaded her way unobtrusively through the traffic.

Last night he'd seen her courage and skill in battle.

Today he'd seen her kindness and chivalry.

She really was magnificent.

Fifty-Five

The first thing was to check their own work, the second was to consult. During the next few hours Charlie and the rest of the Anglo-Australian team did both. They checked and rechecked their calculations, their equipment, and their conclusions. And they consulted furiously: with the European Space Observatory at La Silla, with the Herschel Space Observatory at La Palma, with the Inter-American Observatory at Cerro Tololo, with the Indians, with the Russians, and with absolutely anyone else with qualifications they respected who would talk to them. Each new dialogue seemed to confirm either the calculations or the observations or both.

So it was that finally Charlie felt he had no choice but to inform the government: which as far as he was concerned meant London, Brussels, and Canberra. His duty as a citizen of Europe and of the planet thus done, he told the others that even if the world ended in the next few hours he was not to be disturbed, and went to bed.

As he entered his room it crossed his mind that if he were really the Christian he professed to be, or a real Jew, or a real Muslim, he'd be turning to God, falling to his knees, calling upon the Almighty. Indeed, if he were merely a nicer person, he'd at least be grieving, anguishing over the loss of life and the coming end of all human hopes and dreams. Surely at least that?

But the fact was, following the initial discovery, he and his colleagues had simply worked. They had checked, they had analyzed, they had evaluated, they had consulted. They had done these things because, end of the world or not, that was what they were supposed to do. That was their job. And now, calculations made, alternate hypotheses evaluated and rejected, he for one (he would not speak for the others) did not grieve for the planet nor importune its creator because he was simply numb with exhaustion.

So, "Oh God!" as his head hit the pillow was the closest he came to prayer.

Fifty-Six

Exeter. Later the same morning.

"I'm sorry, ma'am," Verity Jones said. "I'm afraid I'm interrupting you."

Cecilia looked up and smiled.

"You are, thank God."

"Well then, here you are, ma'am. We've checked on the book and the people you filmed and we've found details for most of them."

"Already?" Cecilia said. "That's very good."

"Joseph says your pictures were excellent. He's also made some good stills from them, in case we need them. The book was easy, of course. A good job you put the money by it so we could see the size. It's obviously a perfect match—just a bit more beaten up. Do we actually have it?"

Cecilia pointed to the plastic bag, which lay on the table.

"I want it sealed, put in the safe, and no-one, I mean *no-one*, is to examine it without my personal permission. If anything were to happen to me, this is the man to consult about it." She handed Verity Jones one of Michael Aarons's cards. "No-one else. Make a note of it, and see my instructions are recorded in the file."

Verity Jones looked curious but took the card.

"Yes, ma'am. I'll see to it."

Cecilia nodded. The fact was, with Wheatley now beyond the reach of human justice, the main purpose for retaining the book was gone. Still, she was uncomfortable about destroying anything so materially connected with this affair until she was sure the whole business was cleared up, and she was by no means sure of that.

"Now," she said, "what about all these people?"

"Right, ma'am! Well it was Joseph, really, who did them for you. What we thought were the interesting ones are on top. Hargrove, the Tory MP—well, you can see about him. He died in the fire—they found his body. The same for Hutton, the union man. The woman you caught leaving is Maria Coleman. She's a bit of a mystery. Apparently she's very high-powered in advertising. She left her coat behind in the building—Temperley London!—a bit charred, unfortunately, but with her name in it. And then they found her car, parked in the street a few meters away from the academy. Lord knows why she left that. It's a Porsche!"

Cecilia, who was turning over the photographs and notes in time with Verity Jones's commentary, nodded.

Verity Jones sailed on. "Wheatley of course you know. Then that one…" Cecilia turned up another photograph. "That's it, the one hanging onto the porch!—he lectures there a bit. Has one of those PhDs you get for dredging up a lot of ill-digested information and then chucking some of it back when there's more than you need. Ah, yes" (as Cecilia turned to yet another) "this one's the *real* puzzle. He's simply listed as 'the Chairman.' But there's nothing else about him in the records at all: no name, no background, nothing. Most peculiar."

"Yes, that *is* peculiar. What records are those?"

"Oh, just records… things we were looking at on the web… You know, things…"

Verity Jones appeared suddenly to be very interested in the

wall behind Cecilia's desk. Obviously, they'd hacked into the academy's mainframe. Without a warrant.

Cecilia raised one eyebrow, did her best to look severe, and dropped her gaze again to the papers Verity Jones had given her. There was a principle at stake here.

An awkward silence.

"You *told* us get what we could as quickly as possible, ma'am."

Cecilia nodded and continued to reading. She hadn't told them to break the law. She was wondering how she should say that when Verity Jones said it for her.

"Oh, I know — the problem is, we could come up with something damning we can't use in court because we aren't supposed to have it."

"That *is* the problem." Cecilia laid down the sheaf. "I don't want to stamp on your enthusiasm, but the thing is — if we don't keep the law, who will? *The Queen's under the Law because it's the Law that makes her Queen.* We're officers of the crown, so that applies to us, too. I know it can be frustrating but it's actually what we're here for."

She looked directly at her crestfallen colleague and of course relented. Over-enthusiasm could be a problem, but it was infinitely preferable to its opposite.

"Enough said!" She grinned. "Now look, Joseph ought to send these other photographs to London. They might help the Met know who they're trying to find. If they can't locate that woman — Coleman — they may still be wondering if she died in the fire. Those pictures prove she didn't. Maybe she even started it."

"Yes, ma'am."

"And Sergeant — "

"Yes, ma'am?"

"You've got together a lot of good information here. Good work, both of you!"

"Thank you ma'am!" Verity gave her with brilliant smile.

"And now you at least know what to look for, let's see how much you can find out legally!"

"Yes, ma'am. You've got it, ma'am!" Verity Jones started to leave, then hesitated. "Oh, and by the way ma'am, I just wanted to say I was sorry to hear about your mum and dad's fright last night and I'm glad they're all right. Joseph asked me to send his good wishes too."

"Thank you, Verity. That's very kind and they're fine, thank you. And please thank Joseph for us."

She smiled after Verity Jones's retreating figure. She was touched. She'd met a lot of concern about her parents this morning, despite the verbal rocket she'd fired off earlier about the suicide watch. Even now reposing on her desk was a large slice of lardy cake with a note from Sergeant Wyatt explaining that Mrs. Wyatt had just been baking and was sorry to hear about her parents' nasty shock and thought she'd send along some cake. Mrs. Wyatt's lardy cake, which Cecilia had sampled before, was *incredibly* good to eat. It wouldn't remain on her desk for long.

Half an hour or so later, when she was drinking tea and munching the lardy cake, it occurred to Cecilia that she herself had ignored the law that morning by failing to book the young man with the dying mother.

Which meant (as her beloved Jane would have put it) that with Verity Jones she had, *like many great preachers and moralists, waxed eloquent on a subject in which her own conduct would ill bear examination.*

Yet when she took the young man to the hospital she'd thought she was doing the right thing. She still thought so. And Michael Aarons had been with her and he seemed to approve, and he was a priest.

But then, she also felt she'd been right to caution Verity Jones and company about ignoring procedures.

Life was very complicated.

She shook her head and decided that under the circumstances the only sensible thing was to turn her full attention to Mrs. Wyatt's lardy cake, which in any case deserved it.

FIFTY-SEVEN

Siding Springs Observatory. Slightly later.

Charlie couldn't breathe. He gasped and choked, trying to inhale. But something was pressing down on his chest, his head, his stomach. *Stop it! Stop it!* He would have cried out, but nothing came. Gritting his teeth, he made a desperate effort and at last, as if forcing himself through mud, came upright—

There was the tower, the domed tower… and now the wind, and the doors. White and gold, there was white and gold everywhere. And pillars so huge he couldn't see around them. That always came now. A painted ceiling so lofty he could only catch glimpses of green and gold through mists that swirled and ballooned above him.

Oh dear Christ, yes. And now the chessboard! In a minute he'd see the man. Yes, there he was, waiting for him. The man whose face he couldn't yet see. Only his long black robe.

And behind him, something else, something dark and looming and dangerous.

Something that waited.

The man turned, as always, mist swirling around the dark robe. And now Charlie saw the face, the eyes dark and kind, but commanding.

And as always, the man's voice. "You must!" Tones low, but urgent. "You must!"

"*Must what?*" he wanted to scream. But he was feeble, a shade, a ghost. He couldn't even whisper.

He woke up.

The bedclothes were the usual tangle and his pajamas as ever wet with perspiration. But at least he was awake and the Dream was gone.

Except that now there was that thing he didn't want to remember... what was it? Oh yes: Mickey the cat was dead, and he still missed his old friend terribly.

But it was all right to grieve for him.

Wait a minute, though. Now there was yet another thing. The world was going to end.

And it was all right to grieve for that, too.

FIFTY-EIGHT

A small hotel in London. Sunday, November 2.

Maria Coleman sat in her hotel room on the edge of the bed and considered the contents of the black briefcase. In it, essentially, was the alternative identity she had created for herself over the last four years. There was her Argentinean passport, in the name of Maria del Carmen Rodriquez — all perfectly legal and genuinely hers, for Maria del Carmen Rodriquez was the ten-year-old girl (then speaking no English) who'd come to Britain with her mother thirty years ago, subsequently becoming Maria Rogers as her mother assimilated, and later becoming Maria Carnell and finally Maria Coleman through two marriages.

There, too, were details of Argentinean bank accounts to which she had over the last four years transferred sufficient funds, all in untraceable bonds, sufficient to keep Maria del Carmen Rodriquez if not in fabulous luxury at least in perfect comfort for as long as she chose. There was the key to the tiny but elegant apartment in Buenos Aires she had rented in the name of Maria del Carmen Rodriquez two summers back and kept ever since. There was an Argentinean credit card in her new-old name. And, finally, there were more than enough pounds and euros in used currency to cover her immediate needs.

One detail would need further attention. The woman in the Argentinean passport was dark—her natural color—and no one in Britain had seen Maria as anything but a blonde for twenty-five years.

But still, the briefcase contained the keys to a new life, if she chose to use them. And there would surely never be a better time to do it, for those from the academy who would normally have pursued her for revenge or spite were themselves either dead or in disarray.

And there was another factor.

On the night of the ceremony, once she found herself clear of the temple and still in one piece, she had simply walked, driven by fear—but also, as she now realized, by an instinct wiser than her wisest calculations might have been. Finding herself on the Bayswater Road, she'd turned towards Lancaster Gate, then down Gloucester Terrace, right at the Craven Road, and so to Paddington Station.

The key to her deposit box had been, as always, on a chain around her neck. She removed the brief case and furnished herself with money from it. Then she hailed a taxi, told the driver that she found herself unexpectedly in London without luggage, and asked him to take her to a small, respectable hotel where she could await its arrival. At the hotel, she explained her situation in the same terms, booked a room for two nights, paid cash in advance, and went to bed.

Throughout the following day, which was a Saturday, she made discreet purchases—some clothes and other personal items and a small lightweight suitcase of good quality. Everywhere she paid cash.

She also watched television. And scanned the newspapers.

A fire at an educational institute might not have been a national story, but a Member of Parliament and a prominent trade unionist among its victims made it news. What mattered to Maria, however, was that evidently nobody knew what had happened to *her*. Pictures of Maria Coleman leaving the academy did not appear until the evening newscasts, but when they did, they gave her a fright. Whoever took them evidently knew what they were doing. They were night shots, but they were quite good. And of course the police were appealing for witnesses. Surely it was possible that someone here at the hotel would recognize her and notify them?

So here was her choice.

On the one hand, she loathed and feared most of her colleagues at the academy. And even to think about that final ceremony still terrified her. She remembered very well what she'd said as she ran down the stairs: "*Oh God, if I get out of here I'll never come back!*"

And she had got out.

Such were the arguments for disappearing.

On the other hand most if not all of those she feared at the academy appeared to be dead or to have disappeared. And although the fire had interrupted the academy's plans, it would by no means put a stop to them. If she chose to share in the harvest she would have to be there to reap it. No doubt she'd have to explain herself, to answer questions, but she had, after all, committed no crime. She'd panicked at the fire and gone to ground in a small hotel for a few days. People might call her foolish or hysterical, but it was hard to see what other accusations they might make.

That, then, was the argument for going back.

She sat for some time.

At last she nodded.

"*Ya sè lo que voi a hacer,*" she said aloud.

It was time to take a shower and wash her hair.

***

At ten' o'clock that Sunday morning the quiet woman, who had arrived at the hotel in the middle of the night with a black briefcase but no luggage, checked out.

She had two strokes of luck.

The first was that the young man who booked her in and was the only member of the staff to get a good look at her never watched anything on television except sports.

The second was that when she came to pay her bill, he wasn't on duty. She was now wearing a coat and a crimson silk headscarf. The receptionist, who thought her rather attractive, happened to notice a dark curl that escaped from the headscarf. The young man, had he been on duty, might well have remembered that the woman who had arrived coatless, scarfless, and hatless, had been a blonde.

FIFTY-NINE

New York. Wednesday, November 5.

Charlie Brown started to look at his watch for the fourth time in five minutes and just managed to stop himself. He knew perfectly well what time it was. Well after midnight by his inner clock, and in view of tomorrow's meeting he ought to be in bed. Instead, he was standing in the middle of a roomful of people he didn't know, behaving—and feeling—like a nervous adolescent. Well, he *was* nervous. To his soul he was an academic, never happier than when at his studies or in the throes of scholarly debate, but the discovery at Siding Spring Observatory had landed him in a world as alien to him as it was unexpected. No. "Landed" was hardly the word. It was more that he'd been plunged into it and was now being swept along by it like a twig in a torrent.

Within hours of their original discovery he, Zaziwe, and Thaddeus had been summoned to the British High Commission in Canberra, there to sign the Official Secrets Act in the presence of the high commissioner himself. The Australians involved— Tom Daniels and the rest—had, he gathered, received similar instructions from their own government. Zaziwe and Thaddeus and Tom then returned at the joint request of the British and Australian governments to continue monitoring events with the Australians at Siding Springs. The observatory itself, to the evident irritation of everyone involved, had already become a restricted site—which meant that no one could get in or out without permission of the Australian military.

Charlie might have accepted this regimen without complaint. Those inside were, after all, fed and warm and free to get on with their work. But for him there was no such peace. As the senior British scientist involved, he had to be heard and seen by various powers-that-be, and that meant no-notice flights from Canberra to London, then to Brussels, then Washington, and now New York. True, he was given first-class seats on the flights and admission to VIP lounges that had never been open to him as a mere academic. But still it made his head spin.

So here he was in Manhattan, appointed by her majesty's government to observe and evaluate a United Nations committee meeting scheduled for the following day. In the meantime he was attending a diplomatic reception. Quite why he was attending was unclear to him, save that two young men from the British Foreign Office who had apparently been assigned to run this part of his life evidently thought he should. Absurd. He was here because he and his colleagues had persuaded the powers-that-be that they were facing a crisis without parallel. So what did they ask him to do? Stand around and chat, drink in hand, as if nothing were happening!

He stepped back to avoid a harassed-looking waiter who was trying to pass him with a tray—and bumped into something soft. That was another thing. There were far too many people here. He turned to face whoever he'd all but knocked down.

Large brown eyes under long lashes. Fine, tawny hair. Tip-tilted nose. Small, slender, and elegant.

"I'm sorry," he said. She smiled.

"You're welcome!" Voice low and pleasant. American. From the look of her he'd thought somehow she'd be European. Perhaps French.

"Er — I'm Charlie Brown," he said. "As in *Peanuts*." Why was he babbling? It must be jet lag.

"And I'm Natalie Lawrence." Again she smiled. "Lawrence as in 'of Arabia.'"

He grinned back. She was nice enough to treat his daft remark as if it deserved a response and quick enough to cap it.

Conversation prospered for several minutes. He learned that she was a consultant translator for the US government at the UN and told her he was an astronomer working on a project for the British government.

"Doesn't the UN have translators of its own?" he said.

"Of course they do — good ones! But we're Americans. We don't like to think anyone else can do anything as we can, so we have our own. Me! And Erich over there" — she nodded towards a man at the other side of the room — "and a few more. Just to keep the others honest. At least, that's what we think."

"So you're fluent in dozens of languages?"

"Well, I only do the European stuff. I'm quite good at French, I suppose. And my Italian and my Spanish are decent. German's a bit weak but I cope."

"What she *means*" — this from a willowy, rather beautiful young man with long blond hair and a slight accent that was probably Russian — "is that Mademoiselle Natalie Delage D'Amblimont Sumter Lawrence speaks French so perfectly that she is regularly taken by the French to be a *contesse* — and indeed she really *is* a descendant of Capetian kings. Her Italian and her Spanish are somewhat marred by the fact that she speaks them with a slight and, in the opinion of many, rather charming French accent. And as for her German! — that, I fear, is so poor that when excited she's occasionally been known to make a tiny grammatical error. In other words our Natalie is not only beautiful but a genius. Thank God she never studied Russian or I'd be out of a job. Try the canapes with the green things on top, lovely lady. They're delicious."

The willowy young man passed on his way.

"Sounds like an admirer," Charlie said.

She grinned. "Not a very dangerous one. Boris is gay."

"And is all that really you? I mean, you do have a wonderful name! And wonderful ancestors!"

"Yes, I do, don't I? The result of a long and complicated family history in South Carolina and three continents. But don't even *try* to remember it! Natalie Lawrence is what everyone calls me. It just that Boris is Russian, so of course he loves long names nobody can remember. And he loves the fact that lots of my name is French. I sometimes think all cultured Russians really want to live in Paris."

He laughed. "Quite a lot of them do."

Then came the man he understood to be their host, dragging them both away to people they "must" meet. Hers was an American industrialist. His was a German scientist.

Natalie Lawrence found herself listening for what seemed an age to the industrialist, who was hot on the subject of a new soft drink from which the world in general and his company in particular would greatly benefit.

"What about the problems with the economy?" she said when at last there was a break in his flow. "Isn't this quite a difficult time to launch a new product nation-wide?"

"You're talking nonsense, honey. Everyone knows there are no *real* problems with the economy. It'll swing up in the next few weeks, well before RockPop is on the market."

"Thank you," she said. "I do so enjoy it when my contribution to a conversation is dismissed as not even worth discussion."

"You're welcome, honey. No, what's important, what *you* need to understand, is marketing."

Amazing.

"Never touch anything, honey, unless you're sure of the marketing. But this'll be a big one. Even Coke and Pepsi. You watch. They're going to suffer."

"Amazing," she said, when he paused for breath, "Simply amazing," and excused herself.

And now, just for a minute, she would stand by herself in this corner, sip her wine, and recover.

"Hiram J. Cornelius, ma'am. Admiral, United States Navy."

"Hello, I'm Natalie Lawrence."

"Delighted to make your acquaintance, ma'am. Of course, I'm retired now, just an old sea dog. Went through the whole of World War II in the Pacific, though."

"Really!"

"Yes ma'am. Midway, Guadalcanal, the Philippines. Just about every significant action, Hiram J. Cornelius was there. It's quite a story."

Oh Lord, he was going to tell it.

He was.

He was a very old man—indeed, if what he said was true, though still hale, he had to be in his nineties or at the very least his late eighties. And he had been a hero. So, being of a kind heart (she hoped), she would listen as best she could. And indeed the war in the Pacific was more interesting than RockPop.

Finally, having arrived at Japanese surrender and the USS *Missouri*, she felt able to excuse herself without being ungracious—only to be engulfed by two large young men from Yale who began without apology to describe for her their roles in the Yale eight, of which one was stroke and the other bow.

At this point it occurred to her that she had certainly drunk all the wine she needed and perhaps rather more (her glass had been regularly replenished throughout the sailor's narrative, and she, now she came to think about it, had not been especially cautious in emptying it) and so now she was entirely ready to go home.

Carefully she put down her glass, waved away the waiter who immediately approached to refill it, and waited.

"Excuse me," she said when one of the young men finally paused for breath, "I think I ought to tell you something."

She had their attention. In fact they were staring at her.

"Unlike you," she said, "I am not a great athlete. Nor a war hero, nor an industrialist about to make millions for … well, for anyone. I do, however, do *something*, and I'm very proud of it."

"Of course," said the taller of the two young men. "What is it?"

"Well, now, I'm so glad you asked me. I was beginning to think you never would. I am…" She stood up very straight. "A *translator*. If you're negotiating an international treaty, everybody'd better know what everybody else is talking about. So translators are *extraordinarily* important. And I happen to be an *extraordinarily* good one. In fact, I'm brilliant. Everyone says so. Everyone. Without exception. Including Boris, who is tall and beautiful and *extraordinarily* good at Russian. In fact it's his native tongue. And now would you please go and find me a taxi?"

The two young men stopped staring at her, looked at each other and then, without a word, obeyed.

Charlie had glimpsed her twice. Once being chatted up by an old fellow with gray hair and once with two strapping young men. He didn't like the look of the young men at all. They oozed virility.

Now he looked for her in all the public rooms, twice in each, and she was nowhere to be seen. Obviously she had left. His only consolation was that the two strapping young men were still very much in evidence, so at least she hadn't left with them.

Still he was annoyed, and even though the young men were still around, he found himself imagining all the other smooth, sophisticated blokes she might have left with—leaving him, naturally, the idiot knight, alone and palely loitering.

He *must* be jet-lagged.

Or losing his mind.

He'd been sent here in a situation of extreme urgency to

discuss what might be done about the probable destruction of all life on earth, indeed, the likely end of the solar system.

And here he was having fantasies about a woman he'd just met.

Didn't he just possibly have anything *more important* that he ought to be thinking about?

Resolutely, he determined to banish Mademoiselle Natalie Delage D'Amblimont Sumter Lawrence from his thoughts. He also determined to tell his Foreign Office minders, whom he could see propping up the bar, that he needed to leave. It was late, and presumably they'd like him to have such wits as he had about him for the UN meeting tomorrow morning.

It was interesting, though, that he'd remembered the whole of Natalie Lawrence's name, having heard it only once. Funny what tricks the mind will play when it ought to be concentrating on something else.

And end of the planet or not, nothing could alter the fact that in his opinion Mademoiselle Natalie Delage D'Amblimont Sumter Lawrence was absolutely bloody gorgeous.

That was not negotiable.

SIXTY

Exeter. Joseph Stirrup's apartment.
Thursday, November 6. 12:03 a.m.

"I've got to get to the bottom of it if it takes me the rest of the year. It happened on my watch and it'll drive me crazy till I can sort it."

Joseph was on the phone. He'd shared his hopes over the computer break-in with Alan Sanders, a young Jamaican now working for the FBI in Washington who also specialized in computing. Alan listened as a friend should and made sympathetic noises. Then he went further.

"Joseph," he said, "I think we just may be able to help. No promises, but let me make some calls and then get back to you in a half-hour or so."

It was already gone midnight, British time, but Joseph Stirrup was never early to bed.

"I'm not going anywhere," he said. "I'll be here. And thanks!"

"I haven't done anything yet," Alan said. "Talk to you later."

"Cheers."

Joseph replaced the phone, took a sip from his lukewarm coffee, and went back to his computer. He reckoned he could get in a couple more hours before he turned in.

Half an hour later to the minute his phone rang.

"Hi, Alan. You're a man of your word!"

"I won't beat about the bush. Of course you know about Carnivore?"

Indeed he knew—Carnivore and its predecessors were software programs designed to sniff out invasive techniques and store evidence of them according to criteria set by the FBI. All were very expensive. And all, to a greater or lesser extent, had failed.

"I know about Carnivore, but I'm not sure it'll do," he said. "Not unless…"

"Unless you could get access to 2.0 or even 3.0?"

"Well, yes."

"We can do better. This is 3.2. It's top restricted. But for you—well, the boss thinks we still owe you over the Lexis business, so if you could use some time on it we'll fix it. It'll get you where you're trying to go in a tenth of the time. Now, there's just one problem—at least from your viewpoint. If you use this, it means of course that we'll be able to access whatever it is you're handling. Is that a problem for you?"

"None at all. This isn't classified material. In one way that's what makes the whole thing so frustrating. There is—there was—absolutely nothing here we couldn't show Interpol or the FBI. Or you."

"Then you're on! And believe me, this one's good. It's the best they've developed yet. Trust me."

Joseph laughed. "Enough! I believe you! When can we start?"

His phone call completed, Joseph sat back in his wheelchair and chortled. Carnivore 3.2! He'd told DI Cavaliere he'd get her intruder if it took him a year.

Maybe now he'd be able to manage something a little quicker than that.

SIXTY-ONE

New York. Thursday, November 6.

The multicolored flags outside the United Nations Headquarters flapped and strained at their halyards. A tug hooted mournfully from the East River. The air above New York City was tense, gray, and gusty, and perhaps something other than fancy led Charlie to see that tension reflected in more than one of the representatives who now emerged from oversized and beflagged limousines to attend a meeting of the United Nations Scientific and Economic Liaison Committee scheduled for 3:00 p.m. He walked slowly, trying to look as if he were as at home with the situation as his companions from the Foreign Office.

He had visited New York on other occasions—once while on holiday and once for a scientific congress. But this was the first time he'd been so close to the United Nations complex. He paused, craning his neck to take in the thirty-nine-storied slab of the Secretariat Tower, its side a green-tinted mirror reflecting the dull Manhattan sky.

One of his Foreign Office handlers noticed his gaze.

"Mangled Corbusier," he said. "Not exactly great archi-

tecture, but certainly a remarkable experience. Come on. We'll
be late."

Still walking slowly, Charlie Brown followed.

The United Nations Scientific and Economic Liaison Committee
(UNSELC) is one of the less-publicized sections of the UN. It is,
to be precise, a confidential subcommittee of the Economic and
Social Council, whose function, according to Article 62 of the
UN charter, is to make suggestions and submit reports "with
respect to international economic, social, health, and related
matters." To such a subcommittee the Secretary General may
choose to pass matters of particular delicacy for consideration
and non-binding recommendation.

On this occasion UNSELC had chosen to keep the session
closed and confidential.

"Can this really be kept secret?" Charlie said to one of the
Foreign Office men as they went in. "With so many in the know
already? Surely there'll be a leak somewhere?"

The man raised an eyebrow. "Leaks are an instrument of government, Dr. Brown. Governments can keep secrets when they
want to. They do it all the time. And this time they want to. It's
in everyone's interest. No one wants panic on the streets. You
watch. There'll be no leaks. Unless someone like you decides to
blab to the media."

"And then?"

The man shrugged. "Then you'd be discredited and dis-
graced, so no one would believe you. There'd be plenty of
ways to do it. In this case it would be especially easy, because
of course no one would want to believe you anyway."

"Is that a threat?"

The Foreign Office man laughed. "Not at all! We know who
we're dealing with, Dr. Brown. You've signed the Official
Secrets Act and you've given us your word. And you're a man

who takes his word seriously. You'll keep it. We know that. You wouldn't be here if we didn't."

"Oh." The fact was, the man was right. They knew their man. In a way, he was rather impressed.

On the other hand, it *was* a threat, however nicely they chose to put it.

The British delegation was early. A brief meeting to confer over papers — to note that there was nothing new to note — and by general agreement they went to their places. Several delegations were already there, including the French and the Americans.

The committee gathered quickly and with surprisingly little noise for an assembly so large. Such murmur as there was died rapidly as the group responsible for this afternoon's presentation filed to the platform.

The main presentation was brief. Indeed there was, in one sense, little to say. All knew why they were assembled. On November first an Anglo-Australian team of astronomers using the Schmidt telescope at the Siding Spring Observatory on Mount Stromlo in New South Wales had photographed what was at first taken for a supernova. Subsequent observation led to the conclusion that it was in fact an early manifestation (from the earth's point of view) of an explosion at the nucleus of the Milky Way. The instrument had, as it happened, been trained on that segment of sky for some time, and so, by a comparison of photographic plates taken throughout the period, the astronomers were able to mark the appearance of the phenomenon to within six hours. Siding Star (so someone had named it, and the name stuck) had appeared between 01:20 and 07:20 UT (GMT) on 1 November. Other observatories had later confirmed both the observations and their interpretation.

The trouble appeared to have begun 27,000 years ago, with an explosion at the heart of our galaxy. In the universe as a whole, such explosions are, of course, not uncommon. The center of the explosion being 27,000 light years distant from our planetary system, its results were just now beginning to show up and would escalate over a period of months. First (the speed of light vastly exceeding anything else) we should see the star: indeed, instruments powerful enough could see it already. The light would become brighter. After a while it would be visible to the naked eye that looked for it. Later still, it would be visible to anyone who looked at the sky.

Behind it were likely to come other, dangerous phenomena: a hail of high-energy particles and electromagnetic radiation whose effect on our planet could not be calculated. There were no precedents—and too many unknowns. At one extreme some theorists expected the earth's atmosphere to be torn away and all life to be extinguished. At the other, many claimed that interstellar gas along the path of the advancing wave would act as a shield, minimalizing the effects of the radiation particles. Needless to say, there were various positions in between. A view expressed by some was that the best chances for survival would be the northern part of the northern hemisphere—the theory being that since the southern hemisphere was directly facing the explosion, it would receive the full impact, whereas the northern would be relatively shielded. Charlie conceded the possibility but wondered what sort of planet, even in the north, would greet any who managed to survive.

There remained the matter of breaking this news to the world. When? A point would come, if the astronomers' predictions were correct, when the world could hardly fail to notice. Charlie's first calculations at Siding Spring, had led him to expect this to happen in no more than a few days. Consultation with colleagues had led to a revision of these figures. On the best evidence now available it looked as though for about a hundred days there would be no way for the world—other than the world of major telescopes—to know what threatened it. Then, about mid-February, the light would brighten. It would begin to look like a planet. By late February it would begin to look like Mars — Mars in the wrong segment of sky. By then every amateur with a passing interest would be able to see it and, surely, question it. By mid-March it would begin to illuminate the night sky: a pinpoint of light (technically) but as bright as the moon. Then, within two or three days, the particles would come.

So. What was to be done?

There were, as the chair pointed out, no precedents.

Charlie sighed. No, there weren't. At least, not in the records of the UN.

Ragnarok, perhaps?

Götterdämmerung?

The Book of Revelation?

Maybe it was time the diplomats turned to the seers.

Or the prophets.

It ain't over till the fat lady sings.

He shook his head and turned his attention back to what was happening.

Various delegates went to the rostrum. There were questions. Reactions. Suggestions. Most of the presentations were low in key. They represented various conflicting interests and ideologies — developed and developing, Asian, Islamic, and Third World. The rhetoric varied. But it seemed to Charlie, as he listened, that the burden was constant. And the Foreign Office man obviously knew what he was talking about. From those who declared that the whole thing was a western-Zionist-anti-Islamic plot to those who called it a cover for Islamist terror, every speaker was basically invested in the same thing. Panic must be avoided. It was too soon to terrify the world. If the interstellar gas theory were correct, very little would happen anyway, save an opportunity when it came to view some unusual night skies. It would be best, for the moment, simply to monitor the situation.

But later? If the environment did begin to disintegrate? If a moment came when the world began to see for itself? The possibility was raised, only to be dismissed. Here again there was virtual unanimity. This situation, several different speakers declared, was for the moment hypothetical.

Charlie found himself no longer surprised they all remained calm. What they chose to contemplate was relatively trivial. What was not trivial, they chose not to contemplate. *Humankind cannot bear very much reality.* He sighed and shifted in his seat.

Mercifully, the session ended a few moments later.

Afterward, inevitably, there was another meeting with the other members of the British delegation. All solemnly agreed there was no more information to be shared and therefore nothing, for the moment, to be done.

Charlie was becoming increasingly uncomfortable with the easy assumption, as it seemed to him, that secrecy must be maintained. He raised the issue.

"For myself, I've always been clear that if a doctor knows I'm likely to die soon, I expect to be told. There are things I'd like to do. Reconciliations I'd like to try for. That's the only way death can be a human act. So what if the chances are the human race is likely to die? Is no one going to consider giving its members a chance to prepare? To think? To repent?"

Apparently not.

"Dr. Brown," one member of the delegation said to him, "I think we all respect your concern. Speaking for myself, I certainly do. But let us be frank: you scientists as a group don't agree as to what's going to happen, do you? So let's say we do release this information now, and then the 'interstellar gas' theory proves correct. What will we have done? We'll have created an international panic—indeed this news will create *chaos*—and it will all have been for nothing. Dr. Brown, can even you look me in the eye and declare categorically that the 'interstellar gas' theory will turn out to be wrong?"

Of course he could not. There were very few things about

Siding Star he could declare categorically, and that certainly wasn't one of them.

Eventually they emerged.

Then to his surprise — just when he wasn't thinking about her at all — there was Natalie Lawrence at the far corner of the hall. She was standing with Boris and Erich and several others. But why should he be surprised? She'd told him she worked here. She was wearing a dark suit and looked serious. She was what fashion magazines would describe, he supposed, as *petite*. And even in the cold light of morning — which, alas, does not always replicate the warm glow of evening — she was still gorgeous.

And since he didn't see how it would affect the end of the world one way or the other, he might as well go and talk to her. Excusing himself briefly to his companions, he crossed the hall.

"Hello," he said.

She looked up, surprised — then smiled.

"Well, hi! So your 'project' for the British government is in these dark and dangerous corridors! And you're a mysterious diplomat as well as a great astronomer!"

He grinned. "Out of all that, I think I *can* safely say I'm an astronomer."

She laughed.

"Come and meet my colleagues. Hey guys, this is Charlie. He's a friend of mine."

Sixty-Two

Joseph Stirrup took a sharp intake of breath and whistled softly. He'd been through it three times now, and there was no mistake. Carnivore 3.2 had done everything Alan said it would, and more. Then, relieving himself of Carnivore (the Americans were good friends and he was grateful to them, but there was no need for them to know all his little secrets just at present, and in any case he'd reached a point where perhaps there *was* something a foreign government shouldn't know) he'd done a further bit of rather smart intuiting on his own account and now —

He picked up his phone and stabbed a number.

"Verity, do you have a moment to join the boffins down here in their underground kingdom? I think I've got something that'll interest you."

"On my way!"

She was beside him a few minutes later, bending over his shoulder and peering at the monitor.

"Look here!" He went through a succession of moves. "This is where we start. This is where we go. And this is where we end up." She lacked his sheer genius for computers, but he'd taught her a lot over the last month or so.

"Good grief! No wonder we had trouble tracing it!"

"Exactly."

"Can you go any further?"

"I already have." He reached for a scratch pad, tore off a page, scribbled on it and passed it to her.

She read it. "Fantastic! You've nailed the blighter!"

"That I have." He took the paper from her and carefully tore it into tiny pieces before confining it to the wastebasket. "There's just one problem. It's classified. That's why I didn't go in there again to show you that part. No sense in leaving my own footprints all over the place."

"Oh." A pause. "But someone has to tell DI Cavaliere. It simply isn't fair not to. I mean, I realize in one sense it's all water under the bridge, but she really should know."

"I agree. And I promised her myself. She's away at that thing in Middlemoor, isn't she?"

"She's due back Tuesday."

"I'll figure out something. Meanwhile, even on the basis of what's *not* classified, there's no reason I shouldn't send the super a discreetly worded memo. It's time he stopped making snide cracks in his memos about secretarial inefficiency. The fact is, there's absolutely nothing the people in secretarial could have done about this, Verity. Nothing."

"What I *don't* see though, is how you managed to do it so quickly. You said it would take months. I thought that's why you were getting frustrated."

"I did, and I was," he said. "But, well… I get by with a little help from my friends."

Sixty-Three

New York. The same day.

For the next few hours there was, it appeared, nothing for either Natalie or Charlie to do. So they drank quantities of Starbucks coffee and talked.

She was working with a group discussing climate change. She evidently found listening to and translating the debates almost as frustrating as he found his own group, mostly because of her embarrassment over the positions taken by her own delegation.

Then came his moment of embarrassment: he, of course, was not at liberty to tell her what he was involved in.

"Don't worry," she said when he started to apologize, "around here we're involved all the time in stuff we're not allowed to talk about. As it happens, climate change isn't one of them, since everyone knows what's going on, and even the press is allowed in. But that's today. Tomorrow I might be the one involved in something I can't talk about."

Actually, and rather to his surprise, not being able to talk about it was a relief. He was sick to death of Siding Star and sick to death of what the diplomats were doing or not doing about it. So he was happy to have it not exist while he was with Natalie. She almost made that possible.

***

Diplomacy, he decided over the ensuing weekend, seemed to consist of a great deal of sitting around. He wasn't sure Natalie Lawrence fancied him half as much as he fancied her, but she seemed happy to talk to him, so they talked. She'd been born and raised in Charleston, South Carolina, but they talked mostly about Paris, which he had only visited but where she had studied for four years, beginning her postgraduate work at the Sorbonne immediately after graduating from the University of the South; and about Oxford, where they had both studied, she for a year following the Sorbonne, he for the whole of his undergraduate work. They talked about politics, in which sphere they shared a mildly pinkish cynicism. She was cautiously optimistic about the new American President-Elect, who had won the election by a landslide on the previous Tuesday but was evidently about to inherit a mess.

"I supported him and I think he's brilliant," she said. "I just hope we haven't given him a job that's simply impossible."

Charlie was happy enough to applaud her enthusiasm and indeed, like most Europeans, was an admirer of the President-Elect. But then he thought of Siding Star and wondered: would the new President have a chance to do anything at all? He sighed.

"What's the matter?"

"Oh, nothing."

On one occasion he did come quite near to revealing something.

"Tell me," he said, "what would you do if you thought all this" (he waved his arm) "I mean everything, everybody, was likely to be ended, killed, destroyed—quite soon? What would you do?"

If she wondered whether his question had anything to do with the project he couldn't tell her about, she didn't say so. She merely gazed at him.

"I think," she said at last, "at least I *hope*, that I should follow John Wesley's advice."

"Which was?"

"Well, someone once said to him, 'What would you do Mr. Wesley, if you knew you were going to die at the end of the day?'"

"And what did he say?"

"He said, 'I'd do exactly what I intend to do anyway.'"

"Oh."

He did tell her about Mickey the cat. She sympathized. A few years back, she'd lost the little gray cat she'd grown up with.

"She was called Misty," she said, and her eyes grew misty as she spoke. "She'd get on the bed in the morning and nuzzle me to wake me up. Then if I didn't do anything she'd play with my hair. And *then* if I didn't do anything she'd sit on my head and start to wash. That usually did it!"

He decided he liked her better than ever.

On Monday the powers-that-be finally decided they had finished with Charlie Brown, so, on his last afternoon in New York, Natalie asked him if he'd like to meet some of her family.

He would indeed.

She took him to visit relatives on her late father's side who lived near the Cathedral of St. John the Divine. The Lawrences were chaotic and delightful. They took him to evensong, gave him a tour of the cathedral, introduced him to the dean and a local rabbi, and finally filled him with sandwiches, cake, and tea.

Then when it was time for him to leave and he mentioned telephoning for a cab, Natalie offered to drive him in her uncle's car to the airport. There at last, when the moment came to say goodbye and enter the departure lounge, he did what he'd been wanting to do for some time. He put his arms around her and kissed her.

He did it rather clumsily, almost losing his glasses in the process.

"I kissed you!" he said.

"I noticed," she said.

Whatever she thought of the kiss, she was still delightfully in his arms and making no attempt to move.

Then she said, "I'm going to Paris for a week after Christmas to stay with some friends and celebrate New Year. I'm planning to leave them on the second. But I'll still have two weeks' more leave. I could come and visit you in London, if you like. You could show me around!"

"You—I could. Of course I could. I'd *really* like that!" He hesitated, then, "You could stay at my house if you want. It's just me there, I'm afraid, but it's quite big and I've got a proper spare room and everything."

She smiled. "Thank you, Charlie. I'd really like that."

"I'll phone you when I get back," he said.

"That would be nice."

Natalie walked thoughtfully back to the car.

Obviously, there was a cloud over Charlie. He'd surely touched on it the other day with his question about the end of everything. It must be the secret UN thing.

She hoped she'd helped.

She really liked him. He was obviously brilliant. But he was modest, too, self-deprecating. The men she met weren't like that.

And he'd actually been nervous about kissing her!

Softly, she quoted Victor Hugo to herself, *Les bêtes sont au bon Dieu ! Mais la bêtise est à l'homme !*

She smiled. Never mind. He might be a little *farouche* just at present, but when the New Year came, she reckoned she could probably do something about that.

Proper spare room indeed!

Sixty-Four

London. Monday, November 17.

With the clear understanding that he accepted the implications of having signed the Official Secrets Act and would be available to the government for consultation whenever needed, Charlie had been returned (like a fish put back into the river!) to his normal pursuits at London University for the closing weeks of the term. After a few days and somewhat to his surprise he found himself immersed pretty much as usual.

He was teaching classes as usual.

He was attending as usual too many committees and faculty meetings in the Senate House, where he found himself bored or nauseated as usual by university politics, futile in the light of what was about to happen—but then, he'd always found them futile.

He was taking the tube every evening from Tottenham Court Road to Edgware Road, buying a paper, and walking from there to the house in Sussex Gardens.

And for the moment, at least, Siding Star and its effects were becoming a little more unreal by the day.

As the term drew to its close he was faced with proofing an article, "Assessing the Age of Large Magellanic Cloud Blue Globular Cluster NGC 2134," which he had written earlier in the year for *Publications of the Astronomical Society of the Pacific*, and with marking and evaluating his students' end-of-term exams. He addressed both these tasks as carefully and well as he could, including making some significant changes to the article in the light of his most recent work.

Quite why did he take such care, when in his view it was extremely unlikely that the article would ever be published or the students ever graduate?

The answer to that was obvious.

Natalie Lawrence was the one factor in his recent experience that did *not* fade. On the contrary, throughout the days that followed his visit to New York, memories of her, thoughts of her, daydreams and fantasies of her, dominated every moment when he was not consciously paying attention to something else.

And he certainly had not forgotten her story: *"'What would you do, Mr. Wesley, if you knew you were going to die at the end of the day?' 'I'd do exactly what I intend to do anyway.'"* So he proofed his article and graded his papers, making a point of doing it all as well as he could.

A telephone call from Jodrell Bank and a couple of summonses to conferences at the Department of the Environment served to remind him, nonetheless, that Siding Star was still there. At both these conferences, he met with representatives from the Ministry of Defense. His opinions and advice were sought, but he had the distinct impression that he was being told nothing—certainly nothing of any substance.

Three times in six weeks he had the Dream. More and more it seemed to center on the man in the black robe. The man behind whom there was something else, something dark and looming. And now for the first time—perhaps for no other reason than the obvious reason that it was on his mind—he found himself wondering if it all had anything to do with Siding Star and the threat it presented. How could anything he did affect a galactic explosion 27,000 years ago? He had no idea. Yet it was always the same man, and he always gave the same command, "You must!" And now when Charlie heard it he found himself thinking, "Siding Star! I must do something about it," as if there *were* something he could do.

But then, as always, he awoke, flustered and frustrated, the big question unanswered: "Must what?"

Sixty-Five

The first person Cecilia saw when she arrived in the car park at the Heavitree Police Station on Tuesday morning was Verity Jones, who was walking towards her car. Although she'd evidently been on duty for much of the night, her suit (silver-gray today) looked pristine. As for her hair? In heaven's name, how did she do it? Cecilia's dark curls seemed to lead a life entirely of their own.

"Joseph is waiting to see you, ma'am," Verity Jones said as they passed. "He looks *extremely* pleased with himself!"

"Does he?" Cecilia said, just managing not to laugh at her young subordinate's hopeless attempt to allow Joseph to give her his news himself. She was willing to bet he'd found their hacker.

His wheelchair was parked right outside her office and the expression on his face was indeed wonderfully smug. She held the door open and he fairly zoomed in.

"I've solved your little problem," he said once she'd closed the door.

"That soon!"

"I got help from some pals in the FBI who owed me one, and to be honest I got lucky. It happens sometimes."

"I'm all ears," Cecilia said.

"Well, as Verity said, it's not surprising it took us so long—it was the Ministry of Defense. I found traces of two of their security codes embedded in the encryption."

That certainly made sense, in view of all that had happened.

"Thank you very much indeed. Well done!"

Joseph beamed.

"Look," Cecilia said, "I know it's a lot to ask, but—do we happen to know just *who* in the M.O.D. did this?"

"The answer is, yes and no. As I say, I found traces of two of their security codes—one for the department that made the entry to our system, the other for the particular official who authorized it. But there's a problem. The M.O.D. says that just *what* and to *whom* those codes refer is classified, and they won't tell us. In other words, ordinary coppers simply can't be trusted with stuff like that. We might sell it to Osama bin Laden or one of his mates, I suppose." He glanced at his watch. "Well, I must go. Meeting time! But I just thought you'd like to know where I'd got to."

"You were right. I do—like to know, I mean! Thanks again, Joseph!"

"My pleasure!" Again she held the door for him, and as he trundled through it he turned in the chair and held out his hand—which, though surprised, Cecilia took. "As I say, nothing that's on a computer can be hidden forever if you know how to look for it. And I mean *nothing*. Take care. Catch you later." And he was away, shooting his wheelchair down the corridor, adroitly avoiding a tea trolley, and cornering at the far end on a penny.

Cecilia closed the door and only then became aware of the two post-it notes that had been pressed into her palm.

She looked at them.

On each were a few words, neatly printed in capital letters with a ballpoint pen.

One said, WEAPONS RESEARCH ESTABLISHMENT. HARTON DOWN. The other said, DR. HENRY WHEATLEY.

She grinned.

Classified my foot.

No one can do this sort of thing without leaving a footprint somewhere.

There it was at last, literally in the palm of her hand. The smoking gun! It made her wish—not for the first time, but now for an entirely different reason—that Henry Wheatley hadn't succeeded in killing himself.

SIXTY-SIX

London. Friday January 2, 2009.

Natalie had said to Charlie that he could "show her around" in London. But she'd not been with him more than a few hours before it became obvious that she actually knew the city a good deal better than he did, at least when it came to places to have fun and good food.

"Tell you what," she said on her second evening, after they'd walked in Green Park in the afternoon and then, as it got dark, looked at the brightly lit shops along Piccadilly, "let's go to my favorite restaurant in the world, and I'll buy you a wonderful dinner."

"I'd have thought your favorite restaurant in the world would be in Paris."

"Well, it *is* French, and it's run by two Parisians I got to know when I was at the Sorbonne."

"Then I'd like that very much! Do we need to get a taxi?"

"We can walk. It's not far—just off the Haymarket. But we ought to go now. Later they'll be full, and without reservations we'll be a nuisance."

The walk took about ten minutes.

"Restaurant" said a cream awning that stretched along a frontage just long enough for a pair of tables and their benches, although the evening was certainly too cool for eating outside. "Cuisine traditionelle" announced the window. The room inside was brightly lit and cheerful, with places for about twenty people.

"Oh good!" Natalie said. "They've just opened for dinner. Come on—we're first."

As soon as they entered, a small, dark man behind the bar looked up from the glasses he was polishing, broke into a broad smile, and bustled forward.

"*Alors, ma chère Natalie, je suis contente de te revoir! Denise! Denise!*"

"*Ah, Marcel, moi aussi, ça fait un moment que je ne suis pas venue.*"

A pert, pretty woman emerged from the back of the restaurant, saw Natalie, and all but ran to embrace her.

Natalie hugged her back.

Marcel stood smiling.

"*Et alors, Mademoiselle Natalie,*" he said, "*une table pour deux ce soir?*"

Natalie laughed, then turned and held out her hand towards Charlie, who was still standing in the doorway.

"*Mais oui. Tu vois que je ne suis plus toute seule!* Charlie, these are my friends Denise and Marcel, the owners of *Florimel,* which as I told you is my favorite restaurant in the whole world! *Denise et Marcel, je vous présente Charlie Brown.*"

"*Enchanté, Monsieur.* It is a pleasure to meet you."

Charlie grinned. "*Enchanté,*" he said, painfully conscious of his atrocious accent. But Marcel only beamed as he and Denise ushered them to a corner where there was a table for two.

"*Voilà la carte et comme hors-d'œuvre ce soir nous proposons des huîtres fraîches et succulentes et comme plat principal, un filet d'espadon préparé avec une sauce hollandaise.*"

"*Merci, Marcel.*"

Of all this, Charlie understood not a word except "*merci.*" Natalie translated for him. "Lovely succulent oysters to start, and then swordfish cooked in a hollandaise sauce. How's that sound?"

"Splendid!" He beamed at everybody. Denise fussed over him, carefully arranging his cutlery and napkin, which to him appeared to have been perfectly well arranged already. Then she smiled at Natalie.

"*Alors, Natalie, qui est ton nouvel ami?*"

"*Nous nous sommes rencontrés aux Nations Unies. Il ne parle pas un mot de français.*"

"*C'est bien ce que j'avais compris. Dis-donc, il est mignon!*"

"*Et toi, tu es très flirt! Attention, il est à moi!*"

"Excuse me," said Charlie at last, "would one of you be kind enough to translate?"

The two women looked at each other and laughed.

"Certainly not!" Natalie said. "One of the things I like about you is that you aren't conceited."

Halfway through the oysters, it occurred to Charlie that he was happy. Simply and idiotically happy.

Surely he had no right to be, with the world ending? Should he not be praying, or at least worrying? What of the Dream? The call of the man in the black robe was so urgent. It wasn't logical, it wasn't scientific, but what if there really was something he ought to be doing? Something he *must* do? He really —

"*Don't!*" Natalie said, laying her hand lightly across his.

Charlie looked up at her. Her expression was as serious as he'd yet seen it.

"You'll know what to do when it's time, Charlie Brown, and you'll do it. Meantime, if something makes you happy, be happy."

He looked at her astonished.

"Are you a mind reader? Do you know what's going on?"

"I'm not and I don't. And I don't want you to break your promises and tell me. But I do think perhaps I know something about *you*. And whatever's going on, Charlie Brown, I'd say you'll do your duty when you have to. And in the mean time, there's no reason not to be happy with what God gives you. In fact, it may be rather rude not to be. Rude to God, I mean."

"Oh." For some reason tears were welling in his eyes. He blinked. "All right then."

"A promise?"

He nodded. He could hardly speak.

"A promise," he said at last.

The truth was, despite Siding Star, he was ridiculously happy. And Natalie was the reason. And without Siding Star, he'd never have met her.

So where did *that* chain of reasoning get him?

To his hors-d'oeuvre, he decided.

"These oysters," he said after a few minutes, "are incredible."

"Didn't I mention this was a good restaurant?"

SIXTY-SEVEN

St. Andrew's Vicarage,
Holborn Circus, London. Saturday, January 3.

VANDALISM LINKED TO POWER FAILURES

Homes, businesses, and shops in London's East End have yet again found themselves without power, after suspected vandalism caused major fire damage to high voltage electricity cables. This is the district's eleventh power outage since November 1st. A spokesperson for EDF Energy UK said this morning that properties in Poplar, Bethnal Green, Stepney, and the southern part of Hackney lost power supply at 0156 GMT. Engineers have restored power to some areas but it may be another 36 hours before electricity is restored to all. The Royal London Hospital was also affected by the power cut, though a back-up generator started working immediately, a spokesman said. This was a marked improvement on the situation in early November when a power outage was accompanied by a failure of the hospital's own generator.

"Complicated and difficult" work

According to EDF Energy, the fire seriously damaged

five major electricity circuits on a cable bridge, and one of the bridge supports. "There looks to be evidence of vandalism. This morning the locks were broken on the security gates at each end of the bridge."

EDF Energy said the work involved in restoring power had been complicated by the necessity to ensure that the bridge itself was safe before the engineers could begin repairing the damaged electricity circuits.

EDF Energy's spokesman, when asked whether he connected this outage with the series of power failures and various other outbreaks of vandalism and destructive behavior that have affected East London over the last two months, declined to comment.

Michael sighed and laid the newspaper aside. What disturbed him far more than the power outage was that—however evasive the EDF's response to questions—last night's failure obviously *did* connect to another feature of life in the East End over the last eight weeks: a rising level of casual and even quite meaningless violence.

A few nights ago a mob had actually started throwing stones at firefighters who were trying to rescue people from a burning home for the elderly. Michael would much more easily have believed a story of East Londoners—in his experience among the kindest people on earth—risking their own lives to help the residents. But there was no doubt that the story was true. The police had made a number of arrests, mostly of perfectly respectable young men and women who when interviewed said things like, "I feel terrible. I've no idea what got into me."

The magistrate had no idea either, but that didn't stop him handing out hefty chunks of community service—with a strong recommendation that as much of it as possible be done with the London Fire Brigade. "If," he added, "the London Fire Brigade will have you."

Then, of course, there was other violence whose purpose was only too clear. Racist. Ethnic. Religious. It was only days since in a minor way Michael had come up against it himself. Last Sunday, driving to St. George's, Cannon Street, where he was to preach, he had stopped to chat for a few minutes with Nadia, a Muslim friend who taught mathematics at the university.

"Michael, if I were you, I'd get rid of that flag in your back seat."

"It's just an old Union Jack left over from Armistice Day."

"I know. And it's my flag too. I'm British and proud of it. Doesn't make any difference. If anyone sees that in your car round here, they'll think you're BNP. And you know what that means."

He did indeed. British National Party. Racist. Fascist. Anti-Muslim. Anti-Semitic. Homophobic.

"If you're lucky," Nadia said, "when they see it they'll just smash your windshield. If you're not, who knows? They might set the car on fire. Or beat you up. Get rid of it, Michael. Just so your friends can stop worrying about you." She grinned. "And by the way, it's a Union *Flag*. It's only a Union Jack when it's being flown from a boat."

"I never knew that."

Nadia laughed. "Neither did I, but my kid sister's just joined the Royal Navy. I think it's the first thing they told her."

So when he arrived back home he took it in—it was time he cleared out the back of the car anyway. But it saddened him to think things had got to such a pass that it was actually dangerous in some parts of Britain to be associated with the British flag.

Not, of course, that all the problems were being caused by the BNP, bad though it was. He could tell that from his newspaper. He moved from headline to headline. More suicide bombings in Iraq: yesterday, it appeared, a man had bombed his own family. The Israelis were still knocking hell out of the Gaza strip and declaring themselves ready for "long weeks of action." The

U.S. economy was in chaos with unemployment galloping and an administration in its closing weeks of office apparently incapable of action. Michael pushed the paper aside. This was really depressing. Was the world going mad?

Then he thought again of Nadia (with her kid sister in the Royal Navy!) There were plenty of people like Nadia trying to keep things on track. Police, like the wonderful Cecilia. Social workers, doctors and nurses, railway workers and secretaries and teachers, repair workers and engineers and firefighters, rabbis and imams and priests: keeping the hospitals and the surgeries and the schools open, keeping the traffic and the trains moving, keeping the lights on, putting out fires, saying the prayers.

Soldiers of light. That's what they were. Doubtless few of them thought of themselves like that, but that's what they were, all the same.

SIXTY-EIGHT

Sunday, January 4.

Natalie announced at breakfast that she wanted to go to church. Charlie had thought she might want to attend one of the great churches, Saint Paul's or the Abbey, but no, she wished to attend the 11:00 a.m. Eucharist at Saint John's Wood Parish Church.

"It's easy to get there," she said. "We take the tube from Edgeware Road, change at Baker Street, and it's one stop."

"It's a nice church," he said, impressed by her knowledge of the London Underground. "But why especially there?"

"Because a friend of mine from Charleston is doing an exchange year there, and this morning she gets to be celebrant. Her first ever mass outside the States. I promised her I'd come if I could."

So they went, and after mass he got to meet the celebrant, a dark, rather Spanish-looking young woman who rejoiced in the notably un-Spanish-sounding name of Calhoun Walpole Perkins.

"We went to school together," Natalie said. "And somehow or other Callie and I *just* managed to get through the experience without being thrown out!"

"But let's face it, once or twice it was a near thing," Callie said. They both laughed. "Actually, we were at *two* schools together, one of which has since been closed."

"And the other's wisely decided to change its name," Natalie said. "Still, at least Callie's managed to land a respectable job. Which is more than Mama thinks I have. Did you know, Charlie, that New York is no place at all for a properly brought up Charleston girl?"

Church was followed by an uproarious lunch with Callie in a nearby pub.

"So what have you been up to?" Natalie asked.

"Oh, being virtuous: serving the poor, visiting the sick, preaching the gospel. Actually" — she grew more serious — "it's not as easy here as you'd think. There's a lot of violence about. Quite unusual for Saint John's Wood. One of the curates got assaulted the other day — for no apparent reason. The vicar keeps warning me to be careful. He says he just doesn't know what's gotten into people lately. But whatever it is, it's nasty."

It started to rain just as Charlie and Nathalie arrived back at Charlie's house, and within a few minutes they had a downpour.

"Let's stay in and be cozy," she said.

Assisted by the Doyley Carte Opera Company on a CD, they sang through *Trial by Jury* with a grubby score he'd had at school (Natalie found it in the bookcase in her room). Then she picked Vaughan Williams' *Fantasia on a Theme by Thomas Tallis*, and they listened in a more sober mood.

"That was glorious," said Charlie when it ended.

"It was. And I chose it especially for you! Do you know what Herbert Foss says about it?"

He shook his head.

As she reached for the record notes, her hair caught the light.

"'These nineteen folio pages hold the faith of England,'" she read. "'In its soil and in its tradition, firmly believed yet expressed in no articled details. There is quiet ecstasy, and then alongside it comes a kind of blind persistence, a faithful pilgrimage towards the unseen light.'" She looked up. "How about that?"

There was a pause. He held out his arms.

He was no longer clumsy.

And nothing would ever be the same again.

SIXTY-NINE

So Charlie was persuaded by love to be to be distracted, temporarily at least, from the prospect of annihilation, and if it is true that love is stronger than death, who is to say that he was wrong to be so persuaded? What then of the world's governments, whose representatives had so frustrated him? To do them justice, it would by no means be true to say that they did nothing. On the contrary, in many ways they acted with remarkable vigor, and there was, certainly among the "developed" nations, a quite remarkable degree of cooperation as they took steps to preserve at least what they regarded as the brightest and best.

The hope that the northern part of the planet might be the most promising area for survival naturally formed the focus of much of this effort. So government offices and government servants found themselves called upon without warning or explanation (or, at best, with flimsy excuses—"for military exercises," "in the event of hostilities") to produce contingency plans for the selection and movement of significant groups; for the swift creation of underground complexes—schools, hospitals, administration buildings; for the commandeering of transport.

Naturally all this activity could not go unobserved. In the democracies, questions were asked, in parliaments and congresses, in newspapers and on television. But the explanations were ready. New refineries. New bases. New mines. Contingency against nuclear terrorism. And, of course, massive outlay to stimulate the economy. Indeed, the huge building projects did provide jobs. No one could deny that. And this surely was one reason why the hard questions were not pressed. As one union leader put, "I'll build apartments for the devil himself if it means jobs for my people." Only with time could it become apparent to those with access to information and tools to analyze it that the scale of the operations and their nature went beyond anything the explanations explained. Only with time — and time, like the economy, was not on the side of the questioners.

SEVENTY

Heavitree Road Police Station. Friday, January 16.

Cecilia, dripping from the rain, scurried into her office, hung her raincoat on the hook, made minor repairs to her appearance in her small washroom, and finally approached her desk.

On top of her in-tray was a folder with a note pinned to it in Verity Jones's handwriting: *Thought this would interest you."*

It was a printout of a page from a tabloid newspaper. Attached was another note: *From the digital edition of yesterday's* Hackney Gazette. *See small column headed New College etc.*

Cecilia turned to the article.

NEW COLLEGE PROCLAIMED 'MASSIVE BREAKTHROUGH'

Minister of Technology Praises Cranston

Speaking at a dinner of representatives of the Managerial Institutes of Industry, the Rt. Hon. Robert Dawes, MP, Minister for Technology, referred in glowing terms to the massive breakthrough for Britain represented by developments such as the new Cranston

College of Science in the heart of London's former
dockland, due to be officially opened on January 30th.
Here, he claimed, as a direct result of far-sighted government initiative, Britain has a chance as never before
to benefit from ever-changing technological advances.
The new college is being acclaimed as an outstanding
example of cooperation between government, which
had provided the basic resource; local authority, which
provided the site; and non-statutory bodies.

Why did Verity Jones think she would be interested in this?
Cecilia shrugged and read on.

> The minister referred in glowing terms to the contribu-
> tion of the London-based Academy for Philosophical
> Studies, to whose credit must go the provision of con-
> siderable funding from voluntary sources.

The academy! So they were back in business.

She read to the end, but here was nothing more about the
academy. Then she picked up the phone.

"Verity, do you usually read the *Hackney Gazette*?"

Verity laughed. "Not exactly. I got Joseph to program my
computer for digital editions of the London local press, so the
academy would come up on my screen if ever it got any mention in the press."

"Well that's brilliant. Joseph's a genius—but then we knew
that. Thanks, Verity."

"It's a pleasure, ma'am."

So the academy was back, and from the end of the month an
unspecified number of Britain's and the world's brightest young
brains would be under the influence of an institution approved
and supported by the same group that had not only tried to
murder her parents but if Michael were right had schemed to
bring about an incalculable amount of other damage.

In a general way she'd tried already to warn a few friends in the Met about the academy, but she was well aware it was hard for them to do much when she didn't even know what to tell them to look for. As always, there was nothing concrete to go on. What, in fact, that would stand up in a court, did they actually *know*? Even about October 31st? That the academy had a fire! But that wasn't a crime unless they started it. And now they were providing funds for a technical college. Not exactly criminal activity.

She would talk to Michael about it.

Before the Cranston College opening, if possible. He believed the academy was dangerous, and she'd seen quite enough to feel sure he was right. That said, she had no idea how to prove it. And for the present there wasn't, so far as she could see, a damned thing Michael or she or anyone else could do about it.

Maybe pooling their thoughts would help.

Seventy-One

The same day.

It was Natalie's last evening in London.

They were planning to walk along the Edgeware Road up to the Speakers' Corner, enjoying the last light of the day. As they turned from Sussex Gardens they saw a harassed woman struggling out of a pick-up with parcels and a child. Natalie went and helped her, Charlie happily offering his assistance. The two women allowed him to hold the door open.

He and Natalie walked on, arm in arm.

As they drew close to Marble Arch they saw the flashing lights of police cars.

"Some kind of commotion," Natalie said.

A little further on, and they were passed by a helmet-less policeman supported by two colleagues. He was bleeding from a gash in his cheek.

"Good God," Charlie said, "poor fellow. How on earth did that happen?"

Minutes after that, they were being turned back.

"I'm sorry ma'am, sir," the officer said, "but there's been some trouble at Speakers' Corner, a sort of gang warfare, it seems. We've just about got it under control, but a couple of our lads got hurt, and we'd like to keep the area clear for a bit."

Of course they turned back.

"I feel somewhat embarrassed," Charlie said. "London's not paradise, but it's usually safe enough. Certainly at Marble Arch! You're just not seeing us at our best. I don't understand it."

"Never mind," she said. "Although I'm sure you're person-ally responsible for the whole thing, on this occasion I'll forgive you."

And stretching up, she kissed him.

She meant it to be a light, quick kiss, just for fun, but then he caught her to him and she clung and somehow it wasn't light and it definitely wasn't quick.

In fact it took so long they had to go back to the house so as to finish it properly.

Next day, a Saturday, she flew back to New York.

Before leaving, she told him she was scheduled for two more weeks' leave, which she'd have to take in February or she'd lose them. She realized it was rather soon, but she could come and spend them with him in London if he liked.

He didn't think it was at all soon, and he liked very much.

SEVENTY-TWO

*Saint Andrew's Vicarage,
Holborn Circus. Friday, January 23.*

Michael hung up his raincoat, gathered several letters from the hall table, and climbed the stairs to his study. He'd been attending a long and particularly tedious meeting at Church House, followed by a more than usually slow bus-ride back, and it was good to be home again. Mrs. Owens had put some flowers in his study. His books and papers were, of course, in an untidy heap, just as he'd left them. She had once, some years ago, tidied them for him. A disaster! "It may look like a mess, Mrs. Owens," he'd said. "In fact, let's face it, it *is* a mess. But it's my mess and I understand it. If you tidy it, I'm lost!" She'd never moved his papers since. Bless her!

Michael heard the front door rattle and walked back to the stairs. Down in the hallway stood Jim, officially the church secretary and unofficially responsible for virtually everything practical that had to be done around the place. He wiped his feet, then placed a length of cable and an inspection lamp on the hall table.

"The heating went off in church," he said. "It's all right. We had to poke about under the boards. But it's on again — for now, anyhow."

"Well done!" Not for the first time, he thanked God for Jim. The church heating system was to Michael a mystery whose depths were beyond scrutiny.

Shaking his head at this profound thought, he descended the stairs, went to the vestry, and put on his cassock.

It was nearly time for the Eucharist.

Charlie Brown heard the church bell as he left W. H. Smith's in Holborn, where he'd been on a lunch-time errand. He looked up at St Andrew's clock, then at the church itself. He had passed it a thousand times, noting it as one of many fine churches in that part of London; but he'd never been inside. Well, why not?

His return to bachelordom from the joy of being a lover had been as hard as he expected. True, he now really had a girlfriend, a wonderful girlfriend, who'd said she would come and see him again in only a few weeks. He could email her and skype her and talk to her on the telephone, and already his British Telecom bill was enormous and he didn't care. But still, with her physically gone from the house, it seemed he must again renew at least some of his anxieties. Last night for the second time since she left he'd dreamed the Dream, which now seemed to him ever more closely linked to the Siding Star, though he had no idea how.

It would be good to spend a little time in quiet. He would go into the church.

He negotiated the Holborn Circus traffic, was sworn at by a taxi driver (justifiably, he suspected), and found himself facing a handsome blue notice board with gold-painted lettering. "Holy Eucharist 1:10 p.m. weekdays." Good.

He entered by the south entrance, looked around him in astonishment, saw the priest in a black cassock, and fainted.

SEVENTY-THREE

A few minutes later.

Someone fetched Jim, and between them they easily enough had the young man propped up in a pew.

"Is he drunk?" Jim said. "Drugs?"

Michael smelt his breath, then lifted an eyelid and looked at the pupil.

"Neither, I think. He just fainted. Look, he's coming round."

Charlie Brown blinked. He was seated. The priest was looking into his face.

And there was no mistaking *his* face. It was the face of the man in his dream. And beyond the priest was the great hall— lofty pillars, cream and gold; magnificent black and white flooring, like a chessboard. St Andrew's, Holborn Circus.

"How do you feel? Are you all right?"

The priest was talking to him. Asking the questions anyone might ask. Slowly it dawned on Charlie that he had fainted. He struggled upright, and the conventional reactions of one who hates to cause a fuss came instantly to him.

"I'm so sorry. I seem to have just blacked out. Stupid of me. Yes—thanks. I think I'm fine now. Maybe I could just sit here for a bit?"

"Of course you may. Unless you'd rather be somewhere quieter. Would you like to go to the vicarage? We're just going to have the service here."

"Yes. The Eucharist. Weren't you just going to have Eucharist? That's what I came for."

The priest smiled.

"We were. And if you're sure you're comfortable, we will. Maybe we can have a word afterwards?"

"Yes. Thank you. I'd like that."

"Good. Jim—would you mind lighting the candles? We're a bit late."

The priest went to the vestry. Jim lit the candles. The small congregation went to their places—not without covert glances at their new neighbor—and the service began.

As it proceeded, Charlie felt calm returning. By the time of the consecration he seemed to have quite recovered, and a few minutes later he went up with the others to receive communion.

After the service he remained in his place until the priest came back. He got to his feet and held out his hand.

"Father—thank you for your kindness. My name is Charles Brown. Charlie. I teach at the university."

"And I'm Michael Aarons. You can see what I do!"

"I can. And I'd like to have that word afterwards, please. I think I need to talk to you."

"Of course. Do you drink coffee? Or tea? Have you eaten? Come to the vicarage. Let's see what we can find."

As Michael Aarons led the way through the church, Charlie realized that he was ravenously hungry. So he needed little persuading to the plate of sandwiches that was soon set on the table beside him in the study.

The priest fetched his own sandwiches and coffee, and then placed himself in the armchair opposite.

"What would you like to talk about, Charlie?"

During the service, Charlie had resolved to tell about his

dream. Yet now he came to it, he was less sure. Surely the priest must think his story preposterous?

"I'm afraid that what I want to tell you involves a recurrent dream of mine — a dream that on the face of it sounds ridiculous."

The priest smiled.

"Most dreams do... on the face of it. But why don't you tell me a bit about yourself first? Give your ridiculous dream a context. If you like."

Charlie liked. In fact it made things a good deal easier. He said something of his work as a teacher in the University of London, even a little about Mickey the cat and Natalie. Finally he came to the dream. His questioner was bent forward, eyes fixed on him, fingertips together as Charlie told him how the dream had recurred when he was a child, then declined in frequency, and now, recently, recurred.

He described it.

"And the fact is," he said, "it's this church. And it's you. I've never been here in all my life before today. Yet there I was leaving W. H. Smith's, and the bell rang, and I walked across and decided to come. And it's you. It really is you. In my dream, you're always telling me there's something I must do. And in the dream that "You must" is terrifying, because I believe you but I don't know what it is I'm to do. And there's always something dark and menacing behind you. Here, there isn't. But can you make any sense of it? Or do you just think I'm going around the bend?""

"No, I don't think that. And I think the dream may be telling you something important."

Michael Aarons paused, then looked sharply at him.

"Charlie, I'd like your permission to risk something with you."

"Please Father, risk away."

"I want to make a very impertinent suggestion. I want to suggest that a great disturbance has entered your life recently.

I don't mean the sad loss of Mickey—something I sympathize with since I've lost a couple of cat friends myself over the last year. Nor am I talking about your American friend. She's obviously disturbing you but you're obviously enjoying it! No, I mean something else. Something… menacing? A serious threat? A danger? Am I in any way correct?"

Charlie was astonished. He'd skirted—successfully, he'd thought—the whole business of Siding Star, only now to find himself apparently transparent to Michael Aarons.

"Well—yes, you're right. But I'm in a difficulty."

Michael waited.

"The fact is, I'm pledged. The Official Secrets Act. I've given my word. Signed a paper."

"That's clearly a serious matter." Michael hesitated. "Of course I'm talking about the _moral_ part of it. Revealing the affair to me would also presumably involve you in a _legal_ offense."

Charlie, who had taken some interest in the subject, nodded.

"A misdemeanor under Section Two, I gather."

"Exactly." The priest hesitated again. Then, "Well, I can only say this—there does seem to me to be a certain imperative about your dream as well. And I have the feeling your dream and your secret are linked. Otherwise why would the dream start to come again when the secret emerged —which I take was the case?"

Charlie nodded.

"But you say your dream involves me. In which case, I think you may have to choose between what the Official Secrets Act tells you to do and what your dream tells you to do. I can't tell you _how_ to choose. But I do think you may have to make such a choice. I'm sorry." He sighed. "In case it's any help, I might remind you that an _ethical norm_ isn't the same as a _moral rule_. Of course things like telling the truth and keeping our promises are ethical norms—apart from anything else, society can't really function without them.

"But anyone who understands anything about ethics also

knows that it doesn't follow that, say, telling the truth is also an unbreakable *moral rule* that you must keep when—say—a maniac with a gun is asking you where your baby daughter is so he can kill her. In that case *two* ethical norms—telling the truth and protecting the weak—would be in conflict. So to find the *moral* thing to do in that case you'd have to choose *one* of the two ethical norms, since you obviously couldn't keep them both. Well, you may have to do that here." He almost smiled. "But I'm sure you knew all that."

There was a moment of silence, then Charlie shook his head.

"I didn't, actually. That's a helpful distinction. But as you say—I still have to choose. Look, at the moment I honestly don't know. I must think about it. May I do that—and telephone you?"

"Excellent." The doorbell rang. "And there, I think, is someone I've promised to see."

Charlie got to his feet.

"Now, are you quite sure you feel well enough to go out? You can certainly stay here longer if you need to."

"Oh, I'm fine. Really. I'm not usually a wilting violet. And I've got a pile of students' papers to read through, so I ought to be getting back. And thank you—for everything. I'll think about this. And I'll telephone you."

"I look forward to it. In the meantime I'll pray for you, Charlie."

Seventy-Four

The same day.

Charlie Brown departed — presumably to his university —
and Michael went to his visitor, another young man sent
to him by the Rector of St. Dunstan's, Stepney. He spent an
hour with him, arranged to see him again in a week's time,
then showed him out into the sharp, windy day. As often, he'd
found the time of counsel and prayer exhilarating rather than
tiring. There was something about the sight of a troubled person
struggling to be absolutely honest that never ceased to fill him
with respect for the human spirit — even with awe.

Back in his study, he took out the *Guardian*. Yet again, it con-
tained an article about East London that disturbed him. No vio-
lent outbreaks, no power outages, but disturbing nonetheless.
The brand new Cranston College of College of Engineering and
Technology was receiving substantial private grants from the
Academy for Philosophical Studies.

So the fire on All Hallows' Eve had inconvenienced the academy, but it hadn't stopped them.

As for Cranston College itself, Michael had heard some
odd things about the place, even before he knew it was connected to the Academy. There was, in particular, the story that
a priest friend in Limehouse had told him about two of her

parishioners—young men, brothers, who'd been working on the building site for the new college. Their mother said they'd told her about part of the site's being sealed off, no one allowed to go there because it was dangerous. An old tomb or something, they thought, but the college authorities were very cagey about it. The boys went out the next evening and while at the pub laughed and talked about the tomb, said they were going to visit it, see what the mystery was. Several people heard them—but no one had seen them since. The police had turned up nothing at Cranston, and Michael's friend backed up the mother's conviction that they would never have gone off without telling her.

A new thought struck him. A lot of the East End's troubles, the violence and the power failures, seemed to be centered in the area around Cranston College. Was he seeing a pattern or obsessed to the point of seeing patterns where none existed? He sighed. Cecilia was interested in the academy and wonderfully competent. He really ought to talk to her about it. She'd challenge him if he was letting his imagination run away with him. And if not, well, she had all sorts of resources.

Within a few days the college was to be opened officially. The first full intake of students wasn't planned until the autumn, but in the meantime fifty or so research and overseas students were being allowed preliminary use of some facilities. The opening itself promised to be quite an occasion, including a speech by the Minister of Education. The many distinguished guests included the Venerable Michael Aarons, Archdeacon of Hackney. The invitation stood, copperplate engraving, gilt edges and all, in the middle of his mantel, addressed to "The Venerable and (they assumed!) Mrs. Michael Aarons."

He'd already decided to attend. Perhaps he would learn something.

So what then of his notion of consulting Cecilia? Should he wait to do that until after his visit? Until perhaps he had more to go on? Or should he talk to her now? And then it came to him. He'd invite Andrea and Rosina for a weekend visit — which would be pleasant anyway — and suggest that they bring Cecilia if she was free.

He turned to the telephone and punched in the Exeter code.

SEVENTY-FIVE

The same day.

"No, I'm not on duty this weekend," Cecilia said when Mama called her to the phone. "Thank you, Michael! Figaro and I accept with pleasure."

"Actually, I'd like to talk to you again about the matter you raised with me on your last visit."

"Oh, really? So you too are having thoughts about the opening of Cranston College?"

"That's very clever of you. I'm actually going to it on Friday evening. They sent me an invitation, and I thought I ought to go and see what I could see."

"Verity Jones told me about it—the opening, I mean, not your invitation! She showed me an article in last week's *Hackney Gazette*. But it was your being so very solemn about..." (she mimicked his voice) "'the matter I raised with you on my last visit' that made me guess it was that."

Michael chuckled. One of the sadnesses of his life was that people so rarely made fun of him—or at least, not to his face.

"The fact is," she said, "I was meaning to talk to you about it and would have done sooner, but we've just had the week from hell here and I haven't had a minute. Still, if you've got an official priestly invite to the opening I certainly think it's a good

idea for you to go and see if you can discover any evil works."
Her tone grew more serious. "Actually, Michael, I've tried in
a general way to alert a couple of colleagues in the Met about
the academy — but it's hard for them to do anything when they
don't know what to look for and I don't even know what to *tell*
them to look for."

Michael told her about the two young men who had vanished.

"Any thoughts, Detective ?"

"It's an academy kind of story, isn't it — nothing concrete! Still,
I can inquire how the investigation's going. It'll be Shoreditch
and Hackney. You never know."

"I'd appreciate that very much."

SEVENTY-SIX

The same evening.

Throughout most of the rest of Friday Charlie wrestled with his decision until time came for his usual conversation with Natalie. The call, as it turned out, was cut short. She was involved in a diplomatic conference with sessions that were going on at all hours of the day and night. The conference had been a last-minute demand, and she'd called him from the UN on her mobile. She sounded harassed.

Throughout the evening he continued to reflect on his dilemma. For better or worse, his word once given meant a lot to him. The Foreign Office man had been right about that. Of course talking in confidence to a priest was hardly the same as "blabbing to the media" and the distinction between ethical norms and moral rules to which Michael had pointed was helpful. But at the end of the day, as Michael had also said, he still had to choose.

He closed his eyes.

Almost without realizing it, he found himself praying for guidance.

None came — at least, none he could discern.

It would be nice, God, if you would occasionally give a straight answer to a straight question.

As it was, even Saint Paul had to struggle. *For this thing I besought the Lord thrice...*

The words swam into Charlie's mind. But then the reply to them came at him like a whiplash. *My grace is sufficient for you.*

Yes. No doubt that was all very fine. So Saint Paul had had his problems too. But just how exactly did that help Charlie now?

My grace is sufficient for you.

That, it seemed, was all he was going to get. It had been good enough for Saint Paul. Apparently it would have to be good enough for him.

At last, with some kind of peace, he went to bed.

Hours later he was awake again, gazing at the ceiling. He looked at his watch. 4:10 a.m. A thought struck him.

He got up, dressed quickly in a sweater and jeans, got his old Alvan Clarke six-inch refractor from the cupboard above his bed, and went up onto the roof. It was a fine night. And—yes. It had risen. A red star, barely above the horizon but bright enough to be visible even through the London haze. He set up the telescope, adjusted the focus, and found himself seeing it with a clarity that shocked him. Since last he looked, it had grown, not merely in size but in authority. It pulsed. He felt like Frodo watching the Red Eye of Mordor.

Suddenly he could endure it no more. He told himself haste was absurd, but dismantling the telescope he hastened nonetheless and was relieved to return to the warm depths below.

He read until 6:00 a.m., then switched on the television. He fetched a glass of fruit juice and made himself a peanut butter sandwich, half listening to an actress who was opening in a new play in the West End. Then the anchors introduced an amateur astronomer who had "views" about "the supernova" (as the newspapers were calling Siding Star).

Charlie laid aside his half-eaten sandwich and leaned forward.

As an astronomer the man was evidently something of a crank. He quoted the Revelation of St. John the Divine (to the interviewer's evident amusement) and proposed that the new light in the sky was Lucifer come down to earth. He spoke of the nearness of the End, of a last chance for the nations to repent. He had observed that the new star was approaching from the center of the galaxy, which he interpreted as a sign of coming judgment.

The interviewer thanked him politely and passed on to a politician, whose concerns did not include "the supernova."

Charlie switched off the television.

Yes, by the standards of post-Enlightenment astronomy the man was a crank. Yet if he had lived three hundred years earlier he might have been called a seer. The fact was, leaving aside the metaphysics, he'd just about got it right. Charlie's own most sophisticated projection, using every resource of modern astronomy and mathematics, came to the same thing. The time was short. And crank or not, the man had correctly noted the key factor that had struck Charlie from the first: the thing was coming from the center of the galaxy. If *he* had noticed that, how many others would? How many had heard this morning's broadcast? And how long before others began to make similar predictions, perhaps more scientifically based and therefore more acceptable to the post-Enlightenment mind?

Suddenly Charlie knew that his decision had been made. Almost, it seemed, made for him. *And wasn't this the very guidance for which he'd asked?* What more did he want? The government that commanded him to secrecy would soon have no secret to command. The veil was disintegrating as he watched. And that being so, he must surely follow, as Michael put it, the imperative of his dream.

With that settled, he at once felt better. Certainly, it was a strange world he was entering. Yet it too was a world of facts. The experience of the dream was a fact. Its coincidence with the coming of Siding Star was a fact. St. Andrew's Church and Michael Aarons were real. He would confide in Michael Aarons. Somehow he did not feel that the gentle, somewhat pained wisdom of the priest would lead him astray.

He went to the telephone.

SEVENTY-SEVEN

Saturday, January 24.

Cecilia telephoned the Shoreditch and Hackney Police Station, which occupied (as she never observed without amusement) numbers 4 to 6 in Shepherdess Walk. Her inquiries about an obscure disappearance were not received with quite the zeal she might have desired. She persevered, nonetheless, exercising a blend of patience, sympathy, and refusal-to-be-diverted-until-she-had-what-she-needed that eventually got her to one of the officers who had dealt with the young men's disappearance.

They were pursuing the usual inquiries, of course, but there was really nothing to go on. Cranston College? Yes, well, they'd had a look but seen nothing that was any help. Tomb? Oh—the old site. Yes, well, they'd looked at it—one of the archaeologists had gone with them. Funny old chap. Said they mustn't talk too loud in case they brought the roof down. They'd gone down some steps and found themselves in what seemed like a large hall. Very dank and dreary. Bits of stone lying about. And a horrible smell—couldn't wait to get out of there, but they'd looked round and seen no sign of any missing boys.

Cecilia was about to thank him and end the conversation, when the officer said, "You know, ma'am, we might have missed something. I'm not saying we did but we might. The fact is, ma'am, things have been very difficult round here for the last couple of weeks and I think we're all feeling the pressure."

"I'm sorry to hear that," Cecilia said.

There was a pause. Perhaps he was wondering if he'd been indiscreet?

"Of course I've heard about the power outages," she said. "I saw those on the BBC. Having to clear Poplar High Street in the middle of a Tuesday morning must have been a nightmare."

"Yes, ma'am, it was a bit of a pain. But that's not what's so bad. It's the violence. And half the time there's no sense to it. Not even bad sense. Something really nasty seems to have got into the place."

"I'm sorry to hear that. I thought statistics were showing a *drop* in the crime rate."

"So they may be, ma'am, in other parts of the country. But not in East London and sure as hell not in our manor. As far as we're concerned, I think we're entering a lot of stuff in the records as 'no crime' when in fact there obviously *was* a crime, but we simply can't work out who did it or even why."

"Oh." This was depressing indeed. "It sounds like a tinder box."

"That's what it is, ma'am. That's exactly what it is. A tinder box."

SEVENTY-EIGHT

Later the same day.

It was a fine day and Charlie, after an early lunch, was tempted to walk. On reflection he realized he didn't quite have time for that and compromised by catching the tube as far as High Holborn. He then walked to Holborn Circus, enjoying the crowds and the delicate, chilly sunshine. As he reached St. Andrew's an enormous limousine, no doubt containing some civic dignitary, was just leaving through the green double gates that lead to the vicarage. Inside, Michael Aarons was standing amidst several people by the south entrance to the church. For a moment Charlie hesitated, but Michael saw him, waved and smiled, then nodded towards the open front door of the vicarage. Inside, Jim was sorting letters on the hall table.

"Father will be with you in a couple of minutes." He smiled. "He says would you mind waiting in his study? And would you like some coffee?"

"Thank you. I'd like that very much."

In the study he found both armchairs occupied—one by a magnificent Persian cat who was asleep, the other by a handsome little black cat with green eyes who flicked his tail and stretched luxuriously but made no attempt to move. Feeling he had no right to disturb either of them, Charlie went and stood by the window.

He had arrived a few minutes early, and the hands of the church clock were pointing exactly to two when Michael arrived, still in his cassock and carrying a tray with cups.

"Hello," he said. "I'm happy to see you, Charlie. But not standing! Felix! Marlene! What is going on? Do you occupy the best chairs — illegally! — whilst our guest stands? Off!"

The Persian jumped from the chair, exuding offended dignity, and stalked out of the room. The green eyed little black cat sat up, yawned — and began to wash himself.

"Felix!"

Felix continued to wash.

"*Felix!*" Michael pointed to the floor. The cat, with an expression that clearly said, "Oh well, if you are going to make such a *childish* fuss!" rose to his feet, stretched, and in a leisurely fashion withdrew to the carpet, where he continued to wash.

"I'm sorry, Charlie. As you can see, I've a strict rule that Felix and Marlene are not allowed on the armchairs."

Charlie laughed. "I'm afraid Mickey never took much notice of anything *I* said, either — not unless it happened to suit him. There was never much doubt which of us was in charge."

"Exactly," Michael said. "Anyway, have some coffee and a comfortable chair guaranteed to get cat hair on your trousers. Good. Now let's talk. I rather think you've made a decision."

"Yes, I have. I've thought about this as carefully as I can and I think I must share my secret with you."

Michael nodded. "Though you must already know, let me say that I hear many secrets. Yours will go no further — at least, not without your permission."

"I believe you."

As clearly as he could Charlie told the story of the last few months — of his work with other British astronomers at the Siding Spring Observatory, their concentration on a single segment of sky, and through that, their becoming aware, three months before the world could see it, of the phenomenon that was now attracting the world's attention. Of the theory he had formed and its subsequent support, and of his concern over international refusal to acknowledge the seriousness of the threat or even to inform the world about of it.

When he had finished, neither of them said anything for several minutes.

"Do you believe all this?" Charlie said at last.

"Oh yes, I believe you. You're a person I'd be inclined to trust anyway but as it happens—I hope you'll forgive me—I took the liberty this morning of asking a friend of mine in the university about you. I gather your description of yourself as 'teaching' was modest, to say the least. You're the senior professor in your department and the youngest ever to hold your chair. In the field of galactic structure you're regarded as one of the top dozen people in the world. No, I don't think for a moment that someone like you would make this up. And of course I've read about the supernova, though I haven't yet got round to getting up at four o'clock in the morning to look at it. Look—your coffee's cold. Would you like a fresh cup?"

"Actually, I'd like a glass of water, if you don't mind."

"That's easy," Michael got to his feet. "Do you like ice?"

"Just room temperature out of the tap, if that's all right."

In a few minutes Michael was back from the kitchen.

"Of course," he said as he gave Charlie the water, "I'll admit that what you say is personally threatening. Yet I do already know that the world isn't immortal, and neither am I."

"There's something in that."

"I think I also understand your concern about when the world should be told—yet even there, well, all of us already know we're going to die sooner or later. And it may be sooner." He sighed. "What *does* puzzle me is that if we're to take your dream seriously, which we surely must, and if your dream is connected with the Siding Star—and it does seem to be—then all this also somehow links to me, and there's something that you must do. But how does it link to me? And what is it you must do?"

"I haven't the remotest idea."

Silence.

Apparently, neither had Michael Aarons.

Michael sat gazing into space, turning over the story in his mind. If they were right in connecting Charlie's dream with Siding Star, there had to be a connection with Michael himself. Something that concerned him? All right. Go from there. What was concerning him most at present? The Academy for Philosophical Studies? Cranston College? Cranston seemed to involve a threat to the *future* of the world, so how could it be linked with this threat of universal destruction *now*? As for the academy, since the affair of the *Beriyt et-Mavet* on All Saints' Eve, he could think of nothing that had the slightest —

Then it came to him.

"When did you say this star was first seen?"

"November the first. It appeared between 01:20 and 07:20."

"Do you mean by Australian time?"

"We work by Universal Time — UT," Charlie said. "For all intents and purposes it's the same as GMT — Greenwich Mean Time."

"So you're saying it appeared, British time, during the morning of November the first?'

"Let's see… British Summer Time would have ended the last Sunday in October…yes, you're right. Why?"

The morning of November the first.

The morning of All Saints' Day.

The morning after the fire had stopped the Ceremony of the *Beriyt et-Mavet* — the Covenant with Death.

He looked at Charlie.

"I think I see it. But the boot's now on the other foot. I'm the one who's made a pledge to keep a confidence."

He paused. Charlie was watching him.

"Some friends of mine — one a police officer — were involved with me on the night of October thirty-first in an affair that might be linked to yours. I don't pretend to know how. I've only the coincidence of dates to go on, but it's a coincidence I can't overlook. Now, as it happens, my friends are due to come here on Friday evening." He paused once more, then continued.

"I propose this—I'll telephone them, explain that a very serious situation has arisen, and ask if they're willing to share our knowledge with a fourth person—with you. At the same time, I must ask if *you*'re willing to share your secret with them. I give you my assurance they're a family on whose loyalty and discretion I'd stake my life. They're to stay with me this weekend. If you agree, and they agree, I think we should meet here on Friday evening for a council. If there's something you must do, then surely we're more likely to find it by pooling our knowledge. But the first question is—will you agree to all this?"

To his surprise, Charlie found himself nodding before Michael had quite finished his last sentence.

"I've a late seminar on Fridays," he said. "But I think I can be here by nine."

After Charlie had left, Michael sat alone in his study. What an interesting and impressive man Charlie was! Michael had actually learned more of him from his friend in the university than he'd mentioned—including Charlie's losing both his parents. Well, he could identify with that. Charlie seemed, indeed, to have coped with it better than Michael had. But then he'd been younger, a child. And he'd had the cat. The cat was clearly important—as cats are! And what a long path of brilliance Charlie had then followed to where he was today!

Michael sighed.

And what of you, Michael? What of your path? What odd events and coincidences led you to where you are now? What brought you out of your madness?

Some things, some stages on the way, he could identify.

Coming back to England had been one, certainly. His own first cat, Squeak, who'd appeared on the doorstep the day after his arrival in London and refused to go, had been another. Then there was the battered copy of the Gospel according to Saint Mark he'd come across at a second-hand book stall in Chapel Street Market and picked up for ten pence out of idle curiosity: it still stood in the book rack on his desk. There'd been a conversation with an American soldier on a bus. And finally a moment when he'd fallen to his knees in his bedroom, weeping, and suddenly realized that mum and dad were all right, and that as for him—he didn't quite know how—he'd become a Christian. So he'd got himself baptized and confirmed. Then after a while, not being one to do anything by half measures, there had been theological college and the priesthood.

In many ways it had been made very easy for him. Sometimes religious conversions could be terrible things, with people tearing robes and casting other people off. But nothing like that had happened to him. Generally he'd received nothing but kindness from the Reform Synagogue he'd left and the Anglican Church he'd entered. With all their flaws as human institutions, still he could have nothing but gratitude for the individuals he'd known in both as they'd encouraged him on his way—certainly not a way he or they could have planned!

And now apparently his being a priest mattered: it mattered when it came to Siding Star, if for no other reason than that Charlie Brown had confided in him. But he knew—of course he knew—there was more to it than that.

SEVENTY-NINE

The same day.

When Charlie Brown got back to the house, the telephone was ringing. It was Natalie, rather earlier than they had planned.

She sounded even more harassed.

"Charlie," she said, "I'm really sorry. I hate this, but I just can't make our date on Monday. Mother's ill and I'll have to go to Charleston. I just have to."

His universe fell apart.

He heard himself saying, "Darling, I'm so sorry. What's happened?"

"It's her damned emphysema. They're going to stabilize her in the hospital and put her on oxygen. I wouldn't mind so much if she tried to stop smoking and failed, but I've tried to talk to her about it and she just says she can't change a lifetime habit and she enjoys it, dammit, and which one of us is the parent, and… and…"

"Darling, of course you've got to go to her. We'll get together as soon as you can—as soon as she's feeling better."

"As soon as she's got the hang of negotiating that oxygen tank—I promise! Look, Charlie, I love you like crazy, but at the moment I need to fix about ninety things here. I'll call you from

Charleston. It may be in the middle of the night, but at least then we can talk properly and make plans. Okay?"

"I love you calling me in the middle of the night," he said. "But go now and see to your mother. And give her my best regards—even though I've never met her."

"Oh, but she knows who you are—as soon as I told her I was dating you she looked you up on the London University website, found what books you'd written and everything. And would you believe it? She approves! Apparently you're a good catch. Did you know that, darling?"

"Actually I can't say that ever occurred to me."

"Well, you are. Mother says so. And I assure you, on such matters as these Mother is *never wrong*."

"Oh."

"So take good care of yourself, darling, and I'll come to you as soon as I can. I love you. Have you got that?"

"I've got it. And I love you."

"And that's all that matters. Try to stay safe. Go with God, my darling."

"And you, sweetheart."

Natalie put down the phone.

She loved it when he called her his sweetheart. She was not at all sure that she *was* a sweetheart, except maybe with him, but she loved to be called it, all the same. Like the time when he... but that was enough daydreaming!

She picked up her calendar. If she was going to catch an evening flight to Charleston, there were about five more things she needed to reschedule.

A knock at her door was followed by Boris, carrying a file— the duBois file.

"Quoyt would like you to take a look at this before we send it. He doesn't think Levenson's translation is accurate enough."

"*What*? That's ridiculous. Of course it's accurate."

"Hey, don't shoot the messenger, lovely lady."

"Bad message, Boris! Go away!"

"I go! I go!" He dropped the file on her desk and backed out salaaming ostentatiously.

Poor Boris! She wasn't being a sweetheart to him. She was being a bitch. Fortunately Boris knew she loved him to death. When she got back, on the first Sunday they could both make it, she'd take him for Skazka at Mari Vanna—he always enjoyed that. But Quoyt—she glared at the file —was a pedantic ass. She thumbed through the places marked in red and swore softly. It boiled down to three occasions where the French had used the subjunctive and Levenson had translated with the indicative. It wasn't what she'd have done herself but it was entirely defensible and made no difference at all to the sense. She was damned if she was going to "correct" it.

The note she wrote to Quoyt was not disrespectful but it still boiled down to, "There's nothing wrong with this. Please don't waste my time" —if he had the wit to see it.

Eighty

Friday afternoon, January 30.

The Cavalieres arrived at St. Andrew's with dog beds and suitcases. Pu, whose hobby was food, discovered the cat's bowls within ninety seconds. She was quickly joined, of course, by Tocco and Figaro. Felix and Marlene, to their credit, treated this disgraceful behavior by retiring to the upper part of the house.

Michael, already dressed in his best clericals, showed them their rooms. Supper was laid out for them in the dining room. He expected to be back by half past eight. Charlie Brown was not expected to arrive before nine. And there was time for an early glass of something before he went if they wished. They did. Surely they were all conscious on some level of the meeting they had agreed to have later "because of a serious situation." But no one asked about it, for which Michael was grateful. Sufficient unto the day — or in this case, the hour — was the evil thereof.

While Michael was filling their glasses, Cecilia noticed the Cranston College invitation propped up on the mantelpiece and picked it up.

"There's a spare seat here," she said as he was replacing the stopper in the decanter.

"What did you say?"

"It says 'The Venerable and Mrs. Michael Aarons'."

"So it does. It often happens to me. Everyone still assumes a respectable Anglican archdeacon must be married. Why?"

"Well, who are you going to take?"

"No one, I suppose."

She raised an eyebrow and waited.

"Well, I don't have a wife, do I?"

She continued to stare.

"Oh! Well, I could take you. I mean, if you'd like! Would you like to come?"

"I thought you'd never ask! Of course I'd like. And think how much use I'll be as an extra pair of eyes spotting evil works. I expect I'm better at spotting evil works than you, anyway. After all, it's my job."

"Well..."

"Mama and Papa wouldn't mind being deserted for a bit, would you? There don't seem to be seats for you. But you could stay here and dog- and cat-sit."

Andrea had just completed a long week at one educational institution, followed by a drive from Exeter to London in heavy weekend traffic. The idea of a couple of hours spent quietly with Rosina (not to mention, of course, Tocco, Pu, Figaro, and — should they choose to reappear — Felix and Marlene) was infinitely more appealing than a jaunt to some affair at another educational institution.

"Speaking for myself, I wouldn't mind in the least. Sounds like a good plan. What about you, *cara*?"

Rosina smiled. "Oh, very appealing."

"There you are, Michael," Cecilia said. "Professor Andrea Cavaliere and Senora Rosina Cavaliere both think it's a good idea to stay here, and I'd like to go with you. How about that?"

"I should be delighted."

"Right! I'll change, then. Can you give me fifteen minutes?"

La bella figura! Michael barely repressed a smile.

"We don't have to be there until six. These things never start on time anyway."

Cecilia was almost at the door when she turned back.

"I say, Michael, you're sure you don't mind? I mean — I sometimes forget, not everyone wants a copper barging in on them all over the place. You weren't planning to go and be serious with bishops or something?"

"I make it a practice *never* to be serious with bishops."

Only after she'd left the room did it occur to Michael that he was actually quite excited at the prospect of turning up at Cranston College with Cecilia Cavaliere in tow.

He must be losing his mind.

If Charlie was right, the world was probably going to end shortly.

And in any case a woman like Cecilia Cavaliere must have her pick of eligible men flocking after her.

And he was probably too old for her anyway.

EIGHTY-ONE

Later the same evening.

Cranston College was strikingly, even aggressively, contemporary. Passing through the transparent doors was like entering an airline terminal. Money had been spent lavishly on the décor: thick carpets, concealed lighting, exotic indoor plants, and running streams. The assembly hall held several hundred people, all of whom rose to their feet as the principal entered with the Minister of Education and a number of others whose faces Cecelia didn't recognize.

The first part of the proceedings—the official opening—was entirely formal. Proper things were said. Proper ceremonies were performed. Proper people were thanked. The Minister of Education said nothing in particular for about ten minutes. And the thing was done.

Then came the principal, a heavy, slightly bulbous man in his fifties.

"Mr. Minister, My Lord Mayor, Your Worships, distinguished visitors, ladies and gentlemen..."

His delivery was monotonous, and Cecilia found herself focusing on an enormous indoor plant that stood in front of her. She was good with house plants, but she'd never managed anything like that. How on earth did they do it? It was gigantic. It was magnificent. It was—

Plastic.

She glanced around her. Politely attentive faces. Glassy eyes thinking distant thoughts. Michael's face a mask.

The principal appeared to be reaching his conclusion. He was speaking with fervor and perhaps just a shade louder than the circumstances demanded. She pulled herself together. She had practically made Michael bring her. The least she could do was pay attention.

"At this time, as never before, it is imperative that we be faithful to those principles which life itself has placed so firmly in the grasp of our generation, for in them lies the key to progress. A wise man once said, there is no sin but ignorance, and indeed…"

Was it really possible that this boring man, uttering platitudes that must surely seem overworked by the feeblest standards, was part of a terrible plot? That his college was involved in a dark design? She pursed her lips and frowned. That, after all, was what they were trying to find out. *What we can't show, we don't know.* Hello—what was that? A ladybird was scuttling along the floor. The insect stopped, then turned. It was perilously near to a softly tapping foot in the next row. Turn back, you stupid thing! Oh, no—it was actually going towards the danger! Ah—at the last minute it had spread its wings and shot away. Now where was it? On the wall to her left? Oh, no. Here it was again —

A sudden burst of applause.

He'd finished. Well that, at least, was a mercy.

The principal sat down, mopped his brow, and poured himself a glass of water. The applause continued as he drank it. Several of the audience rose to their feet.

"What did you think of that?" Michael asked as they moved out.

A momentary temptation to prevaricate was resisted.

"I'm ashamed of myself," she said. "After all the fuss I made to come, I wasn't listening to most of it."

Michael chuckled. "I don't think you missed anything."

They made their way through the crowd.

"Michael, before we do anything else, do you mind if we just go outside for a few minutes?"

"Not at all. But why?"

"It seems I've got a ladybird in my hand."

"Is it awake?"

"It certainly *was* awake. It nearly got stepped on."

"That's odd—they're usually dormant 'til March. Then they wake up."

"Well, this one woke up early."

"I suppose it might be the heat in the building. Let's put him outside somewhere sheltered and maybe he'll go back to sleep."

"How do you know it's a 'he'?"

"I don't. I gather even ladybirds get it wrong sometimes."

"Good heavens!"

"Yes, I'm sorry—I should have said, 'he *or* she.'"

"I forgive you."

"Thank you. Now, shall we go and find somewhere to put him *or* her?"

"Yes!"

They deposited Cecilia's ladybird under some leaves in the churchyard opposite and returned to the reception in a further hall.

"Oh good! They've got nibbles," Michael said. "I like nibbles."

But just as he was about to help himself to cashews, Cecilia put her hand on his arm.

"This is no time for *antipasti mediocri*," she said. "There's work to be done." She tucked her arm through his. "This way!"

"Where are we going?" he asked as she steered him between double swing doors and out onto a wide, empty area of open tarmac between the hall and another large building.

"Exploring," Cecilia said. "Looking for evils, of course. Isn't that what you came for?"

"But we can't just go wandering about the place as if we owned it."

"Of course we can. Look at me—wandering about the place as if I owned it!" With that she stuck her nose in the air and flounced ahead of him with a mincing walk that made him laugh. She looked back and grinned. "There you are," she said, "Nothing to it!"

He caught up with her.

"Now, if anyone asks what we're doing," she said, "you just play the idiot priest and leave the rest to me. Let's go over here. Just stroll. Not a care in the world. Chin up. Perfect right to be here. *That's* it."

A few minutes later Michael found himself walking with her through an arch and into a long quadrangle surrounded by what were evidently laboratories, offices, and workshops, a mass of glass and aluminium that gleamed in the yellow sodium glare. Signs of recent construction were obvious. A heap of scaffolding. Several pieces of machinery. It was quiet, though, after the hubbub of the reception. They walked across freshly laid paving.

"A stream used to run under here," Cecilia said, "but they've diverted it into the Thames, higher up." She took a piece of paper from her handbag.

"How on earth do you know that?"

"Google."

"Now why didn't I think of that?" he said.

"I told you, I'm the expert at spotting evils." Now she was lining up her paper with the buildings. "Anyway, I've got help.... Ah! Let's go through here. It ought to get really interesting."

There were lanterns on each side of the porch, and she paused by one of them to peer again at her paper. The light framed her figure, shining on her hair as it fell forward. Then she looked up at him, her dark eyes bright with intelligence and fun.

"Come on!" she said. "This way!"

He followed her.

She led the way to a corner of the quadrangle, through a narrow space, and out into a wide area. There were halls of residence on each side and between them a chaos of rubble, building materials, tools. Fifty yards ahead of them was a high barbed-wire fence with a well-lit sign.

DANGER

THIS IS A HISTORIC SITE AND ITS PRESENT CONDITION IS EXTREMELY DANGEROUS. ABSOLUTELY NO ADMISSION UNDER ANY CIRCUMSTANCES.

GUARD DOGS AND SECURITY MEN PATROL.

"That," she said, "is Hadrian's Grave. It's what your young men who vanished were on about. Apparently it was called that in the sixteenth century—nobody knows why. But nobody thinks the place really had anything to do with *il Imperatore Adriano*. For a long time there was an inn here. Apparently there's a witticism in Boswell about 'making an end at the Grave'. It seems to be an odd name for a pub, but there you are. The place had some connection with the Hellfire Club—though everyone's a bit vague about that. Then it was burnt down and afterwards there was a warehouse." She peered again at her notes. "Oh, yes. Someone found some Roman brickwork while they were building an extension in 1937. I knew the Italians were in on it somewhere. That's all. Come on."

God in heaven—he really *was* losing his mind!

They got within a few feet of the barbed wire. Beyond it were earthworks and a dark entrance, but there was no obvious way in through the fence.

"I suggest we walk along the fence to the left," Cecilia said. "Michael, do you notice—"

"You two! Where the hell do you think you're going?"

A man emerged from the shadows to their left. As he headed towards them the wind seemed to change direction and Michael became aware of a very strong, *very* unpleasant smell.

"Can't you people read?"

Before Michael's eyes, Cecilia became an entirely different person. She fluttered and flapped toward the advancing figure. She oozed good-natured incompetence.

"Oh—*good* evening, we're *so* glad to see you. We seem to have taken a wrong turning."

"Well, this is out of bounds."

"Oh, really? We *are* sorry, aren't we, Father?"

"Ah—"

"This is Father Aarons. He's an archdeacon, you know. Anyway, I'm afraid *I* was feeling a little faint—so very warm inside, you know—and he very kindly brought me out for some air, and we seem to have taken a wrong turning and so as you see here we are. I suppose this is all to be part of the new college? Are those excavations? They look *very* interesting."

"Yes, miss. At the reception, are you?"

"Oh, yes—dear Father Michael, he's *so* interested in education. Only the other day he preached a *very* fine sermon about it. 'Knowledge is the key to life,' he said, and I do think—"

"Well, the reception's back through there, miss."

"Oh, thank you so *very* much. That *is* kind. And I'm feeling *much* better now, thank you. So *very* kind of you. And such a beautiful reception. A *most* interesting speech! *Delicious* hors d'oeuvres. *Everything* of the first quality. Well, we mustn't keep you talking. Come along, Father. *Good* night, then."

Michael padded along behind her. Dear God, she could make a living at this.

Cecilia said nothing until they were back in the car, then she grasped his arm.

"Michael, do you remember what Mama and Papa told us about last November—when that... that *thing* happened at the house?"

"Of course."

"I really think there may be a connection between what happened then and this place. Remember they said there was an awful smell—like something rotting, a *dead* smell, Papa said? Well, did you notice the smell tonight? Just after the man started shouting?"

"Dreadful. I've never smelled anything worse."

"That's right. A sort of... well, Papa's description would fit, a *dead* smell. And there's something else It was in a mass of routine stuff I skimmed through a few days ago because I asked for *everything* on the night of the academy fire no matter how trivial—and there was an odd report by two Met officers quite near here. They said they'd seen something very strange moving along the East India Dock Road—something that disappeared before they could identify it, but at the same time there was a ghastly, unpleasant smell. They reported it mainly because they thought the sewer might need attention, but the moment I smelled that smell back there, I thought there might be a connection. I know it's not much to go on, but it's something. I would have looked further if that man hadn't interrupted us. At just the wrong moment! I could have killed him!"

"You hid your rage remarkably well."

"Oh, well, he was shouting and then we were busy."

"*You* certainly were. An amazing performance! I was impressed."

She laughed. "Oh, you liked my Miss Bates act, did you? With apologies to Prunella Scales! '*Svergognata*'—'shameless hussy'! That's what Mama would call me."

He chuckled, turned on the ignition, and began driving them home.

It was nice that she'd held his arm. It was a gesture of trust.

To be sure, she could have no idea how much pleasure it gave him. Indeed, he rather hoped she *didn't* have any idea.

Still, trust was precious and he could try to deserve it.

That at least was allowed.

Even perhaps required.

Eighty-Two

The same evening.

They had been back at St. Andrew's for about half an hour — time to drink a glass of wine, eat a little more of the cold supper Michael had provided, and tell Andrea and Rosina the latest news — when the doorbell rang. Michael answered it and ushered Charlie in. Introductions were made and the duties of hospitality fulfilled. Figaro and Pu were friendly, but Tocco seemed delighted by Charlie, prancing around, offering kisses, and curling at his feet when he sat down.

The council began.

At Michael's request they started by telling Charlie their stories — all they knew or could guess of events the previous All Hallows' Eve. Then Charlie told his story: the observations at Siding Spring, their likely significance, the Dream and its recurrence, and his meeting with Michael.

At the end of Charlie's recital nobody said anything for several minutes.

Cecilia found herself nonplussed. Almost detached. It was all so absurdly simple. If they were really to believe this quiet young man, then they and everyone else probably had about ten days to live. The policewoman in her appreciated perhaps better than Charlie the real nature of the diplomats' dilemma. She could picture only too vividly the scenes of chaos that would follow when the world knew.

In the meantime, *she* knew. And what of it? Well, it certainly put her little upset with George in perspective. She had thought he'd betrayed their future together. But it was all an illusion. There wasn't going to *be* any future.

"Michael — why have we been told all this?" Rosina said. "Why have you got us here? What's the point of it?"

"Because there's something here that links to you — to what happened on All Saints' Eve."

"How?"

How to put it?

He paused, and seemed to be gathering his thoughts before replying.

"I admit I'm not exactly sure," he said. "But two things make me think there must be a link. First there's the coincidence of dates. The ceremony on All Saints' Eve and what Charlie saw only a few hours later. Next — and it was some time before this occurred to me — the exact match between what I imagine to be the object of the ceremony and what Charlie thinks may actually be happening."

Again he hesitated.

"The point is, as I told you at the time, the ceremony of the *Beriyt et-Mavet* is meant to destroy. It's an assault upon creation itself. Its center, God forgive us, is a formal and considered reversal of the Ineffable Name. If such an intention were coupled with *real* power, if it could actually do what it set out to do, then what Charlie describes is exactly what we might expect. A threat of total destruction."

"But the fire stopped the ceremony," Rosina said.

Cecilia looked at Michael. "I suppose the question is — did it *stop it*, or did it just interrupt it?"

With what was obviously a heroic effort to keep her voice calm, Rosina said, "If the ceremony had been completed, Michael, wouldn't it have — so to speak — got *us*?"

Michael shook his head.

"It was Henry Wheatley only, I think, who pledged your lives. And he died, as I recall, at about six-fifty a.m."

Cecilia nodded.

"Well then. His life for yours. From the moment of his death, you two would no longer be involved. But suppose someone *else* completed the ceremony soon *after* Wheatley died? According to Charlie, Siding Star was first noted at seven-twenty a.m. Greenwich Mean Time on that morning," — he looked over at Charlie, who nodded — "which leaves time — nearly half an hour — for someone to have done it. After Wheatley's death, and before the sighting."

Rosina stared at him.

"And you really think a ceremony carried out on that morning might have led to this... this Siding Star thing?"

"I only say that there seem to be connections of timing and of purpose."

"There's also a difficulty," Andrea said.

The others looked at him.

"Michael, I admit your time scheme fits like a glove — from where we stand. But if I follow Charlie correctly, this explosion actually happened twenty-seven thousand years ago. It's only its *results* that first appeared to us on November first. So how can something someone did in London on that day have an effect on something that happened twenty-seven thousand years ago?"

"I think I can answer that," Charlie said. "Mathematically, at least."

He took a notebook and a pencil from his pocket and started to draw.

"It's to do with dimensions," he said. "The dimensions in which we operate. Just imagine for one minute that you were confined to two dimensions—a flat surface, like this:

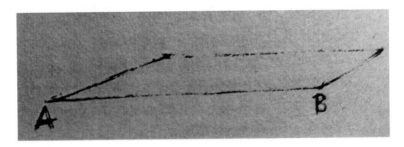

"Now, to get from A to B you'd obviously have to go a certain distance—let's say, since we don't know the scale of my drawing, quite a long way. But then let's imagine the surface curved—as space is, incidentally—so that is was like this:

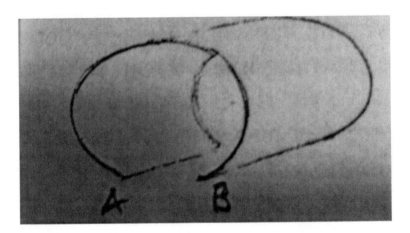

So long, of course, as you were still confined to two dimensions, you'd still have to go the same distance from A to B. But now imagine you've learned a way to get out of two dimensions into the *third* dimension. You could then go by a very brief journey from A to B—like this:

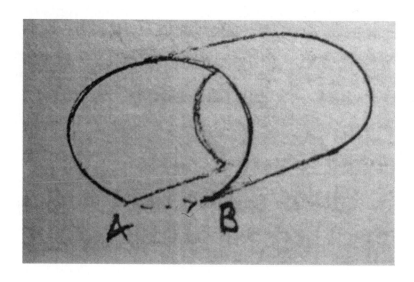

"Do you see?"

"So far." Andrea said.

The others nodded.

"All right. Now, *we* normally operate in *four* dimensions — three of space and one of time. Mathematically, however, it's quite possible to envision a fifth, though of course we don't know how to reach it. But suppose that some immense spiritual — or counter-spiritual — force is unleashed. Perhaps it's precisely through a fifth dimension that it operates. In which case it's perfectly possible to see how a prayer now, or a curse, might effect something thirty thousand light years distant — like a fly crossing from one edge of our paper to the other. Do you see?"

"I'm afraid I do," Cecilia said.

"Of course it's sheer speculation. I'm not actually claiming that's what *is* happening. I'm only saying that mathematically it's possible. Mathematically, of course, as in other spheres of discourse, all sorts of things are possible that aren't actually the case."

"Isn't there something like it in one of Charles Williams's novels?" Rosina said. "Yes — *Discesa all'inferno* — *Descent into*

Hell. I read it some years ago. About a girl in the twentieth century who helps her ancestor who was a reformation martyr."

"That's it exactly," Charlie said. "Naturally Williams doesn't talk about the mathematical side of it, but he certainly saw in another way how the idea could work."

"You know, I think the ceremony must have been completed at Hadrian's Grave," Cecilia said.

"What?" The others were staring at her.

"Hadrian's Grave—the archaeological site at Cranston College. You've shown us how the thing might be possible. And Hadrian's Grave has to be the place where they did it—where they finished the ceremony. They couldn't have done it at the academy because of the fire. But they *did* have time to get to Cranston College. And we know perfectly well they had a connection with the place. We'd already spotted that. What's more, I think it's the right sort of place."

"Why?" Andrea asked.

"It's ancient. And in the past it's had some connection with evil. Michael knows. I looked it up. Wouldn't that be the sort of place they'd use?"

"It would indeed," Michael said, "And then, of course, we noticed the smell."

"Exactly!" She hesitated. *What we can't show, we don't know.* "Of course, it's not proof. But it's surely the best possibility we've got."

"I think it is," Michael said. "Does anyone have any other suggestions?"

No one had.

"So?" Rosina said. "I take it you didn't just ask us here so we could come up with a brilliant theory. Do you think there's something we should do? Something we *can* do?"

"Something we *must* do?"

Michael looked at Charlie, then at the others. Finally, he answered his own question.

"If that place has been claimed for the Destroyer, then my instinct is that someone should go and deny that claim. An exorcism would be appropriate, but it would take time to arrange. Just to go and pray would be something. But if that claim has been made, it should be challenged. After all..." He hesitated, feeling for words, then went on, "If all times are in some way accessible then perhaps..."

Andrea could not help himself.

"Then perhaps all times are redeemable?" he said.

Michael smiled at him.

"Exactly! After all — *God has made all times, and before all times only God is, and time does not antecede itself.*"

"So perhaps, by turning to... to God, we might — or God might — actually change something? I mean — about the star? We might come at things in a different way?" Cecilia spoke hesitantly, but Michael was smiling at her.

"Perhaps," he said. "Or perhaps all it will mean is that when death makes its claim on us, someone will have said, 'No, these things aren't yours. They're God's.' I don't know. But I think we should do what we can. And to say that things are God's is, after all, to speak the truth, which in the end is always stronger than any falsehood, even if it doesn't look like it at first."

"Then I'm sure I have to go," Charlie said. "It all fits. The dream. The church. You. I've got to do it."

"If you feel like that, then I think you must — "

"There!" Charlie's spectacles almost came off as he jerked to his feet. "That's exactly what you said in my dream. 'You must!'"

"Well, yes. But what I was going to say is that since your dream involves me, too, I think I should come with you. I've some experience in these matters, and that may be useful."

"Actually I'd like that very much. I'm completely out of my depth."

Michael smiled. "I think we're all out of our depth. I certainly am. But still, I'll come."

"In which case," said Cecilia, who had wandered over to the window, "it looks as though we're in for a soaking."

"We?"

"Well, you both seem hell-bent on it, pun intended. I don't see how I can let you go blundering about in the dark performing acts of goodwill or saving the planet or whatever all by yourselves. You'll need someone sensible even if it's only to hold a flashlight."

Michael gazed at her for a moment, then collected himself.

"We'll also need all the good will we can get," he said.

"So I'll go and put my jeans back on," Cecilia said.

"I'll do the same," Andrea said.

"And I," Rosina said.

"*Cara*, is this a place for you?" Andrea said. "It's raining, and you've only just thrown off a bad cold!"

Rosina stared at him. "Excuse me, have I not been following this conversation? There are ten days to go to the end of the world and you're telling me to be careful *because I might catch another cold?*"

Andrea grinned and shrugged.

"*Brava Mama!*" Cecilia said, and hugged her, then turned to Michael. "All right, the members of *la forza* are committed. So what's it going to do?"

"I imagine the first problem," Michael said, "is to get in at all."

"Actually," Charlie said with a wry grin, "the place is in association with London University, and I *am* on the faculty. I suppose I could say I thought I had a right to wander in with my friends and look round if I wanted to." He smiled at Andrea, and added, "And of course to extend courtesy to a distinguished visiting professor from another university and his family!"

Cecilia smiled. "I've been handed stories that were worse. And with luck you won't have to use it. Judging by what I've seen of higher education security, if we walk in looking as if we know where we're going, nobody will take the slightest notice."

"They were actually quite strict with us tonight," Michael said.

"That's because they had a government minister and the mayor and God-knows-who there. But that means there'll probably *never* be a better time to walk in than the next hour or so. After getting rid of all those VIP's without disaster, ten to one security will be sprawling about drinking beer and congratulating itself."

"All very promising," Michael said. "But let's be quite clear—if what we've speculated is correct, then after we've cleared that hurdle we're up against something very dangerous. Charlie, when you describe your dream, you always say that somewhere behind or beyond me there's something 'dark and looming'. Isn't that right?"

Charlie nodded.

"And that's the one part of your dream we haven't identified. We don't know what it is, which means we don't know what we're facing. If we go in God's name, intending as best we can to serve God, then certainly nothing can harm us eternally. But physically, temporally—that's a different matter." Again he looked at Charlie. "You've a chief part in this, but I think that has to mean you also face the greatest danger."

"Maybe so." Charlie grimaced. "But—what of it? My girl friend Natalie told me what John Wesley said when someone asked him, 'What would you do Mr. Wesley, if you knew you were going to die today?'"

He paused. The others looked at him.

"Wesley said, 'I'd do exactly what I'm going to do anyway.' So I suppose we'd better go and do it."

Michael smiled. "I can't add anything to that." He looked at his watch. "It's nine-forty. If anyone needs me, I shall be in church for the next twenty minutes. I suggest we assemble in the hall at ten-fifteen."

"Then may I use your study?" Charlie said. "I want to write something."

"Of course."

The decision was made. And it was clear to Michael that all of them were in their own way prepared for whatever lay ahead.

EIGHTY-THREE

Charlie Brown sat at Michael's desk.

He had warmed quickly to the Cavalieres, to say nothing of their beautiful dogs, and he already liked and trusted Michael. But with the stimulus of their presence gone, he found himself depressed and afraid.

He thought of Natalie. 'Keep safe,' she'd said, and that was just what he was about not to do.

There was a scratch at the door, twice repeated.

When he opened it, Tocco stood looking at him until he invited her in, then she walked to the desk and arranged herself by his chair. Charlie was grateful for her company. He sat again at the desk, caressing her head.

He needed to write to Natalie. At least he could do that. He adored her. And she'd given him quite simply the best two weeks of his life. He just hoped she'd forgive him—for not trying to stay safe, as she asked. But then, of course she would. She was the one who'd said, "You'll do your duty when you have to." She'd understand. She was wonderful. He picked up the pen and scribbled for a few minutes. He glanced through what he had written.

"Little enough. But it'll have to do."

When he finished he put the envelope in the center of the desk, got up, and went to the door. Michael was just coming up the stairs.

"I'm ready," he said.

"Then so am I."

For a moment they stood together on the landing.

"Why me?" Charlie asked suddenly.

"It's a mystery. It's one of the two great unanswered questions. Why God? And why me? Theologians call it the problem of election. No one knows. Except God, of course."

"I feel pathetic."

"Who doesn't? But you have good will. A measure of faith. And you're trying to be obedient. So you may have more power than you think. And, of course, you're in love."

Yes, he was. Charlie wasn't sure even now that he understood it, but perhaps that didn't matter. Perhaps the important thing about love was not to understand it but just to be in it.

"Michael—there's something you could do for me. On the desk there's a letter for Natalie. If anything happens to me and you come out of it, could you see she gets it? And explain what happened?"

"Of course."

Together they descended the stairs.

It was already a minute after ten when Rosina and Andrea joined the others in the hall. They had assembled windcheaters, flashlights, Wellington boots, and a piece of rope. Rosina looked curiously at Michael's case.

"It contains the vessels I use to celebrate Holy Communion for the sick. I thought we might decide to say mass there. What better way to reverse the *Beriyt et-Mavet*?"

"Whose car?" Cecilia asked.

"Ours, if you like, Michael," Papa said. "It's an Outback, so we could put all your things in the back."

"Thank you," Michael said. "Now then, let's remind our-selves we're in God's hands."

They gathered around him. Cecilia had thought she would feel awkward about this, it being a very long time since she'd done anything remotely like it. She'd had a religious phase and gone to Mass when she was about thirteen because she'd fancied one of the priests but then the full force of his being celibate had dawned on her and that had so seemed silly she'd given it up. Still, Michael seemed relaxed about it and not to care when her religious phase had been or that it was now over, and somehow that made it all right, so she joined the little circle with every-body else.

She noticed that when Michael finished his brief prayer, Papa and Mama both said "Amen," so she said it too and crossed her-self when they did, though she was surprised. But then, Papa had always said he could recite the creed *ex animo*: it was the institutional Catholic Church with which he had his quarrel. So presumably being with Michael who was an Anglican left him free to indulge the *ex animo* bit.

They left the house a few minutes later. It was raining heavily.

Papa offered her the keys, just as he had whenever they were together from the very first day after she'd passed her test.

"Rosina and I can get in the back with Charlie," he said. "There's plenty of room, Michael. You sit at the front and navigate."

He pulled down the rear door and came around to the rear passenger door, splashing through the puddles.

A few minutes later they were off.

EIGHTY-FOUR

The rain helped. It's a good deal easier not to draw attention to flashlights and a coil of rope if you can hide them under a bulky raincoat.

Cecilia's estimate of what was likely to happen when they arrived at the college turned out to be entirely accurate. The whole reception area had a disorganized after-the-party air. Most people had left but there were still enough to make their entry relatively inconspicuous. Priests were not common here, but Michael was engaged in conversation with Charlie, who looked exactly like the university professor he was, and so little notice was taken even of him.

Cecilia wondered if *all* the plants were plastic. Had she not been so anxious to avoid drawing attention to herself she'd have gone and looked.

Andrea gazed curiously about him. Cecilia was right. It *was* reminiscent of Gatwick Airport. With maybe a touch of the new Euston Station. He continued to gaze curiously as they walked through passages, then splashed across quadrangles that he gathered Michael and Cecilia had already visited that evening. Rounding the last corner, he saw a brightly lit fence.

"That's Hadrian's Grave," Cecilia said to him.

"And that, I take it, is the watchman's hut," he said.

The lights at that end of the fence must for some reason have been off when Michael and Cecilia visited the place earlier, otherwise he didn't see how they could possibly have failed to see the hut at once. Not only was it visible, there was a light inside, and they could see the occupant's head.

"Good grief," Michael said. "I'd forgotten about the watchman."

They sheltered in a doorway out of sight of the hut.

"I could try to talk my way in," Charlie said.

Yes, he could. But watchmen tended to be stubborn and suspicious. It was, after all, what they were paid for.

"Wait," Andrea said. "You can do that if there's no other way." He felt in his pocket. "Rosina, *cara*, you have the *telefonino*?"

She raised an eyebrow but said nothing as she handed an iPhone to him.

"What are you going to do?" Michael said.

What indeed? As the English said: In for a penny, in for a pound!

"None of you wants to know what I am going to do," he said, "and I'll be back in two minutes. I hope."

Cecilia watched Papa walk away from them, back the way they had come, and disappear into the lighted building.

"Do *you* know what he's going to do?" Michael said.

"I haven't the slightest idea," she said. And she hadn't.

Several chilly minutes passed while she stood with the others, watching for Papa and at the same time keeping a wary eye on the watchman's hut. Then, to her surprise, the door to the hut opened and the watchman left. Mackintosh collar turned up against the driving rain, he walked by without noticing them and continued on towards the main building.

Another minute or so passed and Papa reappeared.

"He's gone!" Cecilia said when he got within earshot.

"I know." Papa grinned and handed the iPhone back to Rosina. "Wonderful things, telephones. See the cable—they've even put one in the watchman's hut. Fortunately they also have a highly efficient switchboard: puts you straight through without wasting any time on questions. Very sensible."

Cecilia got it.

"Papa—you *didn't*!" This was a side of him she hadn't seen for years.

"I see there's no watchman in that hut," he said, "so obviously they don't mind people looking round. Shall we go?"

They splashed over to the entrance, then followed a path inside the fence that went to the right. They had to make their way alongside the mound, and the going was not easy. The ground sloped sharply towards the barbed wire and was no doubt slippery at best. Soaked, it was a nightmare. The rain was now falling in sheets, which made it hard even to see.

"My God," Rosina muttered to herself, "maybe I should have taken Andrea's advice and stayed at home." But she clung stubbornly to her flashlight with one hand and her husband with the other, and together they blundered on.

Suddenly the entrance to the mound was there. They plunged into cloaking shadow. It was good, for a moment, simply to be out of the din and the drenching—but only for a moment. Rosina shuddered.

The smell! That horrible smell!

She and Andrea looked at each other. It was the same, the same as the night of the assault. Neither of them would ever forget it. They tightened their clasp on each other's hands.

***

Cecilia noticed their reaction.

"It's the same, isn't it? The smell?" They both nodded. "I knew it," she said. "Along here. It seems to go along here. Oh, God! It's revolting!"

She switched on her flashlight and led the way. Behind her the others lit their own torches.

The passage turned left, then very slightly upwards, then right again, and down steep steps for ten feet or so. At the bottom they found themselves in what appeared to be a plain square chamber that could have held a hundred people.

Good stonework.

Gravel floor.

They shone their lights up, down, right and left. There were no other exits. There was nothing at all to remark on save that smell. And, somewhere, the slow drip of water on stone. It was, after all that had led up to it, anticlimactic.

"Well," Michael said, "we're here."

But somehow Cecilia felt that they *weren't* there, even though she didn't know where *there* was supposed to be.

"I don't think this is it," she said. "There's nothing here."

"What do you think?" Michael turned to Charlie.

"I agree with Cecilia. This isn't it. There's nothing here."

She thought she heard Papa swear softly to himself—and then he called out.

"Here—what's this! I think I've found something."

It was a square of stone that looked slightly different from the others, but nobody would have noticed it if they hadn't been looking for it. Papa touched it. It seemed to Cecilia that it moved, just slightly. Their eyes met.

Was this the place?

He pressed again. Nothing happened. Perhaps she was wrong. Perhaps there had been no movement. He slid his hand to the right and pressed again.

Nothing.

He pressed in another place. This time the wall groaned, and a section of it began to swing back. It moved until it stood at a forty-five degree angle to its original position.

Opened beside it was a dark, narrow entrance.

Cecilia shook her head.

"We might have missed something," the constable had said.

Evidently, he was right.

EIGHTY-FIVE

"Wait!" Cecilia said, as they started to move towards the entrance. "We don't want any accidents. Can you give me a hand?"

With the help of the others she manhandled a piece of stone until it was so placed that the entrance couldn't close on them.

She took from the pocket of her jeans a box of matches, struck one, and held it into the tunnel. It burned strongly, flickering slightly as in a draft.

So far, so good.

She lit another and walked a few yards in. It too burned with the same slight flicker.

"All right. Let's try it."

Within seconds it seemed to her that they had passed a barrier. The walls on each side looked and felt immeasurably older than those they had left. Instead of large, well-squared blocks, there were small, slender bricks.

Papa looked at her, and smiled.

"*Romani,*" he said, with a certain pride.

"*Sì,*" she said, and smiled back.

At one point there was a stone slab set in the wall. It bore an inscription, badly worn. As she shone her torch onto it she could make out two words and part of a third.

DIVVS MITHRAS VEN …

"'Divine Mithras comes — or came'," Papa said.

"We know there was one temple of Mithras in London," Michael said. "Why not another? This would be the sort of place they'd choose, wouldn't it?"

Papa nodded, then shone his torch beyond her and picked up a second slab, again much worn. Most of it was beyond deciphering, but one line stood out:

ET NOS SERVASTI ETERNALI SANGUINE FVSO

"'And you have saved us by shedding eternal blood,'" he translated.

"But surely that's Christian?" Charlie asked.

Michael and Papa both shook their heads.

"I think it refers to Mithras slaying the bull." Michael looked at Papa, who nodded. "But still, let's allow the writers to have said better than they knew."

"Look!" Papa pointed to the wall further along, where the bright beam of his flashlight revealed a painting. It looked ancient, and not all of it was clear — indeed, a major part of it looked to have been vandalized. Splinters of stone lay on the ground near to it, and deep incisions had been cut, it seemed, into the wall itself.

Cecilia looked at her father. He walked forward, knelt by the picture, and stared at it.

"What this once showed," he said at last, "was what the inscriptions say: divine Mithras, the light-bringer, killing the bull. But look at what someone has done to it! And done recently, I think."

Cecilia nodded. The stone shards, even the patterns in the dust, were evidently new. The destruction of such an antiquity had been vicious, wanton, and stupid.

"This is terrible," she said.

"It's worse than that, *bella*. It's a statement. I think that whoever did this understood the painting very well." He sighed, shook his head, then went on. "For Mithras' worshippers, so far as we can tell (for they left no written records) his victory represented the triumph of order and creation over chaos. It expressed their hope—as you said, Michael—for something better than they knew. But now look! It is *Mithras* who has been eliminated! Viciously eliminated—see the deep slashes! Even his knife has been hacked out. What is left is the *bull*. So what was an image of hope has been changed into an image of despair. What it now says is that there is *no* creation, *no* order, only chaos."

The others stood for a moment in silence, surveying the ruined painting. Papa got slowly to his feet.

Suddenly Charlie spoke.

"I think this means we're right. And we're near. I think we must go."

The others followed him.

The way was narrow, curving to the left, and slightly downwards.

And now with each step Cecilia had a sense of moving backward in time, decade by decade into the past.

Without warning the stench, to which she had begun to grow accustomed, trebled in strength. She stopped, nauseated. Shaking her head, she tried to turn away, to find some other air to breathe. There was none. Michael, just behind her, had also stopped and was leaning against the wall. They stumbled against each other. Overcome, unable to move forward or back, they clung together and leaned against the rough stone. Still, his arm around her felt warm and reassuring and she was grateful for it.

Then came the scream—an ear-splitting emanation from the darkness that pierced brain and heart and pulled them inexorably forward. Cecilia found herself being dragged, as if wrenched by a gale. Hair, hands, and body—she felt as if she were disintegrating.

She lost Michael. She seemed even to lose herself.

After a while she again felt gravel beneath her feet, but still she could see nothing. Not "see nothing" in the normal sense of that phrase—but literally nothing. Absolutely nothing. She put her hand to her eyes and moved it inches away and it made no difference. This was blackness so deep it seemed to deny even the possibility of light. Was she blind? She drew breath to cry out, and choked. Yet her choking made no sound. She tried to shout and felt her lips move, but as in a dream there was no sound.

She was sure Michael was near but she couldn't find him.

Suddenly she saw—something! A gleam of white. She strained her eyes, desperate for the relief of vision. The gleam turned to silver and into her view came the last thing on earth she might have expected.

A wolf. A she-wolf.

The wolf was silver—seeming, indeed, to gleam from within with a pale, cool light. Around her, total blackness. Yet the wolf seemed unafraid. Where there was neither dimension nor solidarity, the wolf gave her own. In the instant of seeing her, Cecilia again felt Michael's arm around her shoulders. She pressed against him and received a reassuring squeeze in return. But still she could not see him or the others, so she watched the wolf. She had no idea of the wolf's size, for there was no way to relate her to anything. There was only an impression of joyful, animal strength, an ardent power.

The wolf jumped, as if to a higher level, sat, as if on a flat surface, and looked about. In one way she seemed familiar. And yet Cecilia had certainly never seen such a creature before. To look on her was like listening to a certain kind of music. She remembered once hearing Gluck's *Di questa cetra in seno*, and Mama whispering to Papa, *"Quella è una finestra in Paradiso."* Well, looking at the she-wolf was like that—a window into paradise. She was a creature from Eden.

With a jerk of attention, like a dog called by a well-loved human, the wolf turned, seemed to jump down, and trotted to a place on their left. There she stooped and bent her head. In the faint glow Cecilia could now see the face and form of Charlie Brown, who seemed to be asleep. The wolf was licking his face. Charlie blinked and shook his head, touched the wolf, and said something Cecilia couldn't hear.

Then, slowly, he got to his feet.

Whether there was now light around them, or there had been light all the time and her eyes had not adjusted to it, or, indeed, she saw at all, Cecilia could never be sure. But by some means she was now able to distinguish the others as well as Charlie — who stood, tall and still, his hand on the head of the wolf, and faced the darkness.

As the menace seemed to recede, Michael dropped his arm from her shoulders but stayed nearby. Cecilia moved closer to him but he didn't react, his gaze still fixed on the darkness beyond Charlie. Mama and Papa, who were just beyond him, were staring in the same direction.

Out of the darkness, a voice. Or, rather, the denial of voice.

"How dare you come to disturb us?"

The wolf growled. The darkness seemed, as she watched, to grow — pulsating, summoning, claiming. But then Charlie spoke, and in his voice she heard a grief that seemed older than the foundation of the world.

"This is not your place. You should not be here."

The pulsating darkness wavered. For a long second there was a pause — then the pulsation renewed, and the blackness grew: an infinite void.

"I bring your doom."

Like a drumbeat the last syllable came upon them, and the darkness lapped around them.

Eighty-Six

For some time now, Charlie had known. With Andrea's discovery of the door he had felt again the fear in his dream: the consciousness of something dark and looming, something that waited.

Then came the scream. Lost and blinded, he fell, and might have lain forever had the wolf not roused him and led him forward into the darkness.

And now he began to understand.

Beyond the rage and the danger he saw something else.

He saw loneliness.

Perhaps he saw it because he had been lonely himself.

The creature was lonely.

Whatever its history—a billion years of negation?—the reward of that history was to be alone.

Without hope.

And now, Charlie saw himself.

Infinitely lower in the scale of creation than the fallen angel that he faced, yet possessed of a capacity at that moment powerful.

Compassion.

He could feel compassion: that searing movement by which

the Eternal had been bound to a decaying creation at Bethlehem
and on Calvary.

What, then? Charlie Brown — the fingertip of divine glory?
Ridiculous.

No, actually it wasn't.

But what if he refused?

Had God no other means?

Infinite means, of course.

Another Bethlehem.

A deeper Calvary.

Have I not many words for many worlds?

But all that was at this moment irrelevant. The question that
mattered now was what was *he* going to do?

Of course he was free.

He could say No.

He could abandon the fallen creature.

He could withdraw.

Back behind Michael and the others.

Back to the beginning of the tunnel.

Back to the streets of London.

The underground.

The airport.

New York.

And Natalie. He could go back to Natalie. Who was his
dream, his delight. All that was needed was one decisive act.
An act of which he was, in one sense, perfectly capable: he must
abandon the creature.

He could not.

Why had Natalie gone to Charleston to be with her mother?
Why had she helped the woman with the child in Sussex
Gardens? Simply because she was Natalie — true to a quality in
herself that was the best part of her. And if he abandoned the
creature and went to her now, his going and his union with her
would be founded on a betrayal of that quality. And what was
it that he had just quoted to the others? What would you do

if you knew you were to die today? Why, you'd do what you were going to do anyway.

He must choose the creature.

As he formed that thought, he groaned.

The warm, strong body of the wolf pressed against his thigh.

For a moment he trembled.

Then he grew still, looked at the thing before him, and called it.

He called it as he might have called a well-loved but disobedient dog.

"Come!"

From the depths of a rejection older than time, the creature had known itself approached. Something disturbed it. Something challenged its hitherto impenetrable denial. For a moment its fixed attention to its own perception of ancient wrong wavered. No human word or experience could comprehend what was threatened, for no human word or experience could comprehend its lostness. The creature reared to destroy—but then some not-quite-severed shred of a billion-year-old circuit flickered. Rejection sought, as ever, to support rejection by feeding upon rejection—and reaching, found not enough.

So balked, the creature hesitated. It had been created for angelic charity— sheer intellectual charity. And now a remote survival of that intelligence glimmered, raising the momentary possibility of attention to something other than its own injustice—the possibility, and the infinitely incalculable risk.

Before it stood the biped, disgusting combination of spirituality and matter. Yet from the biped—something. Its mouth moved. It uttered a word. In themselves all words were to be rejected, for all words, however fatuous or malicious, held by their nature some echo of that original Word to which, even now, the creature must concede the very being it willed to deny. Yet fatuity or malice—the denial of intelligence or the denial of charity—could, even through words, have offered the creature the peculiar strength that it sought. Instead there was something else—something affording no handle that could be grasped, no rage or rejection that could be absorbed. Even more dangerous, through the word there came, though faintly, the echo of a call first heard at the dawn of creation. Certainly this was merely the remotest foster-child of that. Yet still, there was something. For an instant, the strain ran true.

"*Come!*"

The creature, poised to destroy, hesitated.

And in hesitating was found.

As Charlie called the creature to himself it seemed to him that they fell. Locked together, they fluttered in a void.

All the follies and self-centeredness, all the treacheries, all the petty betrayals and acts of cowardice in his own life came before him. Between him and the creature lay only the question of degree. Both had betrayed. Betraying in particular they had betrayed the universe. Betraying the universe they had betrayed each other. They were lost.

It seemed that after a thousand years they sank to the final pit of negation. There was nothing. And would be nothing.

Suddenly in that moment they were held—by the One who had created them and who now forgave, assuming their debt and its cost from before the foundation of the world.

See, see, where Christ's blood streams in the firmament. One drop would save my soul. Half a drop, ah, my Christ!

In accepting forgiveness of the One, Charlie accepted forgiveness of creation, forgiveness of the creature. And in knowing that he was forgiven, forgave.

Silence.

The creature had vanished. Yet in the instant before the silence it seemed to the others that they heard—what? A single chord, the restoration of an ancient harmony. For one moment they saw the creature transformed and restored: an angel of the Lord of Hosts. And they might have been tempted to worship, were it not for a voice in the harmony that sang, "I also am a servant. Worship God!" Their spirits soared. The silver wolf bounced and played, and leapt for joy, first around Charlie, then around them all.

Michael could never remember just when he had set out the paten, the chalice, and the book: but now they lay before him and he knew that it was time.

He began the liturgy.

It was such a liturgy as surpassed all memories. Never could they speak precisely of what happened—not because it was confused but because its order was too perfect, not because they were lost but because they were found.

They heard a voice:

Arise, shine, for your light has come, and the glory of the Lord has risen upon you.

Then another voice that spoke with infinite understanding of the world's sorrow:

For behold, darkness shall cover the earth, and thick darkness the peoples,

And another that replied:

But the Lord will rise upon you, and his glory will be seen,

And then a symphonic crash and they themselves were part of an impassioned cry:

Nations shall come to your light, and kings to the brightness of your rising!

Now Michael's voice, quiet but clear:

And the Word was made flesh, and dwelt among us, full of grace and truth; we have beheld his glory.

The Peace was a dance and an exchange of laughter, while the wolf romped in their midst. Someone in a strange cap seemed momentarily to dance among them. Then they and the dance were swept to the altar, in a declaration of the first reality. There was ritual salutation, the demand and acknowledgement of joy, recital of the acts of creation and redemption — and the universe sang in uncounted tongues:

Holy, holy, holy,

Sanctus, sanctus, sanctus,

Hagios, hagios, hagios,

Kadosh, kadosh, kadosh,

Santo, santo, santo!

Then the voice of Michael again:

… Who in the same night that he was betrayed, took bread and gave you thanks…

They ate and drank bread and wine that were the body and blood of their redemption, and gave thanks. Then the priest dismissed them. With his dismissal he blessed them, and as he spoke it seemed that the ground leapt, the solid earth danced, and the walls tumbled to their foundations. The roof was gone so that great bars of golden light shone through the dust. They were swept through the opening like music and caught into light. For one moment it seemed they glimpsed the outskirts of the glory.

They saw and did not see.

EIGHTY-SEVEN

Saturday morning, February 7.

Cecilia's cheek was resting on vinyl, cool and sticky. She opened her eyes slowly.

She saw chrome and more vinyl.

Finally she sat up, focused properly, and looked around.

They were back in Papa's car, parked as they had left it. It was still dark, and the road was illuminated mainly by the yellow sodium glare of streetlights. She was behind the steering wheel. Michael was asleep beside her. Behind them were Mama and Papa, and beside them Charlie, all still asleep. They were where they'd been when they arrived at Cranston College. She looked at her watch. 5:45. Had they fallen asleep when they arrived? Had she dreamed the whole thing? Was she dreaming now?

As she looked at Michael, his eyes opened and met hers. He gave her a sleepy smile. Then he too looked puzzled. She saw memory flowing back and the same questions entering his mind as hers.

"Did you see?" she said at last. "Was I dreaming?"

"That place? The wolf? Charlie?"

"Yes."

"You weren't dreaming," he said. "Or else I was having the same dream. I saw it too."

"And something else. Something dark." She shuddered and then smiled. "But it was all right—it was glorious—in the end. You said mass."

"Yes, it was. I did."

Cecilia began to remember other things.

"I fussed about blocking that door open. That didn't make much difference to anything—just wasted everyone's time."

"Oh, but it might have been important."

"You think so?"

"Absolutely. After all, it was a secret door."

"That's true."

"And with secret doors one just can't be too careful. Everyone knows that."

"Really?"

"Yes."

"Well that's very comforting, Michael. Thank you."

"Don't mention it."

What a kind, lovely man he was. She had a sudden impulse to lean over and kiss him. Not the kind of kiss she normally gave to Mama's and Papa's friends, but a proper kiss.

Whether she would have yielded to this curious impulse cannot be known, for at that moment, Papa stirred. And seconds later, Mama. They sat up and stretched, blinking at her and each other. Both looked sleepy. And both remembered the same things Cecilia and Michael did.

But Charlie didn't wake up. He looked peaceful, he looked happy. But his breathing was shallow.

"Let's get him back to your house," Cecilia said. "If he's not awake by then, we'd better get a doctor."

As she drove away, Mama looked back, then cried out, "Look! Look! Behind us!"

Cecilia stopped the car and turned, as did Michael and Papa. It was an amazing sight. From the center of the college rose a cloud—a heavy pall she at first took for smoke, billowing and monstrous, illuminated from below by the streetlights. Hang on—that wasn't smoke. It was dust. It seemed the archaeologist's fears had been realized. The excavations at Hadrian's Grave had collapsed.

"Oh dear," Papa said, and sighed again.

Cecilia and Mama exchanged a glance.

"Never mind, *caro*," Rosina said after a moment, "perhaps in a little while they can begin excavation again, under someone responsible."

"Perhaps they can." Papa looked at Charlie. "Let's get him home."

Their eyes had been fixed on the cloud, so perhaps it was not surprising that none of them noticed two young men who seemed to have appeared from nowhere and now stood by the college gates. They looked at each other in evident surprise for a few seconds, then set off eastward.

At six o'clock on a Saturday morning the streets of Hackney are quiet. It did not take long to get Charlie to the vicarage and onto a bed. Michael telephoned the doctor, then joined the others by the bed.

Figaro and Tocco and Pu all licked Charlie's hands. He did not stir.

The doctor, who was a friend of Michael's, came within minutes but could do nothing. Mere human physique could not endure the encounter that Charlie had endured and survive.

At 7:20, as the first morning light was streaking the sky, Michael put on his stole, made the sign of the cross, and began the Commendation, *Depart, O Christian soul.*

EIGHTY-EIGHT

Siding Springs Observatory. The same day. 5:51 UT.

Thaddeus Quinn looked hard at the photograph in his hand, then at the previous one. He shook his head. Looked again. Impossible. But there is was.

"Zaziwe," he said, "come and look at this, will you?"

She came and peered at the two images.

"That's impossible," she said.

"I know," he said. "But there it is."

The earlier plate showed Siding Star in all its sinister glory. The second showed the normal constellations. It was as if Siding Star were simply no longer there. Which of course was impossible.

"There's got to be something wrong with the equipment," she said.

Tom Daniels joined them. Looked at the images. Agreed with their conclusion.

But there was nothing wrong with the equipment, and every new photograph they now took showed the same thing. Siding Star had vanished, as suddenly as it had appeared. They quickly learned that the Europeans and the Americans had the same story to tell. They communicated with their governments and with the United Nations. The media soon had the story, and in no time the news was around the world. Siding Star had vanished. Nobody knew why or how. No doubt its explanation would join the disappearance of the dinosaurs and the emergence of the speech gene as a suitable subject for PhD theses. In the meantime, the important thing was that it had gone. And, for those who had known or speculated enough about its significance to panic, the panic was over. Life could return to normal, or whatever passed for normal.

EIGHTY-NINE

New York. Monday morning, February 9.

They brought the special delivery package to Natalie while she was sitting in her office wondering whether it would be a good time to call Charlie. She'd tried twice over the weekend and only been able to leave messages. She had good news — her mother's medication and oxygen supply had been sorted out and the doctor saw no reason why Natalie shouldn't go to England on holiday for a couple of weeks. So she reckoned perhaps she could fly out on Wednesday.

As she was about to open the package the telephone rang. It was a man's voice, with a British accent. He introduced himself as Michael Aarons, a priest from London and a friend of Charlie's. She was, he said, soon to receive a special delivery package. It had just that moment arrived? Then they'd been quicker with it than he expected. Anyway, he was telephoning because he did not want her to receive it without also hearing a voice, without some personal contact.

The priest was, she sensed, a good man, a kind man, even a wise man: but he could not tell her other than what he had to tell her. So she listened, she thanked him, she acknowledged his suggestion that if at any time she wished to talk to him again he would be available, and she replaced the receiver.

For several minutes she sat staring at the telephone. Then she reached for the package and opened it. It contained, as the priest had said, two letters, one from Charlie, the other from himself.

After reading them she sat for while longer.

"Oh Charlie," she whispered at last. "I love you so much."

Suddenly she didn't want to look at the letters or the telephone any more. She didn't want to look at anything. So she put her arms on the desk and buried her head in them.

She wasn't sure how much time had passed when she felt a light touch on her shoulder. She looked up. Boris was bending over her, his gentle face full of concern.

She tried to speak but something seemed to be wrong with her voice, so she pointed to the letters. He picked them up and read them.

When he finished he put them down and took her into his arms.

"Oh baby, baby," he whispered, and rocked her softly.

NINETY

Buenos Aires. February 15.

"Señora Rodriquez! Señora Rodriquez!"

The plump cassocked figure had just emerged from the west door of the Church of the Annunciation and was scampering after a tall, handsome woman who was already half way down the steps. She turned and waited for him.

"Yes, Padre?"

"When you stepped in and organized the entire food distribution last week because Señor Ramirez was ill... You did such an excellent job, Senora Rodriguez."

The woman smiled and shook her head.

"You've already thanked me, Padre."

"Señora Rodriguez, I'm embarrassed to ask you. But... the Catholic Aid office, it's in chaos. The sisters do what they can but they have no idea how to organize anything. Last week the telephone was cut off because no one had paid the bill — and for once we actually had the money to pay it!"

The woman nodded.

"I'll come in tomorrow morning and see what I can do."

"Ah, Señora Rodriguez, we shall be forever in your debt."

She laughed. "Oh, I doubt that."

"Well, then, certainly you shall have our blessings and our prayers!"

"Thank you, Padre. That will please me very much."

NINETY-ONE

In early April, Natalie Lawrence came to England. She went to see Thaddaeus Quinn and Zaziwe L'Ouverture, who told her their experience of a brilliant and wise but quiet and thoughtful teacher they'd come to love. She went to Michael Aarons, who told her what he could of his times with Charlie and their conversations, then suggested she go to Exeter to see "my friend, Detective Inspector Cavaliere" who had also played a part in the last hours of her lover's life.

So, on a sunny morning, Natalie Lawrence and Cecilia Cavaliere met in Cecilia's office. Michael's instinct had been good—they liked each other on sight. Cecilia, to tell the truth, was instantly reminded of Verity Jones.

She told Natalie what she could—as much as she understood, which she was aware was by no means all—about the last hours of Charlie's life and the significance of his death. Yet it was not until Natalie was about to leave that she was emboldened to articulate something that had been lurking at the back of her thoughts from the beginning.

"May I say one thing more about what happened—something rather personal?"

"Please," Natalie said.

"It's this. In the few hours I knew him I think I learned two things about Charlie. One was that he loved you very much. The other—well, it's this: just before we left Michael's house, Charlie quoted something you'd told him—a story about John Wesley."

Natalie nodded. "I remember telling him that story."

"Well, *he* remembered it too. It inspired him. *You* inspired him. And your lover was a man of honor, *real* honor. What I'm trying to say is that some men, just a few, are actually worth breaking your heart over. I think you picked one of them."

Natalie was silent. Then she nodded and smiled, although there were now tears in her eyes.

"I think I did. I truly believe Charlie was the best man I've ever known. I just need to learn to live without him. It might take a while."

Natalie Lawrence returned to New York the following day.

She went on to lead a full and interesting life marked by distinguished service to the republic and the international community. Following retirement, she lived for her last nineteen years in a small apartment in Paris near the Comédie-Française, overlooking the Palais-Royal, with a dog and two cats.

EPILOGUE

It seemed to Charlie that as the mass ended there was ahead of him a light, cool, gracious, and welcoming.

He was still aware of his new friends round him. Of their good will and concern. He felt the dogs licking his hand. He sensed the doctor, competent and caring. He heard the voice of Michael Aarons, "Depart, O Christian soul…"

By all these good people and creatures he felt himself at once supported and released.

He was being released toward the light.

He heard a voice. "Come, Charlie!"

He drew nearer, and as he did so the light brightened and became glorious, and suddenly before his eyes there was spread the universe that he had loved and, in his own way, served. There was the earth, a tiny blue and silver planet with a single moon. There was the solar system. There the Milky Way, a blazing spiral disc with, at its center, something disordered, a sound misplaced, a light quenched before its time.

Then as he watched and listened there came from the blue and silver planet a voice, a breath. The sound was taken into harmony, the light reborn.

He understood. The blue and silver planet had played its part, and he had shared in that. And order was restored.

Still the vision grew. Other galaxies. And others. The Magellanic Cloud. M31 in Andromeda. M81 in Ursa Major. And others. And others. The cosmos itself, a single beloved jewel, beloved dust, a precious adornment in the dance before the throne.

And he heard.

He heard the music of the dance, the festival of all things, a music beyond music and the origin of all music. He knew that in a way he had always heard it, always known it, and always longed for it: but now he heard clearly, and tingled with joy.

Again the voice said, "Come!"

He was standing in sunshine on a grassy slope with daffodils. Far below him to his left he could see a vast shimmering ocean stretching to the horizon. Above and to his right the ground continued to rise, steeply at first (but not so steep he couldn't walk up it), then gently, slope upon grassy slope, until at last it met the blue sky. The air was soft and sweet yet exhilarating, and every breath he drew seemed to fill him with life. There were birds singing. And still there was the music, which seemed softer now but was everywhere, like the sunlight and the air, flowing into him so that he sighed with delight. He felt peace as if he were in the holiest of shrines and at the same time zest as if he were about to begin the most exciting of adventures.

He turned eagerly and set his face to climb the hill. Then he became aware of one who was all light and color and joy, a glorious one who barred his way.

"Not yet, Charlie. You will climb the mountain and you will join the others, but not yet. You aren't yet strong enough for that joy and your eyes aren't bright enough for that light. So be still, Charlie, and watch, while your limbs grow strong and your eyes get used to the light. And wait for your friend, Charlie, since she, it seems, chooses to wait for you. Then you can go on together."

For a moment Charlie stood still, somewhat nonplussed.

The glorious one spoke again.

"And now, Charlie…" Was that a hint of amusement in the voice of the glorious one? "Look behind you!"

Charlie looked back. A black tail, upright like a poker, was moving towards him through the long grass. He cried out with pleasure as his old friend bounded toward him—though to tell the truth, bigger and glossier and fuller of life than he'd ever been—now purring loudly and pressing against his feet, warm and solid and intensely alive.

ABOUT THE AUTHOR

Christopher Bryan is an Anglican priest and C. K. Benedict Professor of New Testament at The University of the South. He was born and grew up in London, and was educated at Oxford. He is the author of several non-fiction books, including *Render to Caesar* and *The Resurrection of the Messiah*. He and his wife Wendy now make their home in Sewanee, Tennessee, and in Exeter, England. Find out more at www.christopherbryanonline.com or at his author's page at Amazon.com.

Read the upcoming sequel to *Siding Star*:

PEACEKEEPER

to be published December 2012.

ONE

Near Tintagel, Cornwall.
Saturday, 25 April, 2009. 11.55 a.m.

It was very nearly noon, but the skies were dark and there was thunder in the air.

A gleaming black Mercedes S-class limousine moved cautiously down the narrow, rutted lane, the bright beams of its headlights gleaming on wet leaves, grass, and the occasional eye of a small, curious creature. It came finally to a halt in shadows by an almost concealed gate, and there idled for several minutes, windshield wipers sweeping to and fro. Then the wipers were stilled and the headlights dimmed. After another minute the engine ceased.

There was now only the sound of wind, gusting and sighing through the branches.

"I think this is it, sir," the chauffeur said through the intercom. "I'm afraid I can't get you any closer to the front door. But at least it seems to have stopped raining."

The man in the back nodded. "The car boot," he said, "you can open it from where you sit?"

"Yes sir. The control's here on the dashboard. Do you want me to open it for you, sir?"

"No, not yet. Listen carefully. I'm going to go to the cottage and you are to wait here for me – perhaps an hour, perhaps more. When I return, I will come to the window beside you and tap the glass. You will remain seated while you open the boot for me and I place some equipment in it. I will not need assistance. You will not try to see what I am doing. Then when I've closed the boot and got back into the car, you will drive me back to London. Is all that clear?"

"Yes, sir. Perfectly clear sir. I stay here. I open the boot from here when you say so. I don't watch what you do. And then when you've finished and get back in the limo, I drive you back to London."

"That is correct. Now wait."

The man got out of the limousine, closed the door, and stood for a moment.

The downpour had indeed stopped, but rain threatened again at any moment. He could hear thunder, and it was not, he thought, very far away. He looked around him. To tell the truth, leaden skies suited him. All things die, sooner or later, and dark clouds spoke more realistically of such a universe than did the jovial pleasantries of sunshine and blue skies.

And he was in favor of realism.

He turned toward the cottage.

As he started forward a small dog darted out from the ditch and barked at him—lip curled, eyes bright with fury, barring his approach—then made off, as if answering a sudden call, to disappear in long grass.

The man hesitated only a moment before continuing through the gate and along an untidy path toward the front door.

The woman who answered it looked tired.

"Yes?" she said. "What do you want?"

"I am the chairman," he said. "I wrote to you. I am chairman of the academy."

"Oh yes," she said. "The chairman. The *new* chairman. They come and they go. The last one wanted to destroy the galaxy."

"He overstepped himself. He achieved nothing."

"And now you want to use the cave."

"Yes."

"Why?"

"I would create servants."

She gazed at him.

He was tall and gray-haired, with a bearing that might have been described as soldierly, even distinguished, and piercing eyes that most people could not meet. His English was perfect — though perfect in just such a way as to suggest that English was not his first language.

The woman looked into his eyes and seemed unimpressed.

"Be careful what you want," she said. "It's not been used for ninety years."

"I know."

"And then," she said, ignoring his interruption, "it made a servant that finally killed its master and sixty-five million others with him."

"I know. I was there."

The woman stared at him. Then she nodded.

"So you were," she said. "I recognize you now." She considered him again. "You have the ointment?" she said at last.

"I have it."

"How did you get it?"

"A consultant supplied it. He has advised me on its use."

"And you have a purpose for these servants?"

"I..." The tall man hesitated. For the first time he seemed slightly disconcerted, even confused. Then he said, "My consultant and I, we have devised a plan."

The woman shrugged but said no more. Instead she signaled him to wait, went for a cape, then led him around to the back of the cottage and down through the woods. They made their way along an overgrown path past stinging nettles, docks, and brambles, alongside a stream and out at last onto a bluff. The rocks on the left fell away into a valley and the stream splashed down them over a tumble of stones, leaves, and dead branches. On the right the rocks rose steeply but were still suitable for climbing.

"Up there." She pointed. "Follow the path, you'll find it easily enough. It can always be found by those who look for it. And do not come to me again."

Order your copy of *PEACEKEEPER* at
www.christopherbryanonline.com
or wherever books are sold.